I0687315

NOGGLE STONES

BOOK I: THE GOBLIN'S APPRENTICE

Written and Illustrated by

Wil Radcliffe

Cover by Theo Bain

Noggle Stones, Book I: The Goblin's Apprentice

R Corners Publishing
Coldwater, MI
USA

www.nogglestones.com

For Julia and Rayan.

MAP OF WILLOW PRAIRIE COUNTY.

To THE WINESTAIN MOUNTAINS

STATE LINE STA
RAY P.O.

To CAER COELYN

JAMESTOWN
CROOKED CREEK P.O.

Lake Grange

Willow Lake

High Lake

Big Lake

Cedar Lake

J A M E S T O W N

NEVADA MILLS P.O.

Otter Lake

Marsh Lake

W I L L O W   P R A I R I E

TAMARACK MT.

Pai Tag latho

EGLWYS CACYNEN

Creek

Orange Hall

Crooked Lake

P L E A S A N T   S C O T T   Y

Lake Owensboro

Loon Lake

Cedar Lake

Pigeon Lake

Silver Lake

BROCKVILLE

Fox Lake

To FILENE

Grange Hall

To TUATHAN

T. 38 N.

T. 37 N.

From my flesh I make this scroll.
I draw ink from veins that bleed.
With my heart I craft these words;
I'm this book that you now read

In darkness I walk in circles.
In circles I walk forlorn.
Yet in you I live forever.
For when you read, I am reborn.
(Unknown goblin author, Age of the Bending Oak)

CHAPTER 1
GOBLINS AND GAMES

The bee danced within its glass jar prison, and the embers in the fire died to dull orange and gray. Bugbear, the keeper of goblin wisdom and culture, pulled his blanket about him and drew in his arms and legs, huddling into a ball on the forest floor. He considered warming himself with a cup of banderberry root tea, but the fire was far too low. Tudmire would need to return with firewood soon or there would be no fire left to rekindle.

Now, sleep tugged at his heavy head. Sleep. Dreaded sleep. Where the dreams were alive and angry. Where faces danced before him, mouths pulled into screams and eyes wet with tears. The dreams... oh, how they had tormented him. Dark visions clouding his mind. Sinister whispers filling his ears. Unspeakable terrors clotting his blood.

And yet it was the dreams that inspired him to search for the lost ruins of Whittlegrip's monastery. It was the dreams that sent him on his scholarly journey into the study of Non-Logical Thought.

And it was the dreams that had brought him here, huddled in the forest at night before a dying fire, a bee in a jar his only companion. The dreams... how he craved them and how he loathed them. The inspiration they granted, and the terror they inflicted. He wanted to deny them... to evict the torment from his head. Yet they always came, like unwanted dinner guests with dreadful eating habits.

As the bee's buzzing drilled into his head, fitful slumber fell upon him, like an assassin, killing him a thousand times. Dark shapes slithered and slunk. Evil voices bellowed and shrieked. He wandered alone in a world of gray, a colorless landscape stretching to the limits of his sight. In the sky above, images formed... dim and dreary like drawings etched in mud. He saw an archer, drawing her bow against an unseen foe. And he saw an animal, loping along upright like a goblin. And he saw something even stranger... a monstrous face, obscure and unclear, yet somehow important... somehow burnt into his skull. This image forced Bugbear's dreaming mind to recall an illustration of an odd and forgotten race he had seen in one of his books of ancient lore. They were called *humans*, and a more ridiculous myth he had seldom studied. The three images then turned to him and pointed, speaking as one: "*You should wake up. The game has begun.*"

With a gasp and a shudder, Bugbear found himself awake. The fire was rekindled, and Tudmire had returned... with three unexpected guests. Large people. Ten feet tall. Pale purple skin. Big warty ears. Small red eyes. Long spotty noses. Ogres.

Tudmire crouched with them before a Noggle Stones board, moving pieces here and there. The ogres watched on with dumb amusement, a bag of copper coins on the ground beside them.

"Gambling," Bugbear hissed.

Bugbear threw his blanket aside, tucked the bee jar into his coat-of-many-pockets, and stormed over to his cousin. "Tudmire!" he barked. "I sent you for *fuel*, not for *fools!*"

Tudmire turned back to Bugbear and waved him off. "Shush, you mouthy mouse! I'm about to win!" And with a surprisingly nimble movement of his thick fingers, Tudmire slid his three white stones over the opposing black stone.

"Ha!" he blurted. "I'm the Noggle Lord!" He stood and danced about the bewildered ogres and the grumbling Bugbear. His voice reached high into the night, filling the air with echoes of laughter and gloating. Then he stopped before the ogres, holding out his hand and smiling with all the teeth he could muster. "My winnings, if you please!"

The ogres shrugged as one. The largest passed the bag and a yellowed scroll over to Tudmire. "Goodly gamings, little gobling," he said with a smile. "Thanks you for the invitings."

Tudmire swept into a deep bow before the ogres. "My pleasure! Unlike some goblins, I appreciate and enjoy the company of ogres!" As Tudmire rose, several black, white, and gray stones tumbled out of his sleeves. He stood for a moment in the light of the campfire, sheepish and uncertain.

The red eyes of the ogres fell upon the pile of stones. Slowly the dim light of realization swept over them and their faces turned from masks of confusion to reflections of rage.

"Cheaterings!" the largest blurted as he overturned the board and sent stones showering into the air.

"Cheaterings!" the other two shouted.

"Smasherings!" the largest yelled as he advanced on the trembling Tudmire.

"Run, you fool!" Bugbear commanded as he took Tudmire by the hand and pulled him off into the thick tangles of brush. Pockets and paths unfolded before them, as Bugbear imagined they might. For he had placed his mind in a Non-Logical state where possibilities in thought could become truth in reality. And so they scurried, scampered, and scrambled, the green things opening before them and closing behind them.

Until finally, his thoughts exhausted, Bugbear collapsed in a worn-out heap. Tudmire squatted down beside him as the leaves and branches covered them in a canopy.

"Cheating at Noggle Stones, Tudmire?" Bugbear huffed at his cousin. "Did you really think you could slip extra stones on the board without being noticed? Honestly! If you were going to cheat, you could have at least been more original and less obvious about it."

"Cousin," Tudmire began, "they're bloody ogres. How was I supposed to know they'd gather enough wits to see through my... uhm... *misinterpretation* of the rules?"

Hoarse voices thundered behind the goblins. Oak trees groaned and splintered as the ogres rampaged through the night. Nocturnal animals scurried, fluttered, and slithered from the chaos. Even the moon and stars seemed to take shelter behind the heavy gray clouds.

"Where for you going with our treasures, little goblings?" one brute yelled. "You been taking advantage of our good natures with your trickeries!"

"Where for you going with our treasures, little goblings?"

Bugbear brushed a few branches aside to peer into the gloom. He could see the silhouetted ogres, savaging the forest with their tantrums. Slender fingers of fear began prickety-pick-picking at his brain. Out there in those huge callused hands death waited. He shook his head and exchanged his fear for fury.

"Gambling with ogres anyway," he hissed. "What were you thinking?" He turned back to his cousin and squatted into hiding.

"They didn't even have anything of value... just a few coppers and a tattered, old parchment."

Tudmire pulled the bag of winnings close to his chest. "You don't understand gambling. It's not *what* you win, it's *that* you win."

"Maybe I don't understand gambling, but I do understand dismemberment. And so do those thugs out there."

The goblins glared at each other, each shifting in place with aggravation. For being cousins they presented a striking contrast. Bugbear wore the clothes of a gentleman... cleanly pressed olive colored coat, spotless white shirt, bright plaid vest, matching olive breeches, and buckled brown shoes, whereas Tudmire wore a stained gray shirt, fraying suspenders, dusty brown breeches with patches at the knees, and scuffed black shoes. Even their hairstyles were as different as right and wrong... Bugbear's a frazzled tangle of thick brown from the top of his head all the way to the unruly mutton chops which sprouted from his cheeks... and Tudmire's a wispy clump of haphazard strands combed over the top of his head to hide an ever expanding baldness.

"You never listen to me," Bugbear said as the confrontation continued. "And now see what comes of it!"

"Angry you making us!" another ogre shouted. "Your bones we be crushering for these flustrations!"

Bugbear snatched the parchment from Tudmire's hand. "We'll give them back their things, apologize, and get out of this with skins intact."

Tudmire protested, trying to snatch the parchment back. "It's my property. After all, I cheated them fair and square."

Bugbear's leathery skin crinkled into a mass of angry wrinkles and his eyes widened into bloodshot saucers. Even in the gloom of the night, his face lit with his rage. He shook the parchment before Tudmire. "Listen, they'll have their valuables back whether we hand them over now, or they pry them from our dead hands. We're barely a fourth their size, Tudmire. We don't stand a chance against them unless we use reason."

Tudmire continued to flail and grab at Bugbear, trying to wrest his ill-gotten treasures from his cousin's keeping. "Reason is for those who lose the game. Winners get the loot!"

While Tudmire tugged and tore at Bugbear, a small object slipped from his vest and fell to the forest floor. It was nothing special, or magical, or profound in any way. It was but a simple tin, unmarked and unadorned. And yet when it skittered to the ground Bugbear's eyes exploded like sparks in the Devil's furnace. "My medicine!" he gasped as he fell to his knees and carefully lifted the dull tin. "It's the only thing that keeps the dreams away," he practically sobbed. Carefully he slid the tin back into his pocket, licking his lips and closing his eyes as if in some starving man's trance. As he did so, the parchment fell from his grasp. It unrolled at his feet, unleashing such an unnatural and brilliant light that the goblins fell back as though struck by a thunderbolt.

"What did you do?" Tudmire yelped. "The ogres are certain to see that!"

"I didn't do anything," Bugbear gasped. "The parchment... it has some kind of peculiar luminous quality."

"You mean it's magic?" Tudmire said.

"No. I've told you before, magic is a foolish superstition. Like Snaggy Mary Tittle-Top, or human beings."

"But Grand Uncle Crick says..."

"Grand Uncle Crick is a dear old soul," Bugbear interrupted, "but he lives in the past. This is the Year of the Dappled Beetle in the Age of the Unstrung Harp. We live in modern times. With modern sensibilities. Science rules, magic fools!"

Bugbear picked at the scroll with dainty, uncertain fingers, until, with a sudden rush of conviction he pinched the vellum at a corner and lifted it. "No. This is a purely scientific phenomenon," he said, examining the strange paper. "Perhaps it would be hasty to turn it back over to the ogres just yet. After all, as I was appointed *Bugbear* by the High Council of Ysgol Gwybod, it is my duty to expand and improve upon goblin culture and knowledge."

"There you go flaunting that fancy *Bugbear* title of yours again," Tudmire snorted. His baggy face then perked with curiosity. "What are all those squiggly lines there?"

"That would be writing, you dullard," Bugbear said, with a dismissing wave of his hand. "Although, I'm not certain what language. It has a structure similar to dwarfish, but less harsh. More fluid, like elfish in many ways. But then again it has a goblin-like boldness to it as well. Given time perhaps I could..."

"Die, you thieverous little greaselings!" The three ogres ripped the brush away from the goblins, exposing them in the dull moonlight. Two of the brutes reached down with ham-like hands, grabbed the stunned cousins by the scruffs of their necks, and hoisted them into the air. The third hissed at them, "Your little feets carries you far from us, and you hides well behind your things of green. But we sees the big flashings and lightnings! And you speaks all too loudish!" The fiend snatched the now unlit scroll from Bugbear's grasp. "Be giving us the rest of our belongings! Else we crushes your bones evers so slowly and not nearly so fastly."

"Oh, you festering fool!" Bugbear yelled at his cousin. "Now we're done for, thanks to your grubbering greed!" He twisted and turned in the ogre's grasp, trying to reach Tudmire with his wild slaps and punches.

"Shut your bloody gob!" Tudmire countered. "If you hadn't been wasting our bloody time with that bloody scrap of bloody paper, we wouldn't have been bloody surprised, you bloody twit!"

"Oh, blame me!" Bugbear said. "Blame me! At least I was interested in *scholarship* rather than *dollarship*! That's something worth dying for, I'll tell you!"

"There's no profit in death!" Tudmire yelled. "Unless it's yours!"

"I doesn't know, Loomis," one ogre said to his leader. "Maybe we be saving us troubles if we lets these goblings killing each another for us."

"They does seem to have a powerful hateness for each one of the other, Nigel" Loomis remarked. "But they is goblings, and goblings is filled of trickeries. We kill them ourselfs, to be safety. But firstly we best be collectoring our thingies post hastal, boys. We doesn't wants gobling bloodieness all over its. You shakes them and I'll sortify what falls loosely from them."

"Did you hear that?" Tudmire whined. "They're going to shake us clean and kill us!"

"Yes," Bugbear said. "I tried to warn you. Ogres tend to do things like that."

The ogres turned their prisoners heads-over-toes, and the shaking commenced. From Bugbear's oversized coat pockets dropped all manner of books, papers, gadgets, contraptions, odds, and ends. Calculations, journals, experiments... delicate pieces of a scholarly puzzle he had studied for years, now lay scattered upon the forest floor. His saucer eyes doubled in size, for even he was amazed at the volume of items he had gathered, and even more amazed that his stunted little body was capable of carrying it about all this time.

"Blimey, Loomis!" the third ogre gasped. "This little feller has more ownings than a museum!"

"Right you be, Dubbin," Loomis said. He rummaged through Bugbear's belongings. "But they is mostly worthless things."

"I beg your pardon?" Bugbear said. "You just happen to be looking at a lifetime of scholarly study!"

"Well, if this is all you gots to be showing for it," Loomis laughed while holding up the bee in a glass jar, "then I says you been wasting yourself a lifetime."

"Do not mock me!" Bugbear exclaimed, a rage boiling through his veins. "You cannot even begin to understand the importance of my work!"

Loomis picked up a small tin, opened it, and fingered through a fine powder. "And where in do you finding the impotence of this?"

"That is my medicine. Nothing more!" Bugbear blurted. "You need not concern yourself with it."

Loomis sniffed and snorted and tasted the powdery stuff. "Not bad. Try some, boys."

The other two ogres snickered and dropped their stunted prisoners. "You stay putses!" Nigel ordered the goblins. "We be eatings, but we also be watchings!" They gathered about Loomis and picked at the tin. "Let us be tasting this new pleasure."

"My tea," Bugbear whined as he pulled himself from the dirt.

Tudmire crawled to his cousin's side. "Are you all right?"

"My banderberry root tea," Bugbear sighed. "They're eating it."

Tudmire brushed the pine needles and dust from his clothes. "At least we aren't dangling upside-down anymore," he said, slicking back his few strands of hair.

Bugbear gripped his cousin about the shoulders. "I need it, Tudmire. I need my medicine. I don't think I can endure another dream."

Fear seized Bugbear. Oh, how he dreaded seeing those wretched, alien creatures again. The dreams... the nightmares... only the tea had staved them off. It was Duergar, the village gardener, who had told Bugbear of the healing properties of the banderberry root. But now Duergar's gift was being devoured by the ogres. And Bugbear's mind was being devoured by unfettered rage.

"I shall crush the heathens with my bare hands!" Bugbear exclaimed. He lurched forward, veins bulging like willow roots, teeth grinding like millstones. "Lowly, insignificant buffoons!"

"Shush," Tudmire cautioned as he caught his irate cousin by the coattails. "They'll hear you."

"Faugh! Even if they can hear me, they lack the intellect to understand my brilliant oration!"

"Listen, Bugbear," Tudmire continued in soft, soothing tones. "My dear, dear Bugbear. You aren't thinking straight. Your mind's all askew, like a spinning coin that can't decide which side to land on. Please," Tudmire said, tugging at Bugbear's sleeve, "come sit and wait. Maybe when they're done with your tea, Loomis and his brothers will show a bit of pity and let us go."

"No," Bugbear hissed. He stared at the brutes as they feasted on his tea. And from the midst of his disordered mind, a small strand of sanity wormed its way to the surface. "I have a plan." Bugbear shook Tudmire's hand from his coat and stepped forward to confront the ogres.

"O' great merciful Lady Luck!" Tudmire gasped. "The little maniac has a plan!"

As they saw Bugbear approach, the ogres wiped the powder from their mouths. "What be you wanting? We gives no permissions for you to be movementing!"

"I was just wondering if you'd be willing to reconsider…"

"No!" Loomis barked. "Go backs over there and waits to be killt!"

Bugbear turned to Tudmire. "You were right, cousin," he said. "They aren't interested in negotiating. But, I suppose we can at least take consolation in the fact that they'll never find where we hid the Treasure of Eglwys Cacynen!"

The ogres stared at Bugbear with mouths agape. "What Treasure of… whatever it was you just says?"

"Yes," Tudmire said, his loose face tightening with delight, "what Treasure of Eglwys Cacynen?"

"Oh, you remember, cousin," Bugbear continued. "The vast horde of goblin wealth that we hid away before we were captured."

"We never…"

"Of course you remember. Gold coins. Rubies. Sapphires. Emeralds. And the magical cauldron. Certainly you remember the magical cauldron."

"Be showing us your gobling treasures," Loomis demanded. He cast aside the tin of tea as he and the other two ogres lumbered forward.

Bugbear eyed the fallen tin with drooling desire… but then remembered himself and his clever plan. "Oh, dear," he sighed. "I've given away our secret, cousin. What a fool am I. Can you ever forgive me?"

"Well, I… I… I," Tudmire stammered.

"Yes, of course you can," Bugbear continued. "Anyhow, the treasure is right over there." Bugbear pointed to a hollow log laying alone in a stream of moonlight.

"Be fetching it for us," Loomis demanded.

"I should say not," Bugbear said. "Tudmire and I strained our weak little bodies severely enough putting it there. I don't believe we could handle any more such exertion. No. Moving treasure is an honor reserved for those strong enough to bear it. Goblins are better suited for standing back in awe."

"Yes," Loomis agreed. "That making senses. You heard the little gobling, boys. Let's be bearing our honors."

Dubbin shambled over to the cousins. "I be watching these maggots. They may still be filled with more trickeries."

"Good thoughting," Nigel said.

Loomis and Nigel confronted the log, like cautious, scavenging animals hovering before some unknown carcass.

"Puts your handses in there," Loomis ordered. "Sees if the gobling is truthful."

"I tain't putsing my handses in there!" Nigel balked. "There coulds be nasty anermals in it! Log lizards, and wood winkies, and rot weasels, and such!"

"Bah!" Loomis scoffed. "Baby babble! There be nothings in there to be afraidness of!"

"Then you puts your handses in," said Nigel.

Loomis' face curdled with anger. "No! I is the eldest brother! I is the rules maker! And I is making a rule right now! You is putsing your handses in the log to be getting our treasures!"

Nigel grumbled, but as he saw Loomis' massive hand knotting into a fist, he seemed to rethink his opposition. "Well, seeings as how you've mades it a rule and all…"

Nigel wallowed on his stomach as his burly arms reached and clawed and clambered inside the rotting hollow log. "Best be thinkering up some newer rules, boss," he said. "If there are treasures in there, they 'tisn't cooperating with me handses."

Loomis turned to Bugbear, his tiny eyes glowing red. "Why 'tisn't he able to be pulling out the treasures?"

Bugbear shook his head. "Obviously because someone needs to be pushing it to him from the other side."

"Ah!" Loomis gasped with joyous revelation. "Ah! Very cleverly! Yes! This log shall not be outsmartsing us this day!"

"But it's night," Nigel corrected.

"Shuts up with you!" Loomis snapped. "Back to your reachings. I be pushering from the other ending."

And so Nigel returned to his wallowing and turning and straining, while Loomis mirrored him at the other end of the log. Their legs beat the ground as they toiled against the troublesome log, struggling to retrieve their elusive prize.

"Oh!" Bugbear exclaimed. "Oh, they're almost there. Yes. Almost. If only someone had the strength to just give them a right good shove. Oh, but where to find such a someone? Where in all this endless woods?"

"I be someone," Dubbin said.

"Why, yes! Yes you be… uhm… are," Bugbear replied. "But my question is, are you strong enough to push them far enough in to where they can get the treasure?"

"Bah," Dubbin answered. "I be winning the Con Courian County skull crackery two years running, I be." Dubbin pointed to several large bumps atop his head. "Sees them? They's my trophy lumps. No one cracks their skull as well against hard things as I does. Not even Loomis."

"Very impressive," Bugbear said. He addressed Tudmire. "Cousin, I believe we have found our someone."

Tudmire looked to his cousin with a face all skewered up in confusion.

Bugbear smiled. He liked it when only he knew what he was thinking. "Well then, dear champion, I suggest you get to cracking that skull of yours against your brother's backside."

Dubbin nodded like a dumb animal being praised by its master. "Yes. Cracking I will go." The ogre set himself into a solid, charge-ready stance. His breath pouring from his mouth like smoke from a dwarven furnace, he rubbed his feet into the earth for leverage. And then he charged, his considerable bulk a blur of motion as he rammed his lumpy, distorted head into Nigel's backside. There was a great splintering of wood, a great movement of earth, and a great howling of ogres.

"Who be shovering his head up me arse?" Nigel bellowed in a muffled rage.

"I be helpering you finding the treasure," Dubbin groaned, his head wedged inside the log next to his brother's rear.

"Moronics!" Loomis cursed as he found himself jammed inside the log and up against a tree.

"Ha ha!" Bugbear laughed. "Delightful! Delightful!" Like a drunken acrobat he skipped and danced and pranced his way to Loomis and plucked the scroll from the ogre's back pocket. "An excellent manipulation of events!"

"Bugbear, you bloody fool!" Tudmire cursed. "With those big oafs wedged into the log, we'll never be able to get the treasure out!"

Bugbear sighed... sighed in the way that very intelligent folk sigh when confronted with the ranting of very unintelligent folk. "History lesson, cousin." He sauntered over to his scattered belongings and commenced gathering them. "Eglwys Cacynen was a goblin monastery founded ages ago by the venerable Whittlegrip. Legend has it that this order developed a new philosophy based upon the concepts of Non-Logic. They studied bees in particular." He held the bee jar aloft and stared at its prisoner with wide-eyed delight. "Bees, cousin. Creatures that defy logic. They fly even though their fat little bodies are disproportionate to their flimsy little wings. The old tales say that Whittlegrip and his monks actually discovered the secret of the bees... how they use a rotating rather than vertical wing motion to stay aloft. From this startling discovery, Whittlegrip developed the four basic precepts of Non-Logical Thought, which can never be repeated enough. *Number one: Reality is Thought. Number two: Logic restricts Thought and thus restricts Reality. Number three: Abandon Logic, abandon restriction. And number four: Unrestricted Thought equals unrestricted Reality!* It is said that he even performed a series of successful experiments proving these precepts. But then unknown forces rose against the monks and destroyed their ranks. And the knowledge was lost... for a time. But I have taken up the search for this forgotten science! And I am on the verge, dear cousin. Soon I shall rediscover the lost Treasure of Eglwys Cacynen! Do you hear me, Tudmire?" Bugbear found empty air his answer. "Tudmire?"

Bugbear turned about to see his cousin sitting in a patch of moonlight, picking coppers from the ground. "Forty-five. Forty-six. Forty-seven..."

"Bah!" Bugbear grumbled, trying to manage his armful of scholarly treasures. A dull metal skittering met one of his footfalls. "Oh dear!" he cried. "My precious tin of tea!" He fell upon the ground, scattering all but his bee jar as he groped blindly through the dark. "Where is it? For the love of sanity, where is it?" His fumbling fingers fell upon the cold metal edges of the tin. "Ah, my medicine!" he sighed. He tucked the jar beneath his arm and ran a finger along the inside of the tin. "Just enough for one dose." Trembling, he brought the ambrosia-laden finger to his mouth.

From the pile of belongings at Bugbear's feet, the scroll crackled with luminance once more. And once more Bugbear fell back, scattering his remaining tea to the night winds and shattering his jar upon a rock. The bee was free. "My tea! My bee! My tea! My bee!" the goblin screeched.

Tudmire looked up from his copper collecting. "What's that you say? Oh! You've lit up that paper again, have you? Excellent! I can see more coppers now!" And he returned to his greedy endeavor.

"Tea or bee?" Bugbear muttered to himself. "Tea or bee? Which is the most important? Which shall I search for first? Only time for one! The tea or the bee! The tea or the bee!" His head turned from side to side, like the pendulum of a tightly wound clock.

Suddenly in the unearthly glow, Bugbear caught the flitting flight of a small form. With the grace of an airborne ballerina, the bee settled upon the edge of the scroll. Using great caution and care, Bugbear picked up the arcane parchment, gently lifting the bee to meet his gaze. It perched there, waving its antennae, and looking to him with endless honeycomb eyes. The bee brought its forelegs together, almost as if in prayer. And then the parchment exploded.

Light scattered in every direction. The entire world was engulfed in luminance. Bugbear could feel the earth beneath his feet trembling and shuddering as though it was alive... and very, very afraid.

Wave after wave of golden and white lights lapped over, under, and into each other. The sky thundered with primal force, ripping and re-forming, collapsing and growing. It seemed as though the world was ending. Or perhaps it was just beginning.

"What is all this noising?" Loomis barked from the log. "What mischiefs be you tricksterers confoundering out there?"

"Cousin!" Bugbear yelled as he peered into the blinding white and gold maelstrom, "can you hear me?"

"Yes," came Tudmire's timid reply.

"This scroll has done something! I don't know exactly what, but chances are we won't live through it! And before we die, I wanted you to know something..."

"What's that?"

"This is all your fault!"

The lights swirled a few moments more, separated into sparkling grains, and danced away upon the winds. The thunder dwindled into soft, lazy rumbles. And the earth settled once again into its unmoving stance.

Bugbear shook the stupor from his head. Slowly his eyes focused and he again became aware of the forest and the night. The parchment glowed ever so faintly in his hands, and as the bee took to flight, the light died completely. "Whatever it was, it's over," Bugbear gasped.

There came a splintering sound. *C-c-c-cr-aaaac-c-c-ket!* And then there came vengeful voices. "Your trickeries travail you not anymore, little goblings! Soon breaking free we will be!"

Bugbear took up as many of his belongings as he could shovel into his stunted arms. "Tudmire! Enough of this dawdling! We must run!" He scurried into the brush.

Tudmire sprang after his cousin, and soon the goblins were scrambling through the thickets and briars.

"What happened back there?" Tudmire asked.

"I don't know," Bugbear admitted. "Some kind of luminous display, I suppose. Maybe a freak electrical storm. Maybe..."

"Maybe it was magic!" Tudmire gasped.

"Again with the magic? Nonsense! All phenomenon have a scientific explanation, Tudmire! This one just takes a bit more thought is all."

"It's magic," Tudmire said.

"I swear if you say that word one more..." Bugbear stopped. He glanced about the forest. "Wait a moment. This isn't the way to the village." He looked up to the night sky. "The village is west and..." Bugbear's words stuck in his throat.

"And what?" Tudmire asked, looking about in confusion.

"By Pappersnap's toe trimmings! The stars are all out of place!"

"What? That's ridiculous! Stars don't just up and bloody move willy-nilly. Unless they're magic, that is."

Bugbear felt impossibilities ricocheting through his head. "I can even make out stars that don't exist! Madness! Madness! We're lost beyond lost, cousin! Stranded in a strange land!"

The sounds of falling trees and harsh voices shook the goblins to alertness. "We are free, we are! And now you be dead, you be!"

"Time enough for stargazing later!" Tudmire said. He grabbed his cousin by the collar and pulled him into action.

Bugbear ran, as did his thoughts... skimming through a fog, dancing in the twilight, tripping along dusty roads. This was not the world as he knew it. And as he felt the scroll warm and throbbing in his hand, he could not help but think, "*Magic?*"

CHAPTER 2
THE MAGNIFICENT MANCHESTER

Puh-tack! Puh-tack!

It must be raining, Martin Manchester thought as the warm droplets splattered upon his cheek, semi-waking him from his slumber. Funny. He did not remember seeing any clouds before he made camp. No matter. He pulled his bedroll over his head and rolled over with a sleepy sigh.

He considered retiring to the warmth and dryness of his caravan. But he had spent his entire life inside. From his sickly childhood spent in bed, to his wasted adulthood spent in his father's tobacco shop, always he had been inside. Human beings were not meant to be confined in such unnatural ways.

Puh-tack!

Another splatter.

Now finally he followed his dream... a dream that was born the day his Uncle Theodore, the traveling vaudeville magician, visited for Thanksgiving. Oh, he was a colorful character! Full of wild stories and ribald jokes! And he taught young Martin tricks... card tricks mostly, but they were enough to ignite his imagination and stoke his ambitions.

Puh-tack!

Manchester floundered beneath his covers.

Then last month, when word came that Uncle Theodore had died, the old feelings and dreams welled up once again. He knew that he had to get away. He had to finally leave his sickbed and experience the world as Theodore had. His father offered to buy him a train ticket to Addison, as that was world enough for him. But Manchester needed more.

Puh-tack!

Confounded rain!

Uncle Theodore had left his magic tricks, vaudevillian supplies, caravan, and mule to Manchester. That was enough to set the plan in motion. This was 1899, the cusp of the new century... the last century of the millennium! What exciting new discoveries and wonders there would be! An entire new realm of experiences opened up to Manchester! It did not matter that he had no performances scheduled, no dates confirmed, and no contracts signed. It only mattered that for the first time in his life, he had a life.

Puh-tack! Puh-tack!

Blast and bother!

"What 'tis it, Loomis?" a coarse, rumbling voice asked.

A thin whisper of fear twined through Manchester's body. Slowly he lowered his bed roll and turned about to find the source of this voice.

Puh-tack! Puh-tack!

They drooled over him. Twisted, nightmare faces, etched with deep lines and painted with distortion. That is what Manchester saw.

Puh-tack! Puh-tack!

"Too tall to be a dwarf, Dubbin," the largest nightmare said. "Too ugly to be an elf. Too scrawny to be one of us."

"Maybe it being some newly hatched dragon," another offered, pointing to Manchester's bedroll. "Sees how its tails wormses out from its? Asks its something."

"What should we be asking it, Nigel?"

"Asking it if it's seeing a pair of gobling runtses."

One of the creatures pulled itself up into a dignified posture and addressed Manchester. "Please to be telling us, O' wise dragon hatchling, but hast thou fort seen a duo of gobling scalawags?"

"Coo!" one of the other nightmares exclaimed. "Loomis! But the way you talks! Just likely some fairy noble folkses, I declares!"

"Shush with your gusherings, Dubbin!" the leader commanded. "You be offendering the dragon with your crass behaviors!"

The trio of terrors hovered over Manchester. *Puh-tack. Puh-tack.* The light from the campfire danced about the rough, inhuman lines of their faces. Ghastly lumps spotted their bodies and coarse hairs sprouted from them in unruly patches. As Manchester looked upon these monstrosities something dreadful and primeval awoke in his brain, as though he looked through a dirty, distorted window onto a world long forgotten. And he wished he had left his foolish dreams of travel and adventure buried beneath his fears and anxieties where they belonged.

"I'm a simple traveling magician," Manchester sputtered, pulling his bedroll up to his chin and shrinking away from the putrid, steam engine breath of his tormentors. "Take my donkey. Take my wagon. Take whatever you like. Just don't hurt me."

"Now, listens, goodly Sir Dragon," Loomis started, "we doesn't want no donkeys, nor no wagons, nor no nothing else you gots. We wants two gobling thieverous greaselings, that's be all, and nothing mores."

Dubbin grabbed Loomis by the ear. "Isn't dragons supposedly more boldly acting in behaviors? This one cowers like a flange-lipped buttertoad in the midstle of a wourmboggle's nest."

The third creature grabbed Loomis by the other ear. "He saids something abouts being into magicals and simple travails."

"Well," Loomis said, "let's be getting our answers direct from the dragon's mouth." He turned to Manchester. "'Tis you or 'tisn't you a dragon?"

"'Tisn't," Manchester whimpered from beneath his covers.

"What is it thens? It ain't nothing we ever seens before."

"And you knows what that be meaning, Nigel," Loomis said. "We gots to kills it."

"Kills it!" Manchester blurted as he threw off his blanket and scurried backwards. "I haven't done anything to you! Just leave me alone! Leave me alone!"

"Nothings personals, monster," Loomis said. "It be ogre law to kill what's different. Keeps things simple for us. Not as much things to be remembering, understands."

"Then can we eats its donkey?" Nigel asked. "That gobling's powder ain't filling me ups too goodly."

"A dream," Manchester gasped. "It must be a dream. No. A nightmare. Wake up, Martin. Wake up. This never happened. You're at home, working in your father's tobacco shop. Safe, secure, and miserable. Wake up."

"What's he on about?"

"Must be addlepated," Loomis replied. "All the more reasoning to be putsing the poor thing outs of its miseries."

The monsters hovered over him, swaying like trees in an October wind. Flickering red thoughts erupted through Manchester's head. He was waylaid by images of himself finally bursting from his awkward, middle age cocoon in a wild display of strength and courage. But these were lies concocted by an over-active imagination held captive in an under-active life. Manchester let out an odd string of syllables he hoped would somehow protect him. But the mallet-like fists raised high and prepared to strike.

"Oh dear!" a voice cried from a few feet away. "It seems our ogre friends have found a new playmate! How terribly sad for us."

"Wha's that?" Loomis said, pulling away from his intended slaughter. "Soundsing like one of them runtses!"

"Oh, yes indeed!" the voice continued. "And I'm hiding right here!"

"Where's that?" Dubbin snapped.

"Here," the voice answered. "Safely hidden in the campfire."

"I gets the little booger!" Nigel exclaimed as he lunged towards the campfire. The brute reached into the flames, digging and scrounging for the source of the ridicule. "Here he be!" Nigel proclaimed as he held aloft a burning log, the flames crawling up his sleeve and spreading ever so quickly about his body.

"Ignoranormous!" Loomis cursed. "That gobling done trickered you! Now you be all on fired and a frightful sights at thats! Dropping that log and rolling on the dirts afore you be all incinderated or some such foolerness!"

Nigel did as told, falling upon the ground and rolling about until the flickering tongues of fire were extinguished. He then sat upright, his skin all bubbled and blackened, bulging and blistered.

"Ha ha!" the voice taunted. "What great sport you ogres are! To think you'd fall for such an obvious deception when any fool could tell we were hiding inside Loomis all along!"

"Ah!" Dubbin said. "You's out-clevereds youselfs, gobling! Now we knows your where accounts!" Dubbin leapt upon Loomis, a delirious glint in his black eyes.

"Stops with you!" Loomis commanded. "More trickeries!"

The protests dwindled into muted gurgles as Dubbin reached down the elder ogre's throat. "Coming outs, you be, dastardous goblings!" Dubbin shouted. "Not sportsing to be cowerings in my brother's innards!"

Manchester recoiled. He almost preferred that the brutes had pounded him into the hereafter, rather than to have to endure such a disturbing spectacle. He inched away, his unblinking eyes never leaving the embattled ogres. He became aware of his wagon off to the side. A nervous instinct sent him rolling beneath it. There perhaps, he hoped, he could hide from the insanity.

There was a buzzing, at first close, then distant, then close once more. *A bee*, Manchester thought. What a wonderfully mundane threat! He almost laughed as it lit upon his nose. There was something familiar, something real, something sane about its tickling crawl and wispy fuzz upon his skin. *Sting me*, Manchester thought. *Sting me so that I might be shaken back into the real world once more. Sting me so that physical pain erases emotional pain. Sting me.*

"Hold very still," a voice whispered beside Manchester, "or else you might get stung."

Keeping his head stationary, Manchester glanced to the side. He saw naught but the open end of a glass jar easing towards him. "Who are you? What are you doing with that jar?"

"I'm trying to catch my bee," the voice replied. "Hope you don't mind, but I borrowed the jar from your wagon. It's in the name of science, understand."

Manchester could only stare in cross-eyed worry as the jar closed over his nose. The stranger slid it downward, gently inching the bee to the tip of the nose, until finally the insect flew into the jar. A stubby hand quickly snapped on a lid.

"Excellent," the voice hissed. "Back where you belong, my little pet."

Manchester slowly turned his head, as though it moved upon rusty gears,. Then he saw it... an imp. It crouched there beside him, clutching the jar and grinning with a mouth that seemed to cover its entire face.

"Back where you belong," the imp tittered. "By the by," it said as it turned to Manchester, "you may call me Bugbear. You wouldn't happen to have any banderberry root tea, would you?"

"I won't stand for this madness any longer!" Manchester yelled. He bolted from beneath the wagon, a rage boiling from his mouth.

"Blimey!" Dubbin exclaimed as he pulled his arm from his brother's throat. "That there hatchling's got hisself in a terriblous tempering!"

Loomis coughed and sputtered, his face flushed with rage and discomfort. "No more wasterings of our times on this foolershness," he spat. "Kills everything what movements!"

Manchester took up a heavy stick. "You'll kill nothing!" he yelled. "You'll leave! Leave, do you hear me?" He rushed at the trio of monsters, waving them back with wild swings of the stick.

"It's gone nasterous on us, Loomis," Nigel said. "It be scaring me with its mean talkings."

"Relax boys," Loomis said as he recovered his breath. "Whatever this creachture be, it only be one."

Manchester's demented cackle echoed through the night air. "Yes, indeed! I am *one! One* fed up human being who wants his sanity back! And I'm going to start by clearing out a few hallucinations!"

Manchester laid the stick aside Dubbin's lopsided head with a great thud. Manchester followed with a thrust to Nigel's groin and a crack to his chin.

As the two ogres sat upon the ground in moaning heaps, Manchester glared at Loomis, patting the heavy stick in his hand. "Step right up, Mister Loomis. There's plenty left for you!"

Loomis cowered. He bowed his head and whimpered and winced. "Leaves it alone, boys," he whispered to his trembling brothers. "There's something t'ain't right with it. Could be rabid or some such nasterousness!"

The ogres stumbled into the forest, spouting cries of terror.

Manchester followed his enemies. He did not know why. He simply did. His head throbbed, crowded with anger and delirium. *Run!* the nervous needle-like voice cried from the far corners of his mind. *Run! And never stop!* And he may well have never stopped... if only he had paid a little less attention to the voice inside his head, and a little more attention to the ditch beneath his feet.

CHAPTER 3
TOO MUCH PEPPER

"A what?" Tudmire said as he stirred a pan of eggs over the campfire.

"A human," Bugbear replied. "That's the only thing it could be. I mean, look at it. Tall. Awkward. Ugly. Just like the legends say."

"Think it'll live?"

Bugbear squinted. The gray light of an early dawn made it difficult to see clearly. He bent down to check the dressing on the unconscious human's head-wound. As his fingers pressed against the skull, the creature stirred and moaned. "I imagine so."

"Seriously though, it can't be a human. They aren't real. Just bedtime stories."

"Not necessarily," Bugbear said. "In my search for the secrets to Non-Logical Thought I have come upon certain documents containing references to goblin and human interaction. I've even acquired a partial manuscript detailing the exploits of Whittlegrip and a human knight known as Sir Reginald."

"Well then," Tudmire said as he nibbled a bit of egg, "why haven't we seen his like before?"

Bugbear stroked his chin as thoughts swirled through his head. "The legends say that humankind left our world for a distant land of milk and honey that can only be visited in dreams. Of course, we have no scientific proof to support this, but there is usually at least some truth to every legend. Perhaps the humans did leave our reality for another."

"That still doesn't explain how he got here," Tudmire said. "How do you want your eggs?"

"As for the eggs, runny in the middle," Bugbear replied. "And as for how he got here," Bugbear pulled the mysterious tattered scroll from his coat pocket, "who's to say we haven't gotten there? Remember how the stars seemed all out of place last night. Perhaps it is not the stars, but we who are out of place." He motioned to a stack of books discovered in the human's wagon. "And these books seem to document and detail certain flora and fauna. Much of what I've been able to pick and postulate indicates that his world is very similar to ours. Strangely enough after viewing some of their maps, it appears these humans even have their own equivalent of Tamarack Mountain, one of our more sacred sites. Of course, I'm just speculating that from the illustrations, as I can't exactly read any of these strange scribbles. How odd that we can somehow understand the creature's spoken language yet not his written. Perhaps it is a side effect of the strange phenomenon was that caused all of this."

Tudmire looked about at the trees, birds, clouds. His eyes rolled about in his head, and the corners of his mouth turned downward with uncertainty. "I don't know as I care much for the idea of there being more than one world." He grumbled and turned back to his cooking. "Grab a plate. Eggs are done."

Bugbear chuckled as he took up one of the odd metal plates they had found in the stranger's wagon. "Well, whoever is wherever," he said as he shoveled a good portion of eggs onto his plate, "that strange phenomenon last night had something to do with it. Some kind of dimensional transference I'd wager."

"I don't care what world we're on, as long as there's a good card game nearby," Tudmire said. "I have to make up for those coppers I lost."

Bugbear scarcely heard his cousin's mutterings. He had turned his attention to the supposed human, looking at the contours of his alien face and the length of his awkward, monstrous body. Something about him seemed familiar. Not quite the familiar of *'Have we met before?'* but more like the familiar of *'What is your face doing in my mind and how long has it been there?'* The long gangly limbs, the mop of curly black hair, the large comical nose, and the neatly trimmed beard and mustache were fairly new to Bugbear. It was the bearing, aura, and presence of the creature that initiated the discomfort.

"Daydreaming, cousin?" Tudmire said leaning into Bugbear's view.

"Yes!" Bugbear trumpeted. "Yes! The dreams! That's where I've seen him before!"

He scurried over to the unconscious man. While he examined the creature, Bugbear's body twitched like a nervous bug on a griddle. Dimly recalled images stumbled before his mind's eye. "He's somehow important. Yes. Important."

Tudmire placed a gentle hand upon Bugbear's shoulder. "Take it easy, lad. We'll find a chemist soon. Set you up with your medicine."

Bugbear turned about to face Tudmire. He felt a fullness in his head... too many things trying to be thought at once. "I... I'm sorry. I seem to have forgotten myself. Silly nightmares are starting to spill over into my reality now. How embarrassing."

"You said you had seen this human in your dreams?"

"No," Bugbear replied. "No, that would make them divinations rather than dreams. And I will have no part of that." Bugbear pushed the more discomforting thoughts from his mind, leaving only his self-deceptions to reign. He ran his fingers along his lapels and straightened his jacket. "I am a scholar, not a prophet."

A low moan arose from the human. The goblins snapped to nervous alertness.

"He's waking," Bugbear said. "Best to stand back. If his reaction to the ogres last night is any indication, he may become violent."

The goblins backed away a few paces and watched the human stretch and moan. Quaking, quivering, he placed a hand to his head and winced. He then rubbed his eyes, and before long he inched his way upright, sitting and blinking in the rays of the morning sun. "What a horrible day to be alive," he whispered.

"How much do you suppose we could sell him for?" Tudmire wondered aloud.

"Silence!" Bugbear commanded.

The goblins looked back to the human, who by this time had seen them. He stared at the cousins, his face fixed with a blank, pale expression. He sighed and lowered his head into his hands. "Hallucinations," he gasped.

"Bah!" Bugbear snorted. "Let's be off then. He's well enough, and obviously not very inclined for conversation."

"Would you like some eggs?" Tudmire asked, holding the plate towards the human. "They're scrambled. You seem like the scrambled type."

The human peeked through his fingers. He pulled his hands down his face until they reached his chin. "Yes," he said. "I would like some eggs. Thank you."

Tudmire handed the plate to the human, and the human received it with a crooked, partial smile.

"My name's Tudmire. And the more disagreeable one here, he's my cousin Bugbear. You'll have to excuse him. He's been sick."

"There's nothing wrong with me that returning to my work won't cure! Now leave the human alone and let's be off!"

"What's your name?" Tudmire asked the human.

"Martin Manchester," he answered as he spooned a portion of eggs into his mouth. "Pah!" He spat the eggs upon the ground. "Too much pepper!"

"Too much pepper?" Tudmire balked. "Of all the..."

"He's right," Bugbear interrupted. "You do use too much pepper. Now, will you leave this Manchester fellow be? He's been through enough, and we have to be on our way."

"On our way to where?" Tudmire said. "We don't even know if we're on our own bloody world or not! You said so yourself!"

"Don't talk back!" Bugbear thundered. "Let's go!"

"Think for a second, cousin. If we've fallen into Manchester's world, we'll need his help getting about. And if Manchester's fallen into our world, he'll need our help getting about. So, let's just suppose we've fallen into each other's worlds and help one another out until we find out exactly which world we're in."

"Not only is that a preposterous thought," Bugbear said, "but you ended it with a preposition."

"What are you talking about? Falling into other worlds?" Manchester asked.

"That's what we've figured," Tudmire said. "Either you've fallen into our world, or we've fallen into yours."

Manchester scratched his head. "The last I knew this was the planet Earth in the year 1899 A.D."

"And the last we knew," Tudmire replied, "this was the world of Annwfn in the Year of the Dappled Beetle."

"And what about those big fellows? Who's world did they come from?"

"Ours," Bugbear answered. "And those big fellows just happen to be called ogres."

"*Ogres*?" Manchester said. "Then that would make you the pair they were after. *Goblings* they called you?"

"*Goblins* actually," Bugbear said. "They were ogres. We are goblins. And you are annoying! Cousin, let's go!"

Tudmire smiled a broad, bucktoothed grin. "Excuse me a moment," he said to Manchester. "Cousin," he whispered as he pulled Bugbear aside, "I think you're throwing away an opportunity here. If we're in his world, he can show us around, give us information, and introduce us to more humans. If the rest of them are as timid as he is, we'll be running the entire operation within a month. And if he's fallen into our world... well, I'm betting folks would pay good money to see a live human in captivity."

"Tudmire," Bugbear hissed as he threw his cousin's hand from his shoulder, "your capacity for greed is outweighed only by your capacity for ignorance!"

"Ignorant, am I?" Tudmire countered. "Well, you're the one who can't see beyond his own pug nose!"

Bugbear snorted as he pushed a single finger into Tudmire's chest. "I can see beyond my nose, beyond your nose, even beyond the human's ridiculously large nose! And I see trouble, Tudmire! Big trouble!" He pulled the scroll from his inside jacket pocket. "And this scroll is a very important part of it!"

Tudmire swatted Bugbear's hand from his chest and pushed his cousin back over the pile of humanly tomes. "You're an idiot!" Tudmire spat. "You have your mind in cosmic quandaries when it should be on our own survival!"

"Tudmire, your capacity for greed is outweighed only by your capacity for ignorance!"

Bugbear wallowed for a moment within the pile of paper, glaring at his cousin. His left eye widened as his right eye narrowed, giving him a deranged and sinister appearance. "You dare lay hands upon me? I should take one of these books and make you eat it! Not the same as making you eat your own words, but considering the illegible nature of this human drivel, I..." Bugbear's voice stopped as a sudden realization shoved it back down his throat. He stared at the books strewn about him. He stared at the scroll still clutched within his fist. Then he stared at Manchester.

"Do you want to fight or not?" Tudmire growled.

"Not," Bugbear whispered as he clambered to his feet and brushed past his cousin.

Manchester backed away as he saw Bugbear approach. "Stay away! You little men fight amongst yourselves! Leave me out of it or I'll unimagine you all together!"

Bugbear held out the scroll, looking up to Manchester with eyes wide in childlike excitement. "This writing! It's like the writing in your books! It's human writing! What does it say? What does it say?"

Manchester inched a tad closer, peering down at the scroll. "I can't quite make it out. It looks like Latin. I don't know Latin very well."

"Try," Bugbear said with a quivering voice. "Please try. It's very important." He offered the scroll up to him.

The human glanced at the scroll, then to Bugbear. He sighed, shrugged, and reached out to take the parchment.

In the instant that Manchester's hand took hold of one end of the scroll and Bugbear's hand yet held the other end, something happened. Inside Bugbear's brain a cold, harsh, snap echoed. The world faded from his sight and he felt himself ripped from reality and thrust into a bleak world of shades.

He hovered in a sky washed in gray streaks. Beneath him he saw a battlefield upon which two armies clashed. One army was a raging throng of animals, red-eyed and snarling. The other was an angry mob of humans, blood stained and screaming. They met with a flash of swords and claws, axes and teeth, fire and venom. Who was right? Who was wrong? There was no way for Bugbear to tell. He could only watch wide-eyed and aghast as the carnage exploded in scarlet spectacle.

Then a gray mist passed before Bugbear's eyes. The battle image faded. In a swirl of shadow a new scene emerged. Through the dim light of a stonework chamber, Bugbear saw Manchester lying upon a cold, stone altar. Shadows crept up his body, slowly engulfing him in darkness. A maiden stood off to the side, weeping over Manchester's fate, but unmoving and speechless. And as the last lick of shadow covered his stricken form, the image was befouled with an impenetrable darkness.

Moments later a bright ray of light stabbed through the ebony curtain, and a new vision was revealed to Bugbear. He saw himself in his candlelit study, sipping tea and reading his precious scholarly tomes. The horrors of his past two visions melted away as he gazed upon this beloved sight. This is the way it was meant to be, he thought. To be safe. To be content. To be a scholar. He allowed himself a small smile. But then with a rumble, a terrible tremble, the floorboards erupted and twisting black roots wrapped about Bugbear's unsuspecting double. The tendrils constricted his body, pulped his flesh, and crushed his bones. Bugbear could only watch and tremble as the roots twisted and writhed about his other self, covering him totally in a mesh of black strands. And finally when the roots unwound and pulled away there was nothing left of him... but his shadow.

"Bugbear!" Tudmire called. "Cousin!" His stubby hands gripped Bugbear about the shoulders and shook him back into reality.

"I must have had another of my spells," Bugbear gasped, as he blinked before the bright colors of the forest. "But it has passed."

"You're all right then?" Manchester asked. He approached Bugbear, his brow creased with both concern and caution.

"Yes, yes! Of course!" Bugbear snorted with a dismissing wave of his hand. "What do you take me for? Some kind of invalid?

A weakling, perhaps? Bah!" He staggered forward, his body trembling and his face drenched in sweat.

Tudmire grabbed his cousin beneath the arm to offer support. "We must find tea for you soon, Bugbear. Your seizures are getting worse."

Worse? Yes, indeed. Bugbear found these visions the worse yet by far. But what did they mean, if anything? And what of Manchester? What was his importance? Then again, what was Bugbear's own importance that he should be blessed... no, cursed... with these visions at all? The doubts and questions went through his head like wood lice burrowing through rotting wood.

"I could make out a few words from your scroll," Manchester said. "There's a lot of mention of *Reginald* and *Whistlesnip*."

Bugbear sputtered out of his confusion. "Sir Reginald and Whittlegrip?" he blurted. "This is an account of their adventures! It could be invaluable in my research! You must translate the entire scroll! You must!"

Manchester shook his head. "I can't. I don't even think it's Latin like I thought. I mean, the letters look like they're from the same alphabet. But just when I think I've got something translated, it changes. Very frustrating and odd." Manchester looked to the scroll once more, before shrugging and lowering it. "Anyway, the words I could make out don't make any sense. Something about making shadows and children fighting wars."

"Shadows," Bugbear gasped. He trembled, his knees weakened, and he collapsed into a quivering ball.

"Bugbear!" Tudmire cried. With a quickness that defied his bulky nature, the plump goblin rushed to his cousin's side. "We need to get him someplace to rest!"

"Maybe he could lie down in my wagon?" Manchester asked.

"I thought you were going to unimagine us!" Bugbear snapped as he struggled to his feet. "Well, get on with it then! I'd just as soon not exist as put up with your brainless drivel!"

"Now, Bugbear," Tudmire said, "Manchester is just trying to repay a favor. After all, you did tend to his wounds. And you did keep those ogres from ripping him apart when you used your magic."

A sheet of red anger smothered Bugbear's mind. "Tudmire!"

"Magic?" Manchester blurted. "Real magic?"

"Now see what you've done with all your blather about magic?" Bugbear spat. "No, Manchester! It's not magic at all! Now get me to your wagon for a lie down before I turn you both into toads!"

Being nearly three times Bugbear's size, Manchester had little trouble helping him along to the wagon. Bugbear would not let the human help too much though. There was a danger in letting the creature think he was somehow being useful.

"I say, Manchester," Tudmire began, "what's that say there along the side of your wagon?"

Manchester lowered his head. The words struggled from his throat, pausing and halting with partial syllables and unfinished words. He took a deep breath and finally he muttered, "*The Magnificent Manchester.*"

The irony of this title tickled Bugbear from the base of his skull to the pit of his stomach. He could not help but laugh. "Oh what a fine jest, my dear fellow!"

Manchester shrugged. "I... I thought it might sound impressive. Magicians are supposed to sound impressive."

Bugbear continued his laughing. He could not stop. But in a corner of his mind a thought stirred, its voice rising over the merriment. *You've had visions of this human,* the thought said. *You've seen him attack three ogres, alone with nothing more than a stick. You've seen that look in his eyes... that lust for excitement and adventure. Yes, he does not seem so special. But you know there is a spark... a spark, that if fanned, could light the world!*

The laughing stopped. Manchester and Tudmire boosted Bugbear up into the back of the wagon. He crawled in and sat upon the wooden floor, staring back at his two companions with suddenly blank eyes.

"There are some blankets there," Manchester said. He looked to the ground and turned away.

"Manchester," Bugbear called to him.

The magician turned back and raised his eyebrows.

"Thank you."

Manchester nodded and offered a small smile. He then shuffled his way back to the campfire.

"There," Tudmire said as he looked into the back of the wagon, "it doesn't hurt to be nice to the lad, now does it?"

"My mind has a mind of its own, cousin," Bugbear muttered.

"What?"

"It's going in so many places. So many thoughts. It's not just the visions now, Tudmire. Theories. Postulations. Calculations."

"Rest, cousin," Tudmire soothed. "Sleep and forget."

Bugbear pulled a blanket up to his chin. "I shall sleep, but I shall never forget." And he laid down in the back of the wagon, his head swimming with the flotsam of a thousand thoughts and the wreckage of a dying sanity.

CHAPTER 4
THE BARGAIN

Manchester looked over the checkerboard design scratched into the dirt. He tugged at his beard as he searched his mind for a strategy. And then he slid his small white stone to the next square.

"Oh," Tudmire said with shaking head, "bad move, m'boy. Now your last lowly white stone is in place to be taken by my big black stone! If you'd joined your three white stones together at the start of the game, you could have fended off my gray and black stones! It's like that old rhyme I told you:

White, Gray, and Black Stones
Scattered 'Cross the Board.
Now You Must Unite Them
To Become The Noggle Lord!

"Bugbear can rant all he likes about Eglwys Cacynen," Tudmire continued as he pushed his large black stone to take the place of Manchester's small white stone, "but Noggle Stones is Whittlegrip's greatest creation!"

"This Noggle Stones is a hard game," Manchester sighed. "How much do I owe you?"

"I think that brings it up to fifty coppers."

"I have a jar of pennies in the wagon," Manchester said. "I'll go fetch it as soon as your cousin is up and about." He stood up from his cross-legged position, and looked to the wagon. "How do you suppose he's doing?"

"What? Bugbear?" Tudmire said as he collected the stones and carefully put them in a pouch. "He's fine. He just has spells from time to time. Blackouts, you know. He thinks it has to do with some kind of vitamin deficiency. That's why we're looking for banderberry root tea. It seems to help him."

Manchester turned back to Tudmire. "Why haven't I ever seen any ogres or goblins up till now?"

"I don't know," Tudmire answered. "When I was younger my Uncle Crick used to tell me bedtime stories about humans all the time. I suppose humans and goblins interacted quite a bit once. Then something must have happened. Maybe they stopped believing in one another, until finally humans became myths to goblins and goblins became myths to humans. Whatever the case, such pondering is best left to scholars and philosophers like Bugbear."

"So you've never seen a human before?"

"No, m'boy. You're the first. But if the rest of your race is as bad at Noggle Stones as you, I certainly hope you're not the last!"

"There's a whole other world out there then," Manchester wondered aloud. His mind wandered through a montage of exotic images. "Goblins, ogres, dragons, elves," he gasped. "What else, Tudmire? What else is out there? What else has mankind been missing?"

"I don't know," Tudmire shrugged with disinterest. "Your guess is as good as mine. Bugbear's the one who's read up on those matters. He knows."

Manchester's eyes lit up. "And you said he knows magic too. Real magic!"

Tudmire straightened his jacket and looked to Manchester with half-closed eyes. "Oh yes! Bugbear is a fine wizard! You saw his work there last night? Setting that Nigel fellow afire, and then summoning up his familiar, that hellish bee! Oh yes! My cousin is a mighty sorcerer!"

"And my cousin is a mighty liar!"

Manchester spun about to see Bugbear hobbling towards them. "Teach me!" Manchester blurted. "Teach me magic! I'm tired of fumbling with card tricks and top hats! I want to know real magic!"

Bugbear waddled past Tudmire and Manchester and squatted at the campfire. "I don't know magic, Manchester," he sighed as he poked through the embers with a stick. "I'm a scholar and a philosopher. I study the laws of nature and try to find ways around them."

"Sounds like magic to me," Manchester said.

"That's what I told him," Tudmire added.

"No," Bugbear said with a frown. "Magic comes from rituals and chanting and other nonsense. Magic is about asking for help from spirits and gods and demons." A mad glow came into the goblin's eye. "What I do comes from me and me alone! I temper my mind with the fire of knowledge and the hammer of truth! I forge it into a perfect weapon... a sword with which to cleave the fabric of reality!" Bugbear leapt forward, poising the smoldering end of his stick at Manchester's bearded chin. "Are you truly willing to embrace such a discipline?"

Manchester looked deep into Bugbear's wide, saucer-like eyes, seeing dementia and wisdom, knowledge and ignorance, kindness and cruelty. "Yes," he replied, unflinching. "Whatever you call it... magic, philosophy, discipline... I want it. I'm tired of being a second-rate stage magician."

Bugbear pulled the stick back and let it drop to the ground. He turned away from Manchester, gazing into the flames. "Very well," Bugbear hissed. "You shall be my apprentice." The little man paused, and Manchester noticed his stunted frame shudder. "For good or ill, it seems meant to be."

Manchester found the goblin's words cryptic and foreboding. And still other pieces of his mind doubted that Bugbear and Tudmire were truly goblins at all... just four flushing little people in Vaudeville make up. Perhaps there was no magic. Perhaps these tricksters were trying to dupe him out of money, valuables, or something else.

No. No more doubts. Manchester had spent his whole life in the shadow of doubts. Now opportunity had been set before him, and no matter how unusual a package it had been wrapped in, he would accept it. And so the cautious portions of his mind were shouted down by more adventurous instincts. "Yes," Manchester said. "It seems meant to be."

"I hope you realize that as the Bugbear of the goblin race, I'm taking quite a risk by accepting a non-goblin apprentice."

"'The Bugbear of the goblin race?'" Manchester said, not quite understanding the meaning. "Does that mean that *Bugbear* is a title and not your name?"

"Yes," Bugbear said, his eyes suddenly regarding Manchester with suspicion and uncertainty. "'Bugbear' is a title I was given while studying at Ysgol Gwybod. It means that I am the official keeper of goblin wisdom and culture."

"Then what's your real name?"

Both Bugbear and Tudmire turned to Manchester... Bugbear's eyes filled with rage... Tudmire's eyes filled with concern.

"You shouldn't have asked that, m'boy," Tudmire whispered, shaking his head.

"How dare you!" Bugbear screeched as he lurched towards Manchester. "How dare you ask me my real name!"

"What?" Manchester said, backing away from the irate goblin. "What did I say that was so wrong?"

"A goblin's true name is sacred!" Bugbear exclaimed. "Even his parents do not know his true name! For a goblin's true name gives others power over him! Power to torture! Power to enslave! Power to destroy!"

"But I don't understand," Manchester protested. "You know my real name. You can't destroy or control me because of it."

"You are a mere human!" Bugbear fumed. "Goblins have a greater destiny! As the goblin playwright and historian Twistroot writes:

"With song and verse the Creator fashioned the world, and it was with special words that He brought the goblin race into His great design. For He desired a cunning and knowledgeable servant among His people. And for that He required materials outside the mundane.

"That makes us different," Bugbear continued. "For the Creator's words don't just identify us, they define us. We call this our *Cysegredig Rhwym* or *Sacred Bond*. While we take titles and nicknames for everyday interaction, it is through our Cysegredig Rhwym that we are called into life, and one day into death. And it is our Cysegredig Rhwym that shall grant us passage into the great Halls of Cymhendod. Thus a goblin must forever safeguard the word that he is!"

"I'm sorry," Manchester stammered, his brow creased with sincerity. "I had no idea that..."

"Save your apologies," Bugbear spat as he turned away and waddled toward the wagon.

Manchester watched the goblin with wide and mournful eyes. Bugbear stopped and braced himself against the wagon, a soft breeze tickling his nose with pinecone and evergreen. The goblin inhaled deeply and sighed, and with that sigh all of his rage and resentment seemed to evaporate. It was as if Bugbear's already tortured mind had no room for a childish grudge.

"I overreacted," Bugbear said, turning about with a slight smile of reconcile. "Your blunder was made out of ignorance. And that makes it all the more imperative that I begin your lessons, thus replacing your ignorance with knowledge!"

Manchester nodded in blind agreement.

"Lesson number one, my pupil," Bugbear said as he sprang to Tudmire's side. "No more gambling!" He pulled the leather pouch from Tudmire's shirt pocket and tossed it into the fire.

"No!" Tudmire screamed. "Those were my best stones! I had them handmade by a dwarf in Caer Badon!" The rotund little man rushed to the campfire. He picked and pawed at the burning logs in an attempt to recover his precious stones.

"Sorry, cousin," Bugbear said. "I can't have you distracting my new apprentice with any more of your crooked Noggle games. I have more important games to teach him."

Tudmire held up a smoldering remnant of leather. "Ruined," he snorted. "Well, fortunately I have several sets of best stones."

"Lesson number two," Bugbear said, turning back to Manchester, "*the feet of a traveler hold more wisdom than the books of a scholar.*"

Manchester cocked his head a moment. He had gotten the first point about gambling clearly enough. But what did this second one mean? Did Bugbear want him to take off his shoes? "Come again?" he asked.

The goblin sighed. "*The open road opens minds.*"

Manchester felt a tingle of shame crawling along the surface of his brain. All this talk of wanting to be more than a simple stage magician, and he had no idea what Bugbear was on about. "Sorry," he said. "I don't quite understand."

"Hitch your bloody ass up to the wagon!" Bugbear yelled.

"Oh!" Manchester gasped as the realization hit him. "You mean we should be leaving then?"

"Yes! Yes! Yes!"

Manchester's head hung low as he hitched his donkey to the caravan. He hated appearing foolish. And yet compared to such a worldly creature as Bugbear, how could he appear as anything else? All these thoughts and worries made his stomach bubble and rumble. As he fastened the last strap on the harness, Manchester looked ahead to the road, snaking through the forest like some vast, endless wrinkle on the earth's skin. Out there he would find himself. Out there he would prove himself. Out there he would reinvent himself. "Real magic," he sighed.

CHAPTER 5
MOVING RIGHT ALONG

The wheels squeaked and the wagon rocked. As he thumbed through a book on earthly flora and fauna, Bugbear felt like one of Tudmire's Noggle Stones being tossed about. Several times he almost tumbled from his perch at the front of the caravan. If not for the beautiful scenery and the beautiful day that surrounded it, he would have found the journey quite miserable.

Trees arched over the dirt road in a wide, sun spattered canopy. And along the roadside wild flowers grew in multicolored clusters. But of all things, Bugbear found the birds most soothing with their sweet songs and gentle play among the branches. It was with the birds that he found a sudden inspiration along the rough, woodland trail.

"Stop the wagon, Manchester," he ordered.

Manchester reined the caravan to a stop. "What is it?" he asked.

"Everything is connected," Bugbear began. "Typically one would believe that many things happen randomly. The wind blows. A rain cloud bursts. A leaf falls from a tree. But everything that happens, happens because something else happens first. One event is dependent upon another event. Do you understand?"

Manchester shrugged. "Certainly. Actually I'd more or less known that already."

"Yes," Bugbear said. "Of course you did. It's common knowledge. But what you don't know is that when you make yourself the first event, you then control the events to follow."

"Now you've lost me," Manchester said.

"We're lost?" Tudmire yawned as he awoke from his nap in the back of the wagon and poked his head through the front flap.

"No!" Bugbear snapped. "Now be silent! I am attempting to educate my apprentice!" He directed his attention back to Manchester. "As I was saying, the planner, the schemer, the mover controls all those things that move after he moves. And when you understand exactly how other things will react to your move, then you can perform miracles."

Bugbear jumped down from the front seat of the caravan. "Observe." He picked up a smooth, round stone. He held it in his hand, feeling its weight upon his palm and rubbing its side with his thumb. Then he threw it, straight and true into the trees. Several birds fluttered out, squawking their outrage. Then Bugbear picked up another rock, tossing it into a nearby creek. This time his action was answered by the croaking of frogs and the thumping of a beaver's tail upon a log. Next he turned to Manchester's donkey and plucked a hair from its nostril, causing the poor brute to bray. "There," Bugbear chirped. "You see what I have done?"

"You've upset a lot of animals," Manchester replied with a furrowed brow.

"No, no, no! You haven't been paying attention at all!" Bugbear shouted. "You are disobeying the four basic precepts of Non-Logical Thought, which can never be repeated enough! *Number one: Reality is Thought. Number two: Logic restricts Thought and thus restricts Reality. Number three: Abandon Logic, abandon restriction. And number four: Unrestricted Thought equals unrestricted Reality.* Thus, when you accept these four laws, you open yourself up to a whole new world that you would never know if you remained mired within the prison of logic!" Bugbear held a hand to his pointed, oversized ear. "With that in mind, listen…"

Manchester cocked his head. "There's a pattern," he observed. "The sounds are forming a pattern."

"Exactly! It's music! It's music, and I've conducted it! Every action I made was calculated! Every move was part of an intricate plan! By abandoning the restrictions of logic and by moving the first event in a series of events, I have performed a miracle! And now you hear it! A song! The birds are squawking to frighten off predators. The frogs are croaking to find out what has invaded their home. The beaver paddles the log to warn his family of danger. And your donkey brays in protest of a very cruel act on my part. My apologies." Bugbear danced about with an upraised finger. "Isolated they are simply noises. But when orchestrated by an intelligence and heard with a Non-Logical ear, they are music!"

The noises filled Bugbear with a passion he could not deny. Fire danced up and down his spine, suddenly spreading to his brain, his arms, his legs, his heart. And soon the spirited woodland music moved him to song.

> *Robin Goodfellow ran away from home.*
> *Crossed a winding creek upon stepping stones.*
> *Ate from a sack full of day old bread.*
> *Had no butter, used honey instead.*
> *Oh ho ho he's a jolly little soul.*
> *Oh ho ho listen to him crow.*
> *Urrrhurrhurrhurrhurrrr!*
>
> *One day the lad found a scroll on his stroll.*
> *Read it aloud and wonder did unfold.*
> *He conjured things from the thin of the air,*
> *Lyrical miracles beyond compare.*
> *Oh ho ho Robin runs the show.*

Oh ho ho listen to him crow.
Urrrhurrhurrhurrhurrrr!

Robin set forth upon the woodland trails,
Spreading his joy along the hills and dales.
His scroll he used for then and forever
To take what is bad and make it better.
Oh ho ho Robin's on the go,
Oh ho ho listen to him crow.
Urrrhurrhurrhurrhurrrr!

Tudmire had joined in the song as well. And even Manchester, although he obviously did not know the words, tried to contribute with a few whoops and yells.

"You see now, Manchester, how the world can be bent to the will of the mover?" Bugbear asked.

"Yes," Manchester said. "But we also were pulled into your song, weren't we? And in that sense we were as manipulated by the events you started up as the birds, or frogs, or beaver, or my donkey, weren't we?"

A burning tongue of rage licked the underside of Bugbear's brain. Manchester was right. Bugbear himself had felt the unbreakable pull of the song. There was an inherent risk when moving events of being moved oneself. Still, he did not like the idea of the student teaching the master. Manchester would have to be reminded of his place.

"Nonsense!" Bugbear exclaimed. "Your untrained psyche may have been pulled into the event, but I was never out of control! I was a willing participant in the song!" He paused momentarily to lick the sour taste of lies from his lips. "Yet, there is more to controlling reality than throwing stones and pulling nose hairs. The moving of events is the foundation upon which we build our power." Bugbear pointed to his head and gave a cryptic smile. "The power itself resides in here."

"Are we done yet?" Tudmire asked as he fidgeted with his pocket watch.

"Yes," Bugbear sighed. "The lesson is over...for now." Bugbear struggled his way back up to his seat at the front of the wagon. "Our minds have been sharpened enough for now. Time to dull them with Tudmire's dreadful stories."

"Well, I hadn't planned on regaling you with any tales of my exploits," Tudmire snorted, "but perhaps if you're more civil to me, I shall honor you with a yarn or two. After I finish my nap, that is." And the portly goblin then grumbled and retreated back to his nest in the rear of the wagon.

Manchester smiled. "Where to then?"

Bugbear stroked his chin. Thoughts and possibilities swam about his head. Finally something very appropriate settled in his forethought. "You move the event, Manchester!"

Manchester stared at Bugbear for a moment, as if the proposal somehow offended him. But then he chuckled. "Very well." And with a snap of the line he sent the donkey forward. "West is as good a direction as any when you aren't even certain what world you're on."

As he stared off into the cloud cluttered skies, Bugbear leaned back and imagined himself dancing along the woodland trails like Robin Goodfellow, making things right and feeling right about himself. And then he felt a very strong craving for tea.

CHAPTER 6
A WHISPER IN THE SHADOWS

"So I says to Putterpep, 'Putterpep, I am not about to let you out-bid me! I'll see your twelve coppers and raise you three!' And Putterpep just starts a-snorting and a-hollering something fierce! 'You got something up your sleeve, Tudmire!' he screeches!"

As the fire dwindled into a smoldering orange glow, and the night settled in around the camp, Tudmire continued his tale. "And so I says to Putterpep, 'Putterpep,' I says, 'The only thing I have up my sleeve is my arm, and it's fixing to come out and give you a sound thump on the noggin! Because this here's one goblin who can get a real mad-on over a game of Noggle Stones!'"

Bugbear had long ago curled up in a tangle of blankets and drifted off to sleep. And after suffering a few hours (or at least what seemed like hours) of Tudmire's ramblings, Manchester decided that closing his eyes and effecting a false snore might be a good way to end the ordeal all together.

"Hello?" Tudmire said. "Has everyone gone to sleep? Well, it is late after all, isn't it? I'll have to remember where I left off so I can continue the story tomorrow."

Out of the corner of his eye Manchester saw the goblin stir his bedding into a haphazard nest and settle down to sleep. After a few moments of silence, Manchester turned onto his back, and gazed up at the vast night. The stars danced against a curtain of blackness. And the moon hung in their midst, full and fat like a child's face. Perhaps sometime during this apprenticeship, Bugbear would teach Manchester about the stars and the moon and what lies beyond them.

A train whistle broke the silence. Manchester bolted to his feet. He looked to Bugbear and Tudmire who yet drowsed on. The train called again, a shrill summons from beyond the trees and thickets. With a smile Manchester trotted forth.

There were deer trails through the brush and briars, making the hike fairly uneventful. Although, there were a few snapping twigs and muted grunts that Manchester could not identify. Perhaps raccoons, or deer, or coyotes. Not likely to be anything dangerous in this part of the country. But then, there was the question of which country he was actually in at the moment. All the same, nothing hindered Manchester during his trek to the train tracks... tracks which he found concealed in the forest but a half mile from camp.

A bright light opened onto the tree-lined tracks. The train was still a few moments from passing Manchester's observation point in the brush. He felt a newly minted coin in his pocket and with a naughty child's smirk he rushed forward to place it on the track. He felt a rush of anticipation as the train grew closer. And then he felt a burst of excitement as the grinding, pumping, churning wheels pushed the steam-powered bulk onward, over the coin and into the distance.

Manchester watched as the train sped on, a jointed, iron snake twisting into the distance. He stepped onto the tracks, feeling the rumble, the power, the supremacy of the spectacular engine. The moonlight reflected off the coin. Manchester picked it up, and as he expected it was flattened and smooth, all traces of its monetary identity erased. He found the object perfect. Perfectly round. Perfectly plain. Perfectly his.

An inspiration leapt through his head. He pulled one of his magician's lock picking tools from his shoe. With a large rock as a workbench, he ground a hole near the top (or at least what he assumed had at one time been the top) of the coin. Then he removed a slender chain from his vest pocket. Once it held a charm he had won at a ring toss at the county fair. He had lost that charm long ago, but he kept the chain for many years. He never knew why, until now. He placed his precious new charm upon the chain, and then put it about his neck.

He smiled. Somehow he felt the charm represented a bold course his life would take... smooth and perfect. As the train had changed the coin into something new and exciting, so the charm would change him.

A tune whistled from his lips as he set back out upon the woodland trail. It was the little *Robin Goodfellow* ditty... or at least what he could remember of it. There was a fine feeling in the forest that night. None of the dread and foreboding one would expect in a dark woods. The owls hooted. The crickets chirped. The stars winked. And everything behaved most properly.

But then, the shadow came. Like ink spilling from a well, it oozed over Manchester's path. Terror showered his body in a thousand exploding pinpricks.

"An ogre!" he gasped.

But no. As his bulging eyes followed the shadow to its source, he saw that the creature crouching atop the ridge above him, silhouetted against the moon, was too small for an ogre. Pale eyes peered out from a darkened pumpkin head.

"Bugbear?" Manchester whispered, squinting upward against the moon's glare. "I... I just saw a train. Look." He held up the coin by its chain, feeling somewhat foolish. "It flattened this coin into a lucky charm. Do you have trains on your world?"

Silence. The pale eyes blinked once, slowly.

"Well, trains are common on my world. Do you think that's where we are? In any case, we must be getting close to a town by now, don't you think?"

The cold eyes narrowed. "Too close," the creature hissed. And then it leapt.

Manchester stumbled backwards as his attacker fell upon him, a dull whisper of wind trailing after it.

"Too close," it whispered again.

The bitter cold edge of a shovel touched Manchester's neck. He grabbed the wooden handle and tried to push it away, but the creature's strength belied its small size. It pulled the shovel back, preparing for a final, pointed lunge to Manchester's throat.

With a whiz and a thud, a silver arrow drove into the shadowed beast's shoulder. It howled, spun about, and fell back. As the fiend hit the ground, it tugged the arrow from its shoulder and threw the shimmering thing into the brush.

Manchester scurried to his feet. A glint of light dispelled bits and pieces of the darkness. He looked about like a nervous animal, attempting to pierce the obscurity. At the same time, he edged away from the cowering and wounded creature. "Is someone there?" The words strained through his sore throat.

A light willowy outline hovered near the tree-line. Manchester caught glimpses of sparkling, silver eyes... a warm, glowing face... long, dark locks... smooth, tan arms and legs.

A gentle sigh and the soft rustle of a swirling cloak signaled the brilliant figure's departure. Even the dark, squat figure had scurried off, its deep, rattling rasp trailing behind. Manchester sat in a splinter of moonlight, rubbing his hands upon his sore neck, easing away the dull pain.

A trick of the light, he suddenly decided. The moon was full. The shadows had quite a bit of room to play about this night. But then again, tricks of the light were not known to speak in such eerie voices... nor attack with cold, black shovels. A sudden dark fear ripped through him. He had to get back to camp and tell Bugbear of this nightmare encounter.

As Manchester moved his hand to brace his ascent, his fingertips grazed a long, slender object. An eerie shimmer drew his gaze to the silver arrow. He instinctively snatched it up, staring at it, a wonder and awe skittering through his chaotic thoughts. But he knew the arrow itself was not nearly as magnificent as the woman who had lost it.

The fire had almost completely died by the time Manchester returned to camp. He sat down upon his bedroll. Tudmire curled up in his blankets, mumbling in his sleep about Putterpep and his unpaid debts. And Bugbear, poor Bugbear, he shivered in the night air. He had cast his blankets aside and now lie spread out with his arms and legs twitching madly. He muttered now and then about *death* and other unpleasant things. Manchester found both of their slumbers unnerving. What manner of mad creatures had he joined up with?

A pale dawn began melting away the night. Manchester moved over to the sleeping goblins. He was not certain if it was safe to wake them or not, but soon they began stirring on their own accord.

"What are you doing up so bloody early?" Tudmire asked as he stretched and yawned.

"I went for a walk," Manchester answered, the blood rushing through his body at the excitement and terror he had to share. "I came upon a train and..."

"That was nothing compared to the dragon I heard last night!" Tudmire interrupted. "It rumbled across the earth like a thousand earthquakes and howled into the night like a pack of hungry wolves! And dragons are supposed to be extinct! If we could set a trap and catch it..."

Manchester chortled. "That wasn't a dragon, Tudmire. It was a train! I saw it! And..."

Quite suddenly Bugbear cried out as he stirred within his tangle of blankets. "Who are you?" he yelled.

"Oh dear!" Tudmire rushed to his cousin's side.

Bugbear's face contorted. Deep lines of fear and misery creased his flesh, as little beads of perspiration trickled from his forehead and his teeth ground and gnashed.

Tudmire cradled Bugbear in his arms, straining to keep the spasms under control.

Manchester stepped closer to the fitful little man and peered down at him. "Shouldn't we wake him up?"

Tudmire shook his head. "Probably best not to. Let him sleep through it. He has these all the time. And I doubt we could wake him even if we wanted to."

"I wonder what would cause him to cry out like that?" Manchester mused as more worrisome thoughts tumbled through his head.

CHAPTER 7
THE SUBMISSIVE TOAD

"The submissive toad shall swallow the vibrant bee."

The words hissed all around Bugbear, slithering through his ears and twining about his brain. He saw nothing but the darkness of a deep cavern. His nostrils filled with the heavy, acid scent of ammonia. He shivered from a damp cold that penetrated him to the pit of his stomach. Bile spilled up from his throat and washed through his mouth before receding. All of his senses fell under the attack of a dark, shadowy discomfort.

"The submissive toad shall swallow the vibrant bee," the raspy voice repeated.

"Who are you?" Bugbear gasped. His hands groped outward in a desperate attempt to meet with some form of solid reality.

"I am the hidden truth," the voice answered. *"I am that which you know and I am that which you deny. I am your only hope and I am your total doom. I am the beginning of your salvation and I am the end of your existence. Through me you shall live and for me you shall die."*

"Why?" Bugbear sobbed. "Why me?"

"By taking up the mantle of Whittlegrip, you have given yourself to me. As you study the bee, so you shall fall further and further into a destiny beyond your control. So your dreams become a reality, and so your reality becomes a dream. You have chosen the path. You must now walk it, or be hopelessly lost!"

"I just want to learn," Bugbear whined as he fell to his knees. "That's all I want."

"Knowledge has a price," the voice hissed. *"When the time comes, you shall pay for what you have received."*

A sudden rage pulled Bugbear to his feet. He raised a fist to the empty, inky blackness. "I'll pay nothing! I've earned everything I have! I do not owe you or anyone else! If anything, the world owes me!"

"*Indeed?*" the voice chuckled. "*And which world would that be?*"

Bugbear's head popped and bubbled with frustration. He shook and shivered. And finally he unleashed his anger, lunging forward into the darkness. "Stop toying with me!" he shrieked. Then with a thud, he fell to the cold, damp floor.

"*For one so little, you are full of much pride,*" the voice whispered. "*But beware. When pride is all you have, you are left with nothing once it's gone.*"

As Bugbear rose upon trembling legs, the darkness began to splinter, letting white light spill through the cracks. Soon the darkness shattered all together, spreading through the air in tiny black grains, leaving only eye-searing light. Bugbear cried out, cowering into a small heap as he covered his eyes.

"*You stand between shadow and light, Bugbear,*" the voice said. "*Choose wisely lest all existence suffer for your failure.*"

Bugbear's eyes shuttered open, blinking and squinting before the bright morning sun.

"Ah! You're awake!" Tudmire said as he squatted before the fire, poking at a pan of squiddle cakes. "And just in time for breakfast!"

"Bugbear!" Manchester exclaimed. He knelt down beside the rousing goblin. "Are you well? We heard you cry out in your sleep!"

Bugbear squeezed his eyes shut, opened them, and shook his head. "Yes," he whispered. "I'm fine. Just slept on a root."

"I told you he'd be fine," Tudmire said, as he flipped one of the squiddle cakes.

"I saw something last night, Bugbear!" Manchester said as his body quivered and a wrinkle creased his brow. "Actually several somethings. A train, first off."

Bugbear sat in a befuddled huddle. He stared at the ground, marking lazy circles with his naked big toe. "What?" he said under his breath.

"I saw a train! A human device that's powered by steam and moves along tracks."

"Yessss," Bugbear hissed as he raised his head to look at Manchester. "Dwarves use such devices. But only for mining purposes. For what purpose are your *locomotives* used?"

"They carry people and cargo across country."

"And where did you see this machine? Was it out in the open?"

"Yes," Manchester replied. "Just beyond those trees. But that's not all I saw." He ran his fingertips along his throat and winced as he swallowed. "There was a strange, little man. At first I thought it might be you or Tudmire. But he didn't reply to me when I questioned him. He only said, '*Too close,*' and attacked me with a shovel."

"What did he look like?" Bugbear asked.

"I couldn't tell," Manchester said. "He was hidden by the shadows."

"The shadows," Bugbear hissed. A blank glaze covered his face. Then with a sudden resolution, he shook himself back to sensibility. "How did you escape him? Did you fight back?"

"He was too strong for me. But someone else was there. A woman. A beautiful woman. I think she shot him," Manchester held out a bright, silver arrow, "with this."

Bugbear's eyes widened. His mind reeled. *"The draig gwraig!"* he gasped. He snatched the arrow from Manchester's hand. He ran his fingers along the elegant shaft, feeling the ornate markings, admiring the sturdy workmanship. "Do you know what this means? You were saved by one of the draig gwraig! A dragon bride! That means we must be in Annwfn! The dragon brides do not exist within the mundane!"

"But what about the train?" Manchester asked. "That's something made by humans. We must be on earth."

In a swift, fluid motion Bugbear flung the bedroll aside and rolled up to his feet. "Fetch my coat, Manchester! We shall examine the areas where you saw these phenomenon!"

"Yes, sir!" Manchester said, throwing in a sloppy salute.

The bitter broth of Bugbear's thoughts swirled about in his head, and then slipped out his mouth in a slight, wispy curse:

Not shadow nor light
Shall stand in my sight,
For from their dread curse
I quench my mad thirst!

CHAPTER 8
RIPPLES

"Here is where I met the creature," Manchester said. He paused in a small glen peppered with tiny white wildflowers and thick leafy ferns. A small, but well-worn deer trail wound through the area, twisting beyond into a tree-thickened forest. Manchester pointed to a ridge which loomed over the glen. "He was standing up there."

Bugbear cocked his head to the wind and took in a deep breath. "There is a faint scent," he said. "What do you make of it, Tudmire?"

Tudmire's bulbous nose twitched as he inhaled. As he exhaled a sour thought seemed to pucker his face. "Very goblinish, yet not quite."

"That's what I thought," Bugbear agreed. "What could it be then? What is a goblin, yet not a goblin?"

Manchester voiced the thought which had quite suddenly leapt into his head: "Perhaps it is something pretending to be a goblin?"

"Ah!" Bugbear exclaimed with a wide grin. "Yes! Very good, my apprentice! You are beginning to think Non-Logically! But an even more Non-Logical assumption would be that it's a goblin pretending to be something else!"

"Something else?" Manchester said. "Like what?"

"Difficult to say," Bugbear replied. "But if we are to assume that it is a goblin pretending to be something else, we must also assume that we are in Annwfn rather than your world."

"But what about the train?"

"Ah yes! Where did you see that?"

"There are some tracks up ahead," Manchester replied.

"Lead on, apprentice!"

Manchester offered an uncertain smirk as he moved forward through the small thickets, briars, and bushes. What if when they came upon the tracks, Bugbear discovered that the train was a dwarvish invention after all? That would mean Manchester was on some alien world. True, he had Bugbear and Tudmire to guide him and help him survive. But never to see one of his own kind again, never to walk through a human city again, nor to hear a human voice again, never to... Manchester paused in his thoughts. He chuckled lightly to himself as he suddenly realized he did not care if he ever saw one of his own kind again, or walked through a human city again, or heard a human voice again. He now found the company of goblins much more exciting.

The trio broke through the thickets and into the tree-lined path where the train tracks stretched. "This is where I saw the train," Manchester said.

Bugbear squatted. One eye squinted almost shut as the other eye bulged wide open. He bent down over the tracks, scanning back and forth in a rhythmic, almost machine-like manner. "Not sturdy enough to be of dwarf-make. Too plain as well. Not a single rune."

"Then it's human-made?" Manchester said. "We're on Earth?"

Bugbear stood up and brushed the dirt from his knees. "Of that I'm not certain," Bugbear replied. He pulled the arrow from his vestments. "There is this to consider as well. It certainly isn't of your Earth. The draig gwraig are a fey race, created and groomed by the dragons themselves! Even on my world these warrior maidens are rare creatures. And when they do make themselves known, it is usually to interfere in the affairs of others. Consider yourself fortunate the wench did not see fit to do away with you as well!"

"Do you think we'll see her again?" Manchester asked.

"Not likely," said Bugbear. "No doubt she is trying to sort her way through this madness just as we are. She is probably just as alarmed at having saved you as you are at being saved."

"So if the train is human-made, and the dragon bride is from our world, then where in blazes are we?" Tudmire asked. "Are we on Earth, or are we on Annwfn?"

"I'm developing a theory on that," Bugbear said. "Follow me and I'll explain."

Bugbear led Manchester and Tudmire along the winding deer trail and into the forest. Manchester looked about at the tree limbs which arched overhead, the twigs which snapped underfoot, and the birds which flitted here and there. It must be Earth, he thought. Everything seemed so familiar, so normal. And yet he noticed too that it all seemed somehow brighter and starker when contrasted with his memories of what should be normal. It could be the Otherworld. Or it could be a trick of the light, like the shadowy figure of last night. Sometimes Manchester thought everything was a trick of the light. It seemed to make more sense than believing in things of which one was uncertain.

"Here," Bugbear said as he paused at the edge of the pond near their campsite. "Watch this." The little man picked up a smooth round stone.

"You aren't going to start upsetting a bunch of frogs and beavers again, are you?" Tudmire said.

"Bah! Nonsense! I am attempting to explain my theory, if you would but give me a moment!" Bugbear let the stone fling into the water. The smooth surface broke into a ripple. "There! You see that ripple?"

"Yes," Manchester said. "What of it?"

"For the sake of argument, let us assume that ripple is your world, Manchester. Now..." Bugbear took up another stone, casting it in the exact same spot as the previous one. A second ripple appeared following the same pattern and movement of the first. "Let us assume that second ripple is my world. Tell me what you see."

"Your ripple, er... world, is mingling with mine."

"Exactly! They are becoming one! And that is what is happening! We are neither on Earth, nor Annwfn! We are on both!"

"That's just plain loony!" Tudmire blurted. "How can two worlds be in the same bloody place?"

"Perhaps because they were always meant to be in the same place!" Bugbear offered. A small throat-clearing and a great ceremonial posturing then heralded a most dramatic reading from the goblin:

In ages long passed
Two houses once clashed
In a dreaded bloody war.

These battles were wrought
Through treacherous plot
Of a hidden demon-lord.

Till one day arose
Two lords to oppose
The dread demon's wicked snares.

They rallied the good
And steady they stood
Before the shadowed terrors.

With quill put to scroll
They took the earth whole
And sundered it in twain

Till Whittlegrip's pride
And Reginald's tribe
Shall make it whole again.

Bugbear presented a self-satisfied smirk. "One of the more lyrical passages of the Whittlegrip fragment in my possession! And yet more evidence for my brilliant theory!"

"You must still be in one of your fits, cousin!" Tudmire snorted.

"Think about it, you intellectual insect!" Bugbear protested. "Think about the shared cultures! Manchester has heard of goblins and ogres before through legends. We ourselves have legends of human and goblin interaction with Whittlegrip and Sir Reginald! Now that we know humans exist and Manchester knows we exist, we can assume that at some point in the past Earth and Annwfn were one world, and now they are one once more!"

"But how and why?" Manchester asked.

"Both how and why are here," Bugbear said as he removed the mysterious parchment from his vestments and gripped it tightly in his hand. "This scroll has something... *everything*... to do with this! I now believe it is the very scroll mentioned in the verse. If we could only translate it, all our questions would be answered! But alas, we have no way of translating it as of yet. In the meantime, in lieu of the questions *how* and *why*, I believe I have the answer to *where!*" The goblin reached into the oversized pockets of his coat and removed two tattered maps. "I took the liberty of looking through a few of your books and maps whilst you were recovering from your spill the other night, Manchester. And I discovered something very interesting. This is a map of the region as it is in your world. Along side it you will note a map of the region as it exists in my world. Tell me, does anything in particular stand out?"

"This scroll has something... everything... to do with this!"

Manchester looked over the maps, his eyes scouring the details and patterns, the lines and shapes, the markings and colors. He pointed back and forth between the maps. "There are two features that are the same. That mountain there. It's called Tamarack Mountain on my world."

"Excellent!" Bugbear cried. "It's called Tamarack on Annwfn as well! This is further evidence to support my brilliant theory! No doubt Tamarack is the point where our ripples start... the source of the separation of the worlds! Excellent!" The little man let out a long, trickling chortle.

"There were towns near the mountain," Manchester added. "One on the west side in your world, and one on the east side in my world."

"Yes!" Bugbear said. "The ruins of the legendary goblin monastery of Eglwys Cacynen are rumored to be the one to the west! What do you call the human settlement to the east?"

"Peculiar," Manchester observed. "It's not named. But the train tracks lead there."

"Well, whatever its name, where there is a town there is usually a library!" Bugbear said as he rolled up the maps and placed them back in his pockets. "This would be the perfect place to have the scroll translated!"

"And to refill our coffers with a Noggle game or two," Tudmire added.

"Well then, let us break camp and make our way to this mysterious town!" Bugbear piped.

Manchester allowed himself a crooked smile as he began packing up the camp. And yet, he felt a discomfort in the pit of his stomach. The train tracks were taking him to an exciting, new place, as he had hoped. And yet, the thought of such grand and cosmic things as merging worlds and foreboding mountains turned his coursing blood into ice. And he could not help but wonder what had become of his parents and family in all of this turmoil. Were they lost in some goblin's game as he now was? Or was his father selling cigars to ogres and dwarves?

CHAPTER 9
WILLOW PRAIRIE

As the covered wagon creaked and rocked along the rough road, Bugbear curled up in a corner in the back of the wagon. The mental stimulation of the morning's events had worn off, and now the terror and foreboding of the nightmares returned. He remembered the shadows clawing at him, coiling about him, squeezing him, pulling him, tearing at him. He remembered dying a thousand times last night, in a thousand horrifying ways. He remembered the voice, which even now echoed through his head, hissing through the nooks and crannies of his consciousness. And now all he could do was shiver, alone in the corner, a blanket wrapped about him as he stared wide-eyed out the back of the caravan.

"We're coming into that town!" Tudmire called excitedly from the front. "Maybe after we get settled we can look for a chemists. They might have tea, you know!"

"Tea," Bugbear sighed. The word alone sent an awkward tremble of power through his body. "Best come back here, Tudmire. We don't want to frighten any citizens who may be unwise to goblins."

"We've reached a town," Tudmire said as he tumbled into the back of the wagon, "and you want us to hide? Where's the fun in that?"

"Where's the fun in being thrown in a cage and put on display?" Bugbear said.

"From the looks of these people," Manchester said from the front, "I don't think they'd have the ambition to bother with you."

Bugbear moved the flap aside with a hesitant finger. He peered out and saw a tidy little village with cobbled streets, neat shops, and squat white houses, all in the shadow of a large, green-mottled mountain. It reminded him of the village in which he had been raised, except that here the sidewalks and streets were dotted with humans... grim, ghost-eyed humans shambling along with no direction and no emotion. And over the entire village, Bugbear perceived a faint, misty shadow, so vague and so transparent, he could not decide if it was real or some defect of his own senses. "What's the name of this town again?"

"The sign outside of town said it's 'The Kingdom of Willow Prairie,'" Manchester answered. "Which is rather peculiar as I've never heard of any kingdoms in this part of the world."

"Willow Prairie," Bugbear said. "The name is familiar to me. I've read it in ancient scrolls. This may be a human settlement, but it is not unknown to goblin scholars."

"Then if you are familiar with this place," Tudmire said, "perhaps the people are familiar with goblins. And that means we don't have to hide after all!"

"I said that I had read the name," Bugbear said. "Not that I had actually read about the town. And, no. Just because Willow Prairie happens to be mentioned in a few obscure annals, doesn't mean the town is a safe haven for weary goblin travelers. Unless we see other goblins walking about unmolested, I recommend caution."

"Just think of all the Noggle games I'll be missing," Tudmire grumbled.

"Perhaps you should pull over and ask someone where we can get a room for the night," Bugbear called ahead to Manchester. "Tudmire and I shall see to disguising our goblinish features."

"Yes," Manchester replied. "Look through that trunk there. I have quite a few wigs and fake beards and other props that may be useful."

As the wagon pulled to a stop, Bugbear and Tudmire opened the trunk and began sorting through the various disguises.

"What do you think?" Tudmire asked as he held a frizzy beard up to his chin. "Or maybe we should wear short pants and try to pass ourselves off as children?"

"No," Bugbear said. "I've seen pictures in some of Manchester's books. Our complexions are far too unusual and our faces are far too wrinkled to make a believable pair of human children. However, a pair of goblins may make for one believable human adult."

"Aha!" Tudmire exclaimed. "I'll stand on your shoulders and we'll put an overcoat atop us to look like regular human folk!"

"No," Bugbear said as a furrow crossed his brow. "I'll stand on your shoulders and we'll put an overcoat atop us to look like regular human folk."

"Why should you get to be on top?"

"Because those late night lemon cake binges of yours make you much more unwieldy than me!"

Tudmire prepared a retort but his words were postponed by a sudden scuffling outside the rear of the wagon. A pair of odd heads worked their way under the tarp to peek in at the cousins. One head belonged to a cat, which had jumped onto the end of the wagon, and the other head belonged to a dog, which stayed outside with its paws and chin poised on the end board.

"Ugh!" Tudmire blurted at the sight of them. "Vermin!"

"Oh, stop with your foolishness!" Bugbear said. "It's merely a dog and a cat." He stroked the creatures, one with each hand. The cat replied with engine-like purrs, and the dog answered with rhythmic wags of its tail. "And they are very pleasant animals at that."

"Buckshot!" a youthful voice called from outside. "Scratch! Here, Buckshot! Here, Scratch!"

The dog and the cat perked up at the boy's voice and jumped down from the wagon.

"A boy has told me of a boarding house not far from here," Manchester called back. "He says we can get a good meal, hot bath, and warm bed."

Bugbear jerked and turned away from the flap. "Yes," he croaked. "Excellent. Let us go then."

The caravan shook and shimmied into movement.

"What if we took turns being the top?" Tudmire asked.

Bugbear did not answer. He peered out the back flap one last time to see a young boy playing with a frisky black and white dog and a cat with turquoise eyes. He closed the flap and pulled a blanket up around his shoulders.

The wheels creaked to a stop. Manchester looked back from his driver's seat. "We're here. Picked out your disguises yet?"

"Yes, here," Tudmire said. He held up a wide brim hat, long coat, and a fake beard. "What do you say, cousin? This will do, don't you think? I'll even relent to being the bottom half... this time - 'round."

And so with Manchester's assistance the disguise was put into effect. It was an awkward sight...a lurching, swaying creature as tall as a short man, but with stubby, outstretched arms, stumbling little legs, and a patch of hair that covered most of the face. Still, all three of the companions agreed that this one uncanny *human* was less obvious than two unbelievable goblins.

"Up right foot," Bugbear directed as Tudmire brought them up to the porch of the grand three story boarding house. "That's it. Now, up left foot." And so he repeated as Tudmire's feet sought out the steps.

Manchester hit the knocker. "Hello," he called. "Hello. Is anyone t'home? We'd like a room." He peeked through the front window, and then drew his head back as though embarrassed for spying. "I don't think there's anyone here."

"Well, stop thinking, and start looking," came a voice cracked with age.

Bugbear spun about, his movement so rapid that he almost sent Tudmire flailing backwards. Off to the side of the porch he saw the old woman, bent and withered, with small spectacles perched at the tip of her nose. She stared at the companions with one good eye, the other glazed over with a cataract. Bugbear turned away. For with that one eye, the old woman stared deeply, azure facets sparkling and reaching out in a way that seemed beyond normal sight.

"Are you Mother Twitchett?" Manchester asked.

"Indeed, I am," the woman answered. "And who might you be, young man?"

"I am Martin Manchester. And my companion here is... uh, *Mister Overdale*. Your godson, Riley, said you have rooms for rent."

"Yes," the woman said. "I have rooms for rent. How long would you gentlemen be staying?"

"A day," Manchester replied. "Maybe two."

"Oh, that's fine," the woman said as she brushed some dirt from her apron and placed a basket on the edge of the porch. "I've just dug some fine potatoes from my garden. I'm planning on an extra special dinner for tonight. I'm sure you'll enjoy it."

Soon Mother Twitchett led the travelers up the narrow stairs of her grand house to their room. It was a fine room, not overly decorative, but homey and comfortable. Three feather beds sat at three different corners and beside each was a dresser. A window let in a pleasant stream of sunlight, and two doorways at the opposite end led to a closet and a small bathroom.

"I hope you gentlemen find this satisfactory," Mother Twitchett said with a smile. "This is the royal suite."

"Oh," Manchester perked up. "The king and queen stay here?"

"Heavens no!" Mother Twitchett blushed. "We don't have any royalty here in Willow Prairie at the moment. In fact, I don't believe we ever have."

"Then why does the sign outside of town say, 'The Kingdom of Willow Prairie?'"

"Just because we don't have a king at the moment, doesn't mean we aren't waiting for one," Mother Twitchett said with a wink of her good eye. "I'll have one of the neighborhood boys tend to your donkey. Feel free to enjoy the indoor plumbing. The evening paper lies there on the night table. And dinner should be ready in about an hour."

"Uh," Manchester began, "not to seem ungracious, but exactly how much do you charge?"

"I won't charge more than what you're willing to give," the old woman said. "It's not often I get three such well-mannered visitors. Your company is more than enough payment." She nodded, smiled, and closed the door behind her as she left.

"Thank goodness!" Tudmire gasped as he dumped Bugbear from his shoulders and onto the floor. "I believe you've been on a few of those late night lemon cake binges yourself, my burdensome cousin! Oh, my aching back!"

"Bah!" Bugbear snorted as he struggled through the tangle of oversized coat and bothersome beard. "There's nothing wrong with your back that a spine wouldn't cure!"

"Well," Manchester interrupted, "if you two are going to be fussing at each other for a while, I believe I shall take advantage of this indoor plumbing and indulge in a shower."

Something unsettling suddenly found its way to Bugbear's consciousness. "Wait a moment," he gasped. "Did that old woman say '*three* well-mannered visitors?'"

"Maybe," Manchester said as he picked up his satchel and made his way to the bathroom.

"Yes," Tudmire added. "That's very strange... considering you are easily the most ill-mannered goblin in existence!"

"She knows then," Bugbear continued, ignoring his cousin's outburst. "She saw through the disguise! She'll tell someone and then we'll all be done for!"

"I may only be the apprentice here," Manchester said, "but I probably know a little more about human behavior than you two. And I'm telling you, she's just a lonely old woman. And with vision as bad as hers, I doubt she could see through a dirty window, let alone your disguise. Did you notice that basket of *potatoes* she had? All rocks, every last one of them." Manchester removed a small pair of scissors, looked to the mirror and began trimming his mustache and beard. "Maybe she did say three instead of two. But I suppose humans aren't as sturdy as goblins and such. Our minds start to go when we get old like that."

"The boy's right," Tudmire said. "She's an old woman. Just got confused, that's all."

"Perhaps," Bugbear replied. "But harmless or not, she makes me nervous."

"I should only be a few minutes," Manchester said as he closed the bathroom door.

"Well, let's see what kind of town we've stumbled upon," Tudmire said. He picked up the newspaper from the night stand, unfolded it, and set it before Bugbear. "You've been studying Manchester's books. Figured out how to read this human scrawl yet?"

Bugbear took the paper, struggled up onto the edge of a bed, and sat in a hunching pout. Although he could read them, the words simply sat before his eyes in dumb, black and white silence. Like a tide eating away at the shoreline, the nightmare of the previous night seemed to have washed over his mind and taken something from him. His thoughts were thin and small, clouded and wispy. He needed some kind of diversion to sharpen his wits again. And there was Manchester's education to tend to as well. Bugbear would have to find something of true merit to study, examine, and investigate. He thought of the books he had brought with him on his journey. He pondered new ways to approach his old habits. But all that came to him was a pale emptiness. His brain swam in the brackish water of frustration.

Then, quite suddenly, in the secret language of Non-Logical Thought, the words on the paper spoke to him, telling him of missing people and missing livestock.

"What's that?" Bugbear said. "People missing? Livestock missing?" He held the paper aloft in triumph. "Aha!" he blurted. "This is what we need!"

"Oh, yes! Human misery! That's what I've got a taste for!" Tudmire said, his tongue thick with sarcasm.

"You insufferable toad!" Bugbear growled. "It's not the *misery* I'm excited about! It's the *mystery*!" Bugbear continued scanning the paper with hungry eyes. "Oh bother! It seems they have solved the mystery without us! The town constable has secured a suspect. Some silver-eyed witch, they say. Still, there's a trial tonight in the town square. We shall be there! The disguise is still in good shape, I trust?"

"Listen," Tudmire began, "I've had enough of being your bottom!"

A deep, slashing rage bubbled up from Bugbear's spleen and frothed in his brain. His eyes narrowed as he could almost feel fire burning within them. "Cousin," he hissed, "if you don't do this for me, I swear I shall summon up every horrible, wretched, torturous skill I've ever mastered, and turn your puny, little mind inside out!"

"Forget it, Bugbear," Tudmire snorted. "You yourself have admitted you don't know magic."

"What I threaten makes magic seem like parlor games," Bugbear whispered. He held his twisted hands up before Tudmire's face as a deep, guttural voice slid from his lips:

> *You cannot escape this curse I make.*
> *Your soul trembles, your body quakes.*

Tudmire offered a mocking grin. But then he actually began to quake. Fear flooded his eyes.

> *You feel the pain, you know the dread*
> *As your brain swells and cracks your head.*

Tudmire held his head, as he fell to his knees and a tortured gasp escaped his agape mouth.

> *Your lips pull back, your gums turn black*

Your limbs go slack, your bones now crack.

Tudmire began twisting and writhing on the floor. His moans bubbled from his mouth like juice bubbling from a crushed grape.

You are burning, and you are blazing
You are rabid, and you are crazing.

The moans turned into whimpers, and Tudmire flailed as though every nerve in his body were exploding.

Nothing is right, everything's wrong
Beg for mercy, I'll end my song.

Tudmire looked up at his cousin with eyes half closed in delirium. "I yield," he croaked.
"Very good!" Bugbear chimed.

The curse is gone, your health restored
Now you may rise, but balk no more.

Tudmire stood, slowly and with great fear upon his face. He stumbled over to the other side of the room, eyed his cousin bitterly, and curled up on a bed.
Bugbear smiled. He had gotten his way, cowered his cousin, and displayed his *power*... a power which was really nothing more than common hypnosis mixed with a bit of showmanship. But Tudmire had no need to know that.
"Cheer up, cousin," Bugbear said as he collected a sheaf of paper and a fountain pen. "Look on this little expedition tonight as a

game. There's no money at stake. But there is knowledge, dear Tudmire, knowledge!"

"Oh, how wonderful," Tudmire grumbled.

CHAPTER 10
THE QUILL IN THE INKWELL

Manchester felt he had missed something while he was in the shower. For as soon as he stepped out of the bathroom Bugbear twirled about and danced, ranting about newspapers, some trial, and an important lesson. And Tudmire, well, he was hardly himself at all. He remained silent the whole time. And when they were all getting dressed for this meeting, Tudmire immediately got down on his knees for Bugbear to mount his shoulders... not one peep of protest...not one utterance of opposition. He almost seemed frightened of Bugbear. Yes, Manchester had definitely missed something while he was in the shower.

Manchester and Mister Overdale bade farewell to Mother Twitchett. They apologized for not staying for her big *potato* dinner, explaining that they wanted to offer their assistance to the citizens of Willow Prairie in their time of need.

"Oh, well isn't that just the sweetest thing!" she said, her one good eye lighting with delight. "It's so reassuring to find good Samaritans these days! You should have something to eat though. Take some potatoes with you. As soon as I'm through here, I'll more than likely be heading to the trial myself. You gentlemen be sure to save me a seat, now will you?"

Manchester assured the old woman they would do so, and shortly the trio was out the door and into the cool night air. Manchester had seen the town square on their way into town, and as it was only a few blocks away, the companions decided a brisk walk was in order.

Willow Prairie on an early summer evening could fill even the darkest soul with a joyful luminance. The clear, dark blue sky.

The soft cricket songs. The sweet scent of honeysuckle. Every sight and sound and smell seemed wrapped in enchantment.

Manchester felt that this town had a spirit... a bright, glowing life he had never felt anywhere before. If such joy could somehow be his, Manchester would have loved nothing more than to live in Willow Prairie for the rest of his days.

"So," he started with a cheerful crack in his voice, "what's got you so keen about going to this trial?"

"Be silent," Bugbear hissed, his head bent and eyes half closed.

"I'm sorry," Manchester said, still keeping his cheer. "I was just curious. You know, us being strangers in town and all, I was wondering what could be of so much interest to us."

"Yours is not to question my decisions, apprentice!" Bugbear erupted. "If you want to learn, you listen! Otherwise your incessant blather will drown out the wisdom you seek!" The goblin gestured madly, his arms circling and turning and jutting every which where. "So, you do not speak to me again! Not until I give you leave! Else I shall null our bargain and you shall spend the rest of your pathetic life in ignorance!"

The cheer left Manchester, fleeing before Bugbear's rage like a field mouse fleeing a hawk. Manchester hung his head. Where was it? Where was that lasting sense of purpose he had sought since childhood? At first he thought he would find it in books and dime novels about pirates like *Jean Lafitte* and outlaws like *Silas Doty*. Then he thought perhaps the life of a traveling magician would give him what he desired. But both were somehow empty, unreal. It was only when he made his bargain to become the goblin's apprentice that he somehow felt his life was just beginning. But as he looked over at the hunched little creature perched atop Tudmire's shoulders in that ludicrous disguise, he felt the only things he would ever learn from Bugbear were bitter thoughts and bad manners. He clutched his flattened coin charm, sighed, and resolved himself to misery.

The mumblings of a small crowd pulled Manchester from his musing. They had arrived at the town square—a circular area, with a nicely landscaped area of green grass and colorful flowers rounded by a cobbled street. And before them thronged a crowd, moving and twisting like an agitated tangle of marionettes. Some squatted on hastily placed chairs. Others sat upon picnic blankets. And still others stood and milled about. In the center of the square the gallows loomed, skeletal and sinister, darkened with shadows in the twilight gloom. At the foot of the gallows stood the judge's bench, rigid and stark, undecorated save for a carving on its front which said, "*Justice is pain.*"

"Perhaps we had better stand," Bugbear said. "Two goblins stacked atop one another do not make for a graceful combination when placed in a chair."

Tudmire grumbled from beneath the overcoat.

"Stop your complaining," Bugbear snarled. "I feel another song coming on, you know."

Tudmire responded with immediate silence.

Manchester was not certain what this exchange meant. And he did not really care. He simply sat at the end of the aisle next to where the cousins stood.

"Now, Manchester," Bugbear said with a pointing finger, "your lesson tonight is in observation." The goblin motioned about the square. "So observe."

Manchester glanced about briefly. "What exactly am I supposed to be looking for?"

But Bugbear seemed distracted, gazing off into the distance, a peculiar stupor across his face.

"I said, what exactly am I supposed to be looking for?"

"I heard what you said!" Bugbear barked as he snapped from his daze. "Just look for everything! Now be silent! I'm trying to find the word for this place!"

"'The word?'" Manchester said.

"You know!" Bugbear replied. "The one, single word that defines this place at this particular time! Every place, every thing, every one has a word. It's never constant, it's ever changing, but at any given point there's a word." Bugbear went back to his contemplative stupor. He hummed. His head bobbed. And his arms twitched. "*Promising*," he finally uttered. "Promising is the word for this place."

"'Promising?'" Manchester said. He looked about the gathering. Most of the people seemed as irritated and unhappy as his companions and himself. How strange that a town which itself seemed so joyous and alive, should be peopled with citizens of such dark moods. All of them lumbered about, with shoulders stooped, faces grim, and fists clenched. Manchester could think of a lot of words for the town square and the people who crowded it, but "*promising*" was certainly not one of them.

"Oh, Mister Manchester!" A sweet, vibrant voice cut through the anger. "Misters Overdale!"

Manchester looked to the other side of the square. There stood Mother Twitchett, waving her handkerchief, and smiling as wide as her dentures would let her.

"How did she get here so quickly?" Bugbear asked, a quiver of suspicion in his voice.

"Probably knows a back way," Manchester said. He waved back to the kind, old woman, offered a false smile, and turned back to his sulking. He was glad Mother Twitchett seemed to have found a seat elsewhere, as he felt he would have been a poor companion for the evening.

"Tudmire," Bugbear said, "where did you put my pad and pen? I must take notes."

Tudmire replied with a muffled, "*Here*." And from beneath the overcoat a hand slipped up with a sheaf of paper and an ink pen.

Bugbear took up the items quickly. "Oh, could we be any more obvious about it, do you suppose?" he hissed. He delivered a quick smack to Tudmire's hidden head. To the casual observer it must have appeared as if Mister Overdale had just struck himself in the midsection. "Now then, Manchester! You take note of what's on the surface, and I shall delve into the hidden meanings, secret messages, and mysterious innuendo!"

"Very well," Manchester sighed. He turned away from the cousins, his eyes downcast, his face sagging with unhappiness.

"Did you lose your dog too, Mister Manchester?" a child's voice asked.

Manchester looked to his side. There sat the boy who had given him directions to Mother Twitchett's boarding house. "No, young Riley," he replied with a weak smile. "Just have a case of misery is all." Manchester looked at the boy, cocking his head with concern. "Did your dog run away?"

"Yes," Riley sobbed. "And Mother Twitchett's cat did too. Please don't tell her though. She asked me to watch after him. And now I've lost both Buckshot and Scratch!"

"Oh, now. They're probably just rutting through some neighbor's garbage can."

"No," Riley said. "No. They're gone. Just like all the other animals and people. Oh, I hope they get this witch to confess where they are! I love Mother Twitchett! I couldn't bear it if she hated me!"

Manchester put a reassuring hand on the boy's shoulder. "Well, where is this '*witch*?'"

"I haven't seen her yet. But the magistrate is getting ready to start the trial," Riley said as he wiped the tears from his eyes with one hand and pointed to the judge's bench with the other hand.

Manchester's gaze followed Riley's hand. He saw several people gathering near the makeshift court. One of them swaggered. Manchester hated that swagger. It reminded him too much of the bullies from his childhood. What made this swaggering lump worse yet was the fact that he wore a badge marking him as Willow Prairie's constable. Then there was the judge... a small, hunched, thin man wearing glasses and a long, black robe that threatened to bog him down with its weight. Manchester took a dislike to this man as well. He seemed so much like a teacher he had suffered under in school... a bitter little man who picked at his students' small mistakes to cover his own large shortcomings.

After the judge and constable took their places, the deputies escorted the prisoner from the jailhouse, a squat brick building which stood just off the town square. She walked to the defense table in strong, defiant strides. Even the weight of the heavy iron chains that bound her could not oppress her spirit. Strong. Confident. Beautiful. She was everything Manchester was not, and everything he struggled to be. Raven black strands crowned her head, flowing down past her shoulders and framing a stern face... serious, determined, grim, yet filled with other softer traits for which Manchester could not find words. Her skin was copper like the desert sands. And her eyes... Manchester felt he almost lost his soul when she chanced to look his way with those shimmering, exotic eyes. Then with a spark, his mind lit with recognition.

"Bugbear," he nudged the top half of Mister Overdale. "The witch. That's the woman who saved me in the forest. The dragon bride, you called her."

"I thought I told you to keep track of the broad picture and leave the details to me!" Bugbear chastised.

Manchester frowned. He turned away from the irate little man and folded his arms over his chest. He thought about snapping back at Bugbear, but then again, how much did he truly know about this goblin? Within that bitter mouth could wait rows of razor teeth every bit as sharp and devastating as that caustic tongue.

As the dark beauty sat at the wooden table before the judge's bench, the constable's church bell voice rang out, bringing the assemblage to attention. "This grand inquisition shall now be called to order! Our high magistrate, the honorable Dunderbeck, presides! All rise in worship and abject terror!"

The townspeople arose, their faces sheathed in pale fear. Many lowered their eyes like naughty pups just swatted with a paper. Others stared straight ahead, eyes round and dull.

The judge, this so-called Dunderbeck, seemed to bask in this respect, whether it was offered sincerely or not. He allowed the worship to linger a few moments before bidding the citizens to sit with a wave of his slender hand. Then he himself took a seat behind his high judge's bench, pounding the wooden gavel in a few weak thumps.

"Thank you all for coming," Dunderbeck said with a salesman's smile. "It really has turned out to be a delightful evening. The weather is with us. And I'm sure we can look forward to a perfectly super hanging. Now, on with the formalities. As the magistrate, I'll be presiding as both the judge and the prosecutor. Do we have a volunteer as counsel for the defense?"

A low murmur rumbled through the crowd, as if some distant lightning bolt had split the sky and released a roll of thunder. Pale faces turned paler yet.

"I'll be counsel for the defense," Mother Twitchett said with upraised hand as she hobbled to her feet.

Several people gasped. Some shouted outright, *"No!"*

But it was young Riley who protested loudest. "Mother Twitchett! Please don't! I need you!"

Manchester grabbed the young man about his shoulders and eased him back into his seat. "Easy, Riley. She's only volunteering to help that poor girl."

"You don't understand," Riley said as he struggled to get back to his feet again. "The law says that the defense counsel dies if she loses!"

Manchester's grip eased. "You mean if the girl is found guilty, Mother Twitchett will be found guilty too? And both of them will die?"

"Yes!" The tears began streaking down the boy's cheeks. "I've lost Buckshot and Scratch, and now I'll lose Mother Twitchett!"

Manchester turned to Bugbear. "Did you hear that? Mother Twitchett could be killed!"

Bugbear kept his head down, diligently scrawling away on his parchment. "Yes! Fascinating! A culture that is so obsessed with ridding itself of crime that it is willing to dispatch accused parties along with those who would defend them! We are quite fortunate to witness such a rare sociological phenomenon!"

"What?" Manchester balked. "Two people might die!"

"Excellent, Manchester!" Bugbear said as he looked up from his scholarly musings. "You have a superb grasp of the broad picture! Your apprenticeship is coming along quite nicely. If only we can teach you to keep your mouth shut!" With that, the little man returned to his scrawling.

Manchester gritted his teeth until he thought they might splinter. Then he shook his head and turned to comfort Riley. "Don't worry, son. If Mother Twitchett loses the case, I'll make sure nothing happens to her."

Mother Twitchett took her place at the defense table as the crowd mumbled with concern and disapproval. "Hello, dearie," she said as she sat down next to the exotic prisoner. "Don't you worry, now. I'll do my best to get you out of this fix."

The prisoner looked to Mother Twitchett, her silver eyes sparkling and her beautiful face breaking into a smile that would be the envy of angels. Manchester thought his heart would beat through his chest when he saw that smile.

Dunderbeck smiled as well, his crooked horse-teeth spilling out over split, chapped lips. "This is just super," he said. "Let's all give a big hand to Mother Twitchett for being such a good sport!"

Spurts of clumsy applause trickled through the crowd.

"And I'd like to add this is the first time we've had a defense counsel since the *Patterson-Dooley* lynching of '68. So we're looking at a really exciting trial! And that's just super, don't you think?"

Again the crowd mumbled, their voices low and docile as they croaked.

"Then let's get things under way!" Dunderbeck said. "The prosecution calls its first witness, Constable Pawe!"

The constable swaggered from his post beside the judge's bench to the witness stand. His boots clicked upon the cobblestone path leading to the stand, and the light from the kerosene lampposts glimmered off a silver badge upon his duster. His harsh gaze moved over the crowd like a cold, bitter wind. He stood with upraised hand. "I swear to testify as is beneficial to the cause of this court's justice."

"Super!" Dunderbeck said. "Now then, constable, I hear tell that you are the one who arrested the defendant. Could you relate to the court the specifics of this arrest?"

"Well," the constable drawled, "my deputies and me were investigating all these animals and citizens what have gone missing the past two days."

Manchester's flesh skittered and crawled at the constable's words... partly from the harsh, almost inhuman tone of them, and partly because the content struck an uneasy chord. "*The past two days.*" That was how long Manchester had been associating with Bugbear and Tudmire.

"We followed a trail from old man Scuttler's farm," the constable continued. "Some of his cattle and horses had been abducted, and the animals left quite a sizable path through the forest where they was led off. After a few hours we come upon a fearsome sight... an entire clearing filled with corpses... corpses not quite man yet not quite beast, but a mix of both. Twisted and horrible creatures, with hooves and claws, but also with arms and legs like men. And over these pitiful creatures she stood." The constable pointed to the dragon bride. "Her sword caked with black blood and her chest heaving with rage. I might have mistook her for a beast too, the way she bore her teeth and growled at us when we come into the clearing. But I ain't the law in these parts for nothing. Didn't take me long at all to figure she was behind it, using some kind of black magic to mix and match all them poor folks and animals, then doing away with them when they turned against her. So my men and I shot at her. She was a nimble one, sidestepping our gunfire as if we was lobbing green apples at her! But like everyone says in these parts, 'Ain't a critter that runs on four legs or two what can escape

Constable Pawe!' I squeezed off a round and creased the witch's forehead, just enough to knock her out so's my deputies and me could bring her back here for a proper trial."

Dunderbeck grinned and clapped his hands in sharp approval. "Outstanding! We're so fortunate to have the good constable looking out for interests, aren't we folks? What a super job he's doing!"

Again the crowd offered an unenthusiastic response as they muttered their agreement.

"Mother Twitchett," Dunderbeck said as he turned to the defense table, "you may cross-examine."

Mother Twitchett offered a weak smile as she stood and approached the witness stand. "Hello, Virgil," she said to the constable.

The constable scowled. "That's Constable Pawe," he growled.

Mother Twitchett continued her sweet smile. "You've always been Virgil to me and you always will be. Now, I have a few questions for you, *Virgil*."

The constable bristled, but then glared at Mother Twitchett and hissed between clenched teeth, "Ask then."

"Did the defendant attack you or your deputies?"

"No, but her stance was hostile."

"And what of your own stance, Virgil?"

"I was cautious, if that's what you're getting at. I had my gun drawn and pointed at her."

"But the defendant made no hostile movements towards you?" Mother Twitchett said. "It was only her stance that you deemed to be hostile?"

"Yes," Constable Pawe hissed.

"And you determined that she had recently been in a battle with strange creatures?"

"Yes."

"So using your years of experience in deductive reasoning, isn't it logical to assume that the reason her stance was so hostile was because she had just been attacked by a pack of wild monsters?"

"The witch intended to slice us in two! I could see the evil in her black heart!"

"No editorials, Virgil. Simply answer the question."

The constable shook as the veins on his forehead throbbed and his clenched fists trembled. "I suppose that might be 'logical.'"

"Thank you, Virgil," Mother Twitchett said as she patted the constable's hand and smiled. "No further questions."

"Well," Dunderbeck started, "what an outstanding cross-examination by Mother Twitchett! Good job! This is going to be a ripsnorter! You may step down now, Virg... er, Constable Pawe."

The constable grunted and swaggered away from the stand, pausing for a moment to offer a glare in the direction of the defendant and Mother Twitchett.

"With that," Dunderbeck said, "the prosecution rests! Does the defense have any witnesses to call?"

"Yes," Mother Twitchett said. "I would like to call the defendant to the stand."

As the gathering rumbled with yet more gasps and sputters of surprise, Dunderbeck leveled his gavel upon the bench.

"I'd have to object to that, Mother," Dunderbeck said. "The poor thing doesn't even know how to speak. How is she supposed to testify?"

"And how do you know she doesn't speak, your honor?" Mother Twitchett asked. "Has anyone even tried to communicate with her?"

The accused backed away as Mother Twitchett gently attempted to take her by the hand. "It's okay, dearie," Mother Twitchett said. "No one will hurt you. Do you understand?"

She nodded and gripped Mother Twitchett's hand. "Yes."

The crowd gasped. At last the witch spoke, and with that simple, single word, she sent waves of awe, wonder, and shock through the people of Willow Prairie!

Manchester felt something different as the soft, breathy voice danced forth from those perfectly formed lips. He longed to hear more as he moved forward, straining to pick up the slightest murmur or whisper of this exotic enchantress. And even as these pure, dreamy emotions tingled through his body, a certain part of his brain puckered in a sour reaction to such overly romantic drivel.

Mother Twitchett looked to Dunderbeck. "Is the prosecution satisfied with the defendant's ability to testify?"

Dunderbeck tugged at his collar slightly and offered a weak smile. "Of course. Proceed with your interrogation."

"I prefer the term 'examination,'" Mother Twitchett said as she motioned for the defendant to take the stand.

She moved with a determined grace. Her arms held to her sides as her long, slender legs carried her forth in a regal manner. She sat down at the stand, her silver eyes set straight ahead, sparkling like stars set in a midnight sky.

"Tell us your name, sweetheart," Mother Twitchett asked.

"I am Maga Ap Allherahiah, blade maiden of the draig gwraig."

"And what is this 'draig gwraig?'"

"More commonly we are called dragon brides. We are trained from birth to uphold the traditions of the great Dragon-Kings... to be wise in the ways of nature and to protect the good and pure from the evil and corrupt. Or in words your constable might understand, 'We kill varmints and kiss babies.'"

A few members of the crowd burst forth in uncontrolled laughter… laughter which quickly died down as the constable glared into the audience and fingered the hilt of his pistol.

"Oh what a splendid vocation!" Mother Twitchett beamed. "And can you tell us in your own words what happened in the forest before Constable Pawe and his men came upon you?"

"Well, you might as well ask me why wourmboggles smoke grisslum weed," Maga said. "Suffice to say, we dragon brides are attuned to nature. For several days I had felt a change in the world, as if it had suddenly grown twice as big and twice as mysterious. I had been wary as I made my way through the forest, seeking out the center of this disturbance. I was drawn to this place, this town, and your people. It was in the wilderness outside your settlement that I was attacked. So I unsheathed my sword and defended my life. It was at the end of my battle that this 'lawman' and his thugs came upon me. He used his little lead-flinging device to attack me in a cowardly way. And I awoke in your jail, where, by the way, the deputies are crude, the food tastes awful… and the rats are crude and taste awful."

Sputters of outrage and disgust spread through the crowd.

"Oh, it was a joke!" Maga exclaimed. "Haven't you people discovered humor yet? Gracious me! What a depressing little town!"

"And so, you made no aggressive actions against anyone?" Mother Twitchett asked. "Even with these strange creatures, you were merely acting in self defense?"

"Yes. That is correct."

Mother Twitchett smiled as she turned to the judge's bench. "No further questions."

As Mother Twitchett took her seat at the defense table, Dunderbeck cleared his throat and looked down upon the witness stand, his eyes narrowing and his teeth gritting. "You claim to be allied with dragons?"

"Yes," Maga said. "We dragon brides were recruited by dragons. We were trained to be their agents in the world... to travel where they may not and perform good deeds in their name."

"Then you are an agent for an alien power?"

"Well, yes. But..."

"The prosecution rests," Dunderbeck said with an abrupt slam of his gavel. "And the court is ready to render its decision."

Bugbear puttered back and forth excitedly, scrawling away on his paper. "Are you getting all of this, Bugbear?" he asked himself. "Yes, yes indeed, Bugbear! Excellent! Most intriguing!"

Manchester watched Bugbear out the corner of his eye. He felt sorry for Tudmire who was bearing all this fidgeting and twisting and turning upon his shoulders.

Dunderbeck pounded his gavel a few times. "In the case of Willow Prairie versus Maga Ap Allherahiah..."

"Objection!" Mother Twitchett cried out. "The defense has not rested at this time!"

"That is irrelevant," Dunderbeck replied. "The court has made its decision. All other considerations are now moot."

"Outrageous!" Mother Twitchett exclaimed.

"Excellent!" Bugbear said to himself. "A wealth of bitterness and rivalry on which to build my investigation!" Suddenly as he scribbled and scrawled the pen burst, spraying ink over his face and false beard. "Blasted contraption!" the goblin spat. He twisted and turned with rage, and Tudmire teetered and tottered beneath him.

"Calm down," Manchester whispered as he steadied the wobbling cousins.

"How do you expect me to calm down?" Bugbear raved. "I have no way to keep my notes now! Let alone the bother I'll have scrubbing this ink from my waistcoat!"

Manchester was distracted. Maga had stood to address Dunderbeck. Manchester wanted to hear what she said. He wanted to savor every precious syllable from those perfect lips. Yet, if he let Bugbear rant out of control, he knew their secret could be exposed.

"Wait here," he said, slowly removing his hands from the goblins. "I'll find you another pen." Manchester turned first to Riley. "Do you have a pen, young Riley?"

"No, sir," Riley answered. "I bet Mother Twitchett has one. She *always* has *everything* in her pocketbook."

"Thank you," Manchester said. He turned to Bugbear once again. "I'll be right back with your pen."

"Yes," Bugbear grunted. "Yes. And be quick about it, apprentice. This dragon bride is making some excellent points of which I would like to have a written record!"

Manchester grumbled and then stumbled his way towards the defense table, crouching low and taking care not to disturb anyone. The entire crowd seemed most taken with Maga's oration. Manchester caught her words in snippets, but he was enchanted by every elegant, superb, and melodic syllable he heard.

"You make me want to vomit!" she blurted. "You call this justice? This is deception! Fraud! Corruption! Ha! And here I accused you of having no sense of humor! This trial is the best laugh I've had in eons!"

Manchester grew so enraptured with her words that he bungled into a few empty chairs near the front of the assemblage. He was able to snatch them before they crashed to the floor, but in his awkward struggle to upright the chairs, the clanging and banging caused a few people to turn about and shush him.

"Let me tell you a few things, Magistrate Dunderbeck," Maga continued. "Let me tell you how your kind make my stomach turn like a stigger worm during mating season. Let me tell you how dishonest, disreputable, despicable little maggots like you are the reason people give up hope!"

Manchester looked back to Bugbear and Tudmire. Bugbear vibrated with agitation. Manchester could see his lips curling into a snarl and an orange rage bubbling up to his cheeks. And he could see Tudmire's poor little legs trembling beneath the long coat.

"And you," Maga said, turning to the crowd. "What manner of people are you to let yourselves be governed by such worthless miggle gimps? Have you no pride? Are a cock-eyed constable and mealy-mouthed magistrate the best leaders you poor sods have to offer?"

And then Manchester saw it... a quill pen poised within and inkwell, which in turn sat upon a stone shrine in the town square just to the side of the gallows. Probably there for the signing of death certificates and what-not, he thought. Regardless, no one would miss it, and it would more than likely fulfill Bugbear's need for a pen.

"That is all well and good," Dunderbeck said after several sharp pounds of the gavel. "But your inflammatory slander does not change the facts. You are an agent for an alien power. Therefore you are an enemy to the people of Willow Prairie."

Mother Twitchett stood up, her voice ringing out in protest. "Preposterous! All of the evidence has yet to be presented! You have no authority..."

"I have all authority!" Dunderbeck shouted. "The town charter of Willow Prairie gives full and complete power to the high magistrate! The only other individual allowed more power is the king! And we have no king, for in all the years since Willow Prairie was founded, absolutely no one has ever been able to remove the..." Dunderbeck's words stopped in his throat as he looked to stone shrine beside the gallows.

The rest of the people at the stand gasped as well. Soon the entire assemblage had turned about to stare at Manchester.

And Manchester stood there, the quill held aloft in his hand, a shower of light streaming down from on high, and a strange angelic chorus filling the air about him. "Uh, I'm sorry," he stammered. "Am I not supposed to use this? Should I put it back?"

"The king," someone whispered.

"The king," another voice followed.

"The king!" someone bolder exclaimed.

Soon the entire crowd erupted into celebration. People rushed up to Manchester, grabbing him about the arms and legs. Manchester struggled. He felt certain they would lynch him. But then, of all things, they hoisted him upon their shoulders.

"He pulled the quill from the inkwell!" someone shouted. "He's the one foretold by the Nagonene! He is the one, true king!"

At that moment an excited citizen bumped into Bugbear and Tudmire, finally sending the unstable pair tumbling to the floor. They tussled and tangled for a few moments until emerging from the large coat and ink spattered beard.

As the other townsfolk stood in stupor, young Riley crept forward. He looked to the goblins with eyes wide in delicious disbelief and delighted discovery. And then when he was almost nose to noses with the cousins, Tudmire shouted: *"Boo!"*

The boy tumbled and scurried back, his body a jumble of nervous excitement. "Look at this!" he shouted.

"Good Lord!" Dunderbeck exclaimed. "They're freaks! Monsters!"

"Nonsense!" Mother Twitchett chirped. "They're prophecy! They are the advisors predicted to help the king in his rise to power and glory!"

The cousins soon found themselves hoisted upon the shoulders of the overjoyed citizens, bobbing alongside Manchester - in a rhythmic ritual.

Manchester caught Maga's gaze as the townsfolk paraded him past the table. She smiled lightly and he thought he saw a faint glimmer in her eyes. But soon his bearers jerked him away from the town square and into the streets.

"Hail the king of Willow Prairie!" they chanted.

"There," Bugbear said, leaning back with a wide smile upon his face. "I'm typically not one to put much stock in prophecy, but I told you two something worthwhile would come of this trial, now didn't I?"

"Oh, a sweet deal you've landed yourself, m'boy!" Tudmire gushed. "The sweetest deal I've ever been a part of!"

"A king?" Manchester said with disbelief. He touched his head lightly. "I don't even know what size crown I wear."

CHAPTER 11
A ROYAL DILEMMA

Bugbear drummed his fingers along the window sill. Outside, down on the streets he saw the thronging crowds... people milling about, hoping to catch a glimpse of their new king. He saw smiles spreading betwixt rosy cheeks. He saw eyes brimming with hope and moistened with joyful tears. He saw sheep bleating for a shepherd.

"What an inconvenient time of day for an appointment," Tudmire sighed as he placed his elbows upon the long meeting table and sat his saggy face upon his palms. "Far too early in the morning for this kind of thing."

"It's like those humans say, cousin," Bugbear started, "'The early bird catches worms.'"

"But the early bird doesn't have to climb four flights of stairs after a night of celebrating," Tudmire snorted.

Bugbear ignored his cousin's rambling and turned away from the window. "How goes it, Manchester? Feel good to be a king, does it?"

Manchester sat at the head of the meeting table, his face blank as though lost in thought. "Hmmmm? Oh. Oh, well. I'm not quite sure." He stammered and stuttered out his next few words. "Any word on... on the girl... uhm that is, the dragon bride?"

Bugbear shrugged. "I suppose with all the excitement she was taken back to her cell by Pawe. No doubt they shall conclude the trial after your coronation."

"But shouldn't we do something to help her?" Manchester asked. "She's so... I mean, she saved my life after all."

Bugbear took a seat at the table, at Manchester's right hand. "You would be better served by concentrating on our negotiations here, m'boy. You may have pulled that quill from the inkwell and all, but there's still paperwork and mindless bureaucracy to sort out, you know."

"But," Manchester started.

"I will not be denied!" Bugbear growled betwixt clenched teeth. "Your petty concerns are of no significance!"

Manchester backed away. His face seemed drawn with both fear and irritation. He lowered his head to the table, cradling it upon his folded arms as he closed his eyes and sighed.

A thin whisper of guilt rasped against Bugbear's rage. He reached out to Manchester with a trembling hand, intending to apologize for the outburst. Yet just as quickly as the whisper of guilt came to him, it left as he pulled away his hand and made room for a big shout of pride. "While the rest of you were celebrating last night, I wandered off to the town library for a bit of reading, where I discovered some very interesting things about Willow Prairie. For instance, the legends of the original inhabitants of the area, the Nagonene Tribe, tell of a pale shaman from distant lands who established a stone altar for a sacred feather. Interesting, eh? And even more interesting is the name of this pale shaman... *Reginald*. I'm willing to wager it's the very same Reginald who traveled with Whittlegrip, the revered goblin monk and scholar."

"My dad used to tell me we had Nagonene blood," Manchester said, his head still buried in his arms.

Bugbear ignored him, continuing with his proud revelations. "There was also mention of a great battle in the shadows of Tamarack Mountain. Unfortunately the records are quite old, faded, and hard to decipher. But it does raise some interesting possibilities. Just imagine, a time when goblins and humans worked together."

"What happened to them?" Tudmire asked. "Why were our worlds split apart?"

"It's a mystery," Bugbear answered. "But no doubt it has something to do with the battle on Tamarack Mountain. Perhaps it was the working of some ancient, unnamed enemy. But while the rest of the human world forgot about those ancient times when man and myth were one, Willow Prairie not only remembered, but believed. And even prepared."

"Tamarack Mountain," Tudmire mused. "I had some dwarf friends who used to go on about that. They called it 'The Thumbprint of God' or some such thing. I don't even think they knew why. Just one of those silly dwarf things, I suppose. You know, giving a big overblown name to every rock, hill, and ditch in creation."

"Regardless," Bugbear said with an upraised finger, for whenever he had an important statement, he made it with an upraised finger, "as interesting as Tamarack Mountain and the mystery of the sundered worlds may be, our main priority is to help good King Martin lay claim to his throne and tame his kingdom!" Bugbear gave Manchester a solid slap on the shoulder, as if his earlier harsh words had never been spoken. "He is still my apprentice, after all. I'm obligated to see him through this!"

"I've been meaning to talk to you about that," Manchester broke in, finally raising his head. "I don't think I'm quite up to being a king. Even the apprenticeship was beginning to leave a sour taste in my mouth. I... I just want to go home. Back to regular human beings and regular human problems. No more goblins. No more secret kingdoms. No more pressures."

"Manchester," Bugbear gasped as a thousand dreams fled his mind. "No! This is what you wanted... to be more than just a stage magician!"

"You've got a whole town bowing at your feet!" Tudmire added. "It's the golden glabtrabbel, lad!"

"But I'm no king," Manchester protested.

"I've looked into the faces of those people out there, Manchester!" Bugbear exclaimed. "You're the best hope... *the only hope*... they've had in a long time."

"But why me?" Manchester asked.

Bugbear raised his hands and sighed. "I don't know why Sir Reginald founded Willow Prairie, or why he set that quill in the inkwell, or even why after all these centuries you've been the only one able to remove the quill. But I do know that there's some reason behind it, Manchester. Something important! The apprenticeship! The inkwell! This kingdom! It's all leading up to something bigger! If you abandon it now, you'll abandon a destiny grander than any you've ever imagined!"

"How do you know that?" Manchester asked, slowly backing away. "How do you know that Willow Prairie isn't just some town filled with deluded maniacs?"

Bugbear stared at Manchester a moment, then he shook his head and turned away.

"Does it have to do with your dreams?" Manchester asked.

The words seized Bugbear's mind with a cold, dark hand. *Yes!* Bugbear felt like shouting. *Yes, Manchester! The dreams! We are all doomed! Forget the crown! Forget Willow Prairie! Forget your apprenticeship! We must both flee! We must run! Run in opposite directions! Never looking back! Never to meet again!*

But Bugbear did not say these dreadful things. Instead the words swam about in his head like blind, albino sharks feeling through the murk of a black tar sea. He strained to find a less drastic, more rehearsed answer. The back of his throat tingled. The tip of his tongue twitched. The edges of his mouth quivered. *Oh, for the numbing tang of a hot cup of tea!*

Bugbear forced himself into composure and looked to Manchester with cold, lifeless eyes. The proper words had come to him, in a bright, glowing inspiration that dried up the black tar sea. "I don't have to have dreams to know that your destiny is intertwined with Willow Prairie's," he hissed. "Accept your crown, Manchester. Accept your fate... no matter where it may lead us."

A creaking door and the obnoxious scent of cheap cologne intruded upon them. Dunderbeck walked into the meeting room, the swaggering Constable Pawe following close behind.

"I trust you gentlemen are ready to discuss the legalities of Mister Manchester's claim to the throne," Dunderbeck snorted.

"Indeed," Bugbear replied, giving Manchester a narrow-eyed glance. "Quite eager to get at it, we are."

"No," Manchester countered. "No. Before this goes any further, I must say something."

"Of all the times to find his backbone," Bugbear cursed to himself.

"I don't mean to sound ungrateful or irresponsible," Manchester continued, "for I truly do appreciate the hospitality Willow Prairie has shown me. One only has to look into the glowing faces of its people to know that this is truly a special town. I guess the best way to say this is to just say it," Manchester sighed. "I don't want to be your king."

Tudmire gasped.

Dunderbeck smirked.

Pawe chortled.

Bugbear cleared his throat. "Well spoken, Manchester," he piped. "After all, the word *king* is so limiting." Bugbear waddled off his seat and scurried over to Dunderbeck's side. "You see, my dear

Mister Dunderbutt, Manchester wants to be so much more than just a king!"

"That's *Dunderbeck*," the magistrate grumbled as he gave Bugbear a quick sideways glance. "And what exactly do you mean, 'More than just a king?'"

"I...I...I never meant," Manchester stammered with embarrassment.

"He has a hard time putting it into words," Bugbear interrupted, "but he also wants to be a friend, a protector, and most of all a true citizen of Willow Prairie! You should hear him going on about the reforms, the programs, the advances he has in mind! He's a bold visionary! A man to admire and respect! Mister Plunderhead, I'm telling you the greatest day in the history of Willow Prairie was the day Martin Manchester came to town!"

"How reassuring," Dunderbeck said with a forced smile. "However, regardless of Mister Manchester's intentions as king, we must still sort through the legalities of his claim. And again, my name is *Dunderbeck*."

Manchester grabbed Bugbear by the collar and spun him about. "What are you doing?" he whispered. "I told you I don't want to be king. I've had enough of this town with its inkwells and witch trials. Why would I want to be king of a town that treats such a beautiful lady in such a barbarous manner?"

"Because as king you can change that," Bugbear replied. "You can pardon her."

Manchester arched an eyebrow. "I could? Then I may be the only chance she has. If I don't become king, Dunderbeck would have her killed. That beautiful, graceful neck placed within a hangman's noose... the world forever robbed of her beauty and perfection...

those petal-soft lips never to utter another magnificent, lyrical sound."

"Stop waxing poetic, Manchester," Bugbear said. "It annoys me."

"If you two are through sharing your secrets, perhaps we could get on with the negotiations," Dunderbeck broke in.

"By all means," Bugbear replied as he took his seat once again. "Please, feel free to propose your terms, and then we'll respond with our own demands."

"Does our new king have a tongue?" Dunderbeck mocked. "Or does he let strange creatures speak for him?"

"Well now," Bugbear started, "one can hardly expect a man of King Martin's standing to exchange words with a mere commoner such as yourself! After all he has an image to uphold!"

Dunderbeck snorted. "Enough with your insults, little man. Are you ready to hear my terms?"

"The king has consulted with me on his demands," Bugbear continued. "I am fully authorized to speak on his behalf. Proceed."

Dunderbeck's brow furrowed with controlled anger. "Very well. Seeing as how Mister Manchester removed the quill from the inkwell in front of a sizable group of witnesses, I have no choice but to concede his claim to the throne. However, as magistrate I reserve the right to succession until a legal heir is born. I also claim the right to keep my positions as officer in charge of public safety and chairman of the town council."

"The king finds those requests acceptable," Bugbear said. "However, he demands full veto power over the town council, and he wishes to place the Department of Public Safety within a larger Department of Justice to be regulated by another officer to be appointed by himself."

"Unacceptable!" Dunderbeck fumed.

"In addition," Bugbear continued, "the king requires final complete and total authority over any military and police operations."

"Preposterous!" Dunderbeck raged.

"As well as control over the tax system, the treasury, and the highways."

"Never!" Dunderbeck ranted.

"Very well," Bugbear said. He jumped from his seat and grabbed Manchester by the hand. "Come along, my king." With an enthusiasm and force that belied his stubby form, Bugbear pulled Manchester from the table and tugged him awkwardly along to the window. "I think it's time you saw exactly what you were up against, Dunderbreath."

Bugbear opened the window and positioned Manchester squarely in front of it.

The crowd on the streets below erupted. They cheered with a wild, unbridled excitement, like prisoners who were being released from their shackles and chains. Their faces almost split in half with joy. Their voices lifted high in the air, loud and ringing with admiration. "The king!" they shouted.

Bugbear pulled Manchester away from the window and closed it. "You have two choices, magistrate," Bugbear said with a hint of menace. "You either give us what I want, or you tell the people why they have no king."

"Blackmail!" Dunderbeck screeched.

"Actually, I believe *extortion* is the proper term," Bugbear chortled.

Manchester bent down, whispering into Bugbear's large, pointed ear. "I'm confused. I never wanted to be king in the first place. But you badgered, bothered, and bamboozled me into accepting. And now you're telling me to give it up again. You could at least tell me which way we're going so I can make up my mind on whether to be miserable or relieved."

"I'm bluffing," Bugbear whispered in reply. "Something I learned by watching Tudmire. But don't let him know that... or I'll never hear the end of it. Mark my words though, Manchester, you shall be king. And with my help you shall be a greater king than even Sir Reginald could have foreseen."

And as Bugbear and Manchester kept their secret council, Dunderbeck stewed bitterly. "This is unfair!" he whined. "This is not proper negotiation! Negotiation is supposed to be a combination of give and take."

"Yes! You give, Sunderneck," Bugbear said, "and we take! That's the way goblins negotiate!" Bugbear waddled before the magistrate, eyeing him with a frightful glare. "I know your type, I do. Sitting at home alone in a cold, dark room. And beneath the glow of a flickering lamp light you read your books on psychology and manipulation. You dazzle honest folk with your flowery phrases and false flattery. You belittle them in subtle ways. You undermine their lives with lies and treachery. Your tiny mind churns with dreams of conquest and delusions of power. Well, now your dreams are shattered! Your delusions dispelled! For King Martin has arrived! And I am with him! And with me is your ruination!"

The magistrate cowered... something he had probably never done before in his wasted life. His facade of confidence disintegrated. And there he sat, a quivering little skeleton of a man. "Well then," he gasped, "for the good of Willow Prairie, I shall agree to your provisions." He glared at Bugbear a moment, and then stood up, his legs weak and trembling.

"Excellent!" Bugbear exclaimed, dropping his vicious demeanor for a much lighter one. "I shall have my cousin Tudmire draw up the paperwork. He's very good with legal terminology and the like."

Bugbear walked over to Tudmire's side. The blubbery toad had fallen asleep during all the negotiation, his feet propped up on the table, his feathered cap tipped over his eyes, and an obnoxious snore sputtering from his lips. "Tudmire! I say, Tudmire! Up with you!" Bugbear kicked the chair out from under his drowsing cousin.

"What?" Tudmire groaned as he floundered on the ground in a sleepy daze.

"We've reached a settlement!" Bugbear chirped as he helped Tudmire to his feet. "Manchester shall be king of Willow Prairie! And as one of his loyal subjects, I have no doubt he has a special title for you!"

"Oh!" Tudmire beamed. "You don't say! You don't say! What is it, m'boy? Or perhaps I should address that *m'Lord*!"

Manchester stared blank faced at his goblin companions. "I don't know. I suppose Bugbear already has the advisor position. What else do I need?"

"Seneschal," Bugbear said.

"Seneschal?" Manchester said.

"Seneschal," Bugbear said.

"What the wallamaloo is a seneschal?" Tudmire asked.

"You're the one who plans special dinners, banquets, and coronation celebrations," Bugbear answered.

"Interesting," Tudmire mused. "Interesting. If you like service oriented positions, that is."

"You know," Bugbear continued, "you'll also look after the king's household. And that includes the servants, the royal guard... - and the treasury."

"At your service, my liege!" Tudmire said with a crisp bow to Manchester. "I'll get on your coronation celebration post haste! Cousin, you simply must write one of your songs for the occasion! I'll try to scrounge up some musicians worthy of your genius!"

"Yes," Bugbear agreed. "A march through the town square would be most appropriate. I'll work on something for it. And you must work on the paperwork as well. Write up something very legalish. You know, with all the '*parties-of-the-first-parts*,' '*wherefores*,' '*where-with-alls*,' and '*here-to-fors*.' I shall get with you later on the specifics of the settlement."

"Of course, my dear cousin!" Tudmire shouted. And with a heady giggle he scurried out the door.

"Well, then," Dunderbeck said as he rose from his chair, "since our business is concluded, I shall be going to take care of a few minor details in preparation for the transfer of power."

"Wait!" Manchester blurted. "There was one more stipulation. The girl... Maga. I want to pardon her."

"Not gonna happen, son," Constable Pawe said as he stepped forth from the shadows. "She's had her trial. Court found her guilty. She'd already be hung if it weren't for you pulling out that quill."

"But if I'm the king, I can pardon condemned criminals, can't I?" Manchester retorted.

"You ain't king till your little buddy draws up them papers, son," Pawe said.

"He's correct, Mister Manchester," Dunderbeck added. "The constable and his men could execute her now if they wished. Mother Twitchett as well."

"And that's exactly what we have planned soon as I get out of this meeting," Pawe said.

"I see," Manchester sighed.

"Sorry about that, Manchester," Bugbear said with a comforting pat to the shoulder. "I didn't foresee this. But we have negotiated a most excellent situation for ourselves otherwise. The girl and the old woman are small losses compared to what we have gained."

"I will not be denied!" Manchester growled betwixt clenched teeth.

Bugbear backed away as Manchester bolted from his chair and lunged at Constable Pawe. With an unexpected strength, the magician-who-would-be-king slammed the lawman against the hard oak wall and snarled. "I swear to God and everything that is decent and perfect in this world, if you harm that girl or Mother Twitchett in anyway, when I sign those papers that make me king, I will also be signing your death warrant!"

"Now listen here," Pawe said.

"I will not listen!" Manchester shouted. "You will listen! You will listen as I tell you that I am the king of Willow Prairie starting right now, this very moment! And you will listen as I tell you that the prisoner, Maga Ap Allherahiah, is to be released immediately into my custody! And Mother Twitchett is to be left alone! Do you understand, constable? Or will my first official act as king be to order your torture and execution?"

"I.. I understand," the constable replied, trying to control his trembling.

Manchester backed away from Pawe, seeming almost as stunned by his behavior as everyone else in the room. "Very well then," he said. "While Bugbear and Tudmire take care of the paperwork, and Dunderbeck makes his preparations, you and I will go to the jail and arrange for Maga's release." Manchester motioned the constable to the door.

With a grunt Pawe eyed Dunderbeck for a moment, and swaggered out the door. Manchester followed him and closed the door behind them.

"Well, Mister Dusterbed" Bugbear said as he smiled brightly to Dunderbeck, "now do you see why I do the king's negotiating most of the time? He has a vicious streak a thousand cubits wide!"

"Indeed," Dunderbeck said as he gathered his papers. "And the name is *Dunderbeck*."

"Of course," Bugbear replied with a very large Cheshire grin. But the grin hid something... deep, dark worries about Manchester. Bugbear had seen the magician upset, bothered, worried, and unhappy, but never angry... not like this. Even against the ogres, he had behaved more frantic than fearsome. But the way he assaulted Pawe... it was reckless and dangerous. What if Pawe had shot him? And Manchester's demands... so bold, so strong, and so passionate. Bugbear had thought using the dragon bride as a ploy to coax Manchester into his kingship was an impromptu inspiration of genius. But now that he realized just how deeply Manchester's feelings for this woman reached, he was frightened. Manchester needed to concentrate on building a kingdom, not wooing a maiden.

As Bugbear shook his way out of his thoughts, he suddenly saw that he was alone in the council room. He remembered that he should be helping Tudmire with the paperwork for Manchester's coronation. He struggled out of his chair and waddled to the door, abruptly stopping as a thought popped into his head. "Yes," he whispered to himself. "If Manchester can't be trusted to make the right decisions, then I shall have to make them for him." A crooked smile crept along Bugbear's thin lips as he left the council chamber... and tripped over Tudmire who had fallen asleep in the stairwell.

CHAPTER 12
LAYING DOWN THE LAW

"So, the new king has come to supervise the execution himself, has he?" Maga scoffed as Constable Pawe fumbled the keys in the door of her cell.

"N... no," Manchester sputtered. "I've pardoned you. The constable is releasing me into your custody. Uh, that is he's releasing you into my custody."

Maga's eyes narrowed. As the door opened she took a hesitant step forward then looked to Manchester with a wry smile. "Your custody?" she said. "And what do you have planned for me, good King Martin? A stay in your dungeons? Or perhaps a public flogging?"

"Oh goodness no!" Manchester said as he backed away from Maga. "I would never think of doing either of those things to you. Or to anyone else for that matter."

"Too bad," Maga said as she ran a slow, seductive finger up Manchester's shirt. "I might have enjoyed it."

"Now do you see why I was so eager to get her hung?" the constable broke in. "Shameless hussy!"

Like a stream of fire ignited by his heart and raging through the muscles and sinews of his arm, a reflex snapped Manchester's fist into Pawe's face.

The big man fell to the floor in a staggering thud. His hand went to his mouth to soothe the pain of the impact. He looked to Manchester with an expression of outrage mixed with surprise.

Maga too gave Manchester a gaze of awe and disbelief.

But neither Pawe nor Maga could have been as amazed as Manchester himself, who stood over Pawe staring at his trembling fist. This was the second time today he had acted in such a reckless, enraged manner. Something was happening to him. Perhaps it was Bugbear's influence. But Manchester felt it was something more... something deep, personal, and hidden. He quickly remembered himself and his new station. "I suggest you rethink your opinion of Miss Maga, constable," the king said in strong, steady tones.

Pawe turned away. He crawled to his feet, moving away from Manchester and Maga. "You may be king, but you can't tell me what to think," he spat as he wiped the blood from his lip with a handkerchief.

"Perhaps not," Manchester said as he took a step forward. "But I can tell you to clear out your desk. Willow Prairie doesn't need bullies with badges."

"Faugh!" Pawe spat. "You can't go without no law around here? Who you going to get to replace me?"

Without hesitation Manchester replied, "Her." He gently took Maga by the hand.

"Never!" Pawe shouted.

"Part of the negotiation says that I can appoint my own officer in charge of the Department of Justice. I appoint Maga."

"The folks 'round here will never accept her!"

"If they accept me, they'll learn to accept her," Manchester said.

"Y... your Highness," Maga stammered. "I don't think that..."

"This is my second official act as king," Manchester said with a soft smile. "You wouldn't want to make me look foolish by denying my wishes, would you?"

Maga wrapped her hand about Manchester's. "No," she whispered. "I don't suppose I would. I accept your decision."

"Dunderbeck will hear of this!" Pawe exclaimed as he slammed his badge down on the desk.

"The entire town shall hear of it," Manchester said with a scowl. "The king's word is law, after all."

"Some day your words will choke you." Pawe turned about and like an engine with a mighty head of steam, charged out the door.

Manchester looked after Pawe, jaw set firm with disgust. His hand slid along the desk and picked up the badge. "This is yours now," Manchester said as he handed the badge to Maga.

Maga received the badge and smiled. "Where does it go?"

Manchester trembled. With an unsteady hand he pointed to his chest. "You put it here. Well, not *here* on me. But, uhm, *there* on you."

"I've never adorned myself with such a decoration," Maga said with lowered eyes. "Perhaps you could honor me by placing it," Maga pointed to her chest, "*here* on me."

There was a pause... one of those long, uncertain pauses that creeps into those moments when fate is decided. Manchester took in a deep breath. His hands moistened with sweat. His body trembled. His heart pounded in his chest. Then he reached out with the badge, seeking out Maga's vestment with fumbling fingers. He found a soft patch not covered with the scaly armor, and gently slid the pin into the material.

"It's rather uncomfortable," Maga said, wincing as she touched with badge with her fingertips. "Is it supposed to pierce the skin like that?"

"Oh no!" Manchester panicked as he lurched forward to undo his bumbling sin.

Maga snorted with mirth as she playfully shoved the king back. "I was only teasing." Her laughter rolled about her mouth for a few gentle moments before her silver eyes set upon Manchester. "Oh my, you are simply adorable."

Manchester's gaze immediately fell to the floor, then back up to the dragon bride, then over to something hanging on the wall... a something that really didn't matter other than to serve as a distraction from Manchester's true feelings.

"Congratulations," Manchester said, finally turning back to Maga with a voice cracking in nervous tremors. "You're my new chief justice."

Maga's face lit with a soft, canny smile. She lowered herself to one knee and kissed Manchester's hand. "I swear my allegiance to thee, the man to whom I owe my life."

Manchester danced in place with nervous embarrassment. "Really, my dear, there is no need to kneel like that."

"But you are a king, are you not?"

"Well, everyone says that I am. But still, I only did what was right. That trial was a sham. No one should be forced to endure such humiliation and injustice."

"Your words betray you," Maga whispered as she rose to her feet and gazed into Manchester's eyes. "Only a true king would say such things."

"All I did was pluck a silly quill from an inkwell," Manchester said as he turned away. "Kings usually fight for their kingdoms or they inherit them."

"Or they earn them."

"What about you?" Manchester started as he gained the courage to turn back around. "Bugbear hasn't told me much about dragon brides. You look almost human. Well, that is. I mean. Well." Manchester turned away again, attempting to hide his embarrassment with a few chuckles. "I'm sorry."

"There's nothing to be sorry about," Maga said with a soothing hand placed on Manchester's shoulder. "You're not too far off. We are human. At least we started that way. My elders have told me of an ancient time when the dragons were still with us. They were glorious beings. Wise. Kind. Patient. And powerful."

"But I thought dragons were evil. You know, capturing maidens, fighting knights, burning villages."

"Lies circulated by their enemies," Maga said. "In truth, dragons were teachers and protectors for all the races. But as they grew older, they felt themselves being pulled away from our reality to another, greater destiny. So as not to leave the world without their protection and guidance, Allherahiah, the bride of Sir Reginald..."

"Sir Reginald?" Manchester said. "He's the one who founded Willow Prairie and traveled with Whittlegrip the goblin."

Sir Reginald and Allherahiah

"Yes. And his wife, Allherahiah, made a pact with the dragons during a great war against a menace whose name even we dragon brides have forgotten. She gave herself over to the Great Drake so that he might infuse her with a portion of his essence. Hence forth, Allherahiah was the immortal queen of the dragon brides. Every hundred years she would give birth to a new dragon bride, and she would teach and train her children to be wise, patient, and just in guiding others from the path of corruption."

"Fascinating!" Manchester gasped. "So how many dragon brides are there now?"

Maga's head dropped. Her beautiful silver eyes seemed to glaze over with sorrow. "Too few."

"But since Allherahiah gives birth every hundred years, there will be more, right?"

"There shall be no more. I was the last. For when Allherahiah gave me my life, she lost her own." Maga's silver eyes closed for a moment as she sighed, seeming to brace her spirit as a loathsome shadow fell across it.

Manchester felt a sharp, shameful pain in the center of his being. "I'm sorry. But it wasn't your fault. Mothers sometimes die in childbirth."

"Allherahiah was supposed to live forever. Because of me, my entire race will die. There will be no more dragon brides."

Manchester did not know what to do. He never did in such uncomfortable situations. He cursed his feeble mind for feeding such inane words to his mouth. "Maga..."

"No matter," Maga said as she brushed away Manchester's offer of comfort and turned towards Pawe's desk. "I am in your service now. Best to get to work."

"Of course," Manchester replied. He backed out of the doorway, keeping his dewing eyes on Maga the entire time.

Manchester sat on the front step of the jailhouse for a few moments, stewing in a thick, uncomfortable feeling. He had almost begun to believe there was something to all this fuss about kings and quills and such. With all the kind words Maga had been saying to him, his stoop shoulders had broadened, his sullen face had brightened, his glum mood had lifted. He had, for a moment, become this king everyone wanted him to be. But now, he shuddered, his eyes darting about in his head like loose dice in a gambler's hand. He had summoned up something horrible with his questions... shaken loose some unbearable skeleton from Maga's past. A true king would not have upset such a noble woman. A true king would have phrased his questions more delicately, chosen his words more cautiously, or not even spoken at all. Surely when he pulled the quill from the inkwell Manchester was not meant to be king at all, but the village idiot. Yes, the village idiot. There was the position Manchester was meant to have.

Manchester stood up and drew in a breath of air. He set out, his feet tripping along the sidewalk and his eyes wandering about the neighborhood. The birds met him with sweet songs. They lit from tree to ground, picking here and there for morsels between the blades of grass. Further away he could hear children, squealing and playing and laughing. And before him he saw the streets of Willow Prairie, all clean and cobbled. Whether Manchester was worthy of it or not, this was a magnificent kingdom... despite its strange, unstable inhabitants.

A soft sound wound its way to Manchester's ears. Thin, soothing, and elegant, yet also mournful. It was the sound of a fife. Manchester recognized the song as well. It was an old Irish tune, *The Minstrel Boy*. Suddenly the tune stopped.

"The song didn't work!" came a child's woeful moan. "It was their favorite! I thought for sure they would come!" Manchester recognized the voice as young Riley's. And across the street he could see the boy sitting upon Mother Twitchett's porch steps, wailing and crying, a fife dangling loosely from his hand as the old woman rocked him in her arms. "I'm so sorry! I didn't mean to loose them! Oh, my best friends! I'm so sorry!"

"Is the boy okay?" Manchester asked as he took a seat beside them. "Should I fetch a doctor?"

"Oh, he'll be well enough," Mother Twitchett said. "Seems his dog and my cat have gone missing, and the poor lad is taking the blame on himself. Not his fault at all. Not at all. Things are happening. Things that no one person can stop."

"Not even a king?" Manchester whispered.

"Not a king alone, dear boy," the old woman answered. "You'll have to gather all the pieces for this game. All the pieces." The corner of Mother Twitchett's one good eye glistened as it caught a drop of sun.

"Well," Manchester said as he stretched into a swaying stance, "I don't care how many pieces they give me, I'm afraid I've never been very good at games."

"You seem almost as distraught as the boy, your Majesty. Does something weigh on you?"

Manchester ran a trembling hand through his tangle of black curls. "I've upset a beautiful woman," he sighed. "The most beautiful woman I've ever known."

"Ah," Mother Twitchett said with a wry smile. "The dragon bride! You've taken a shine to her, have you?"

"Well," Manchester said suppressing a quiver of embarrassment, "I haven't exactly taken a shine to her. I just don't like to upset people."

"Like Constable Pawe. Or should I say, *former* Constable Pawe."

"How...?"

"Small town," Mother Twitchett answered before Manchester could even finish the question. "Pawe was screeching and hollering about it the second he left the jail. Very brave of you to fire him. Not many folks have ever stood up to him."

"I just did what I thought was best."

"I could speak to Maga on your behalf," Mother Twitchett offered. "I have a way with people. I'm sure I could ease any harsh feelings she might have towards you."

"Could you?" Manchester asked, his face lighting with hope and gratitude.

"I could. If you would but promise me one simple thing."

"Name it!" Manchester piped.

Mother Twitchett pulled Riley to her, covering his ears as he sobbed into her apron. "If anything should ever happen to me, look after my dear Riley," she whispered.

The king's brow arched with worry and shock. "I... I would certainly try. I mean, I don't know much about raising children." Manchester smiled as he watched the tenderness and affection with which Mother Twitchett smothered the boy. "I must say, I am certainly honored that you'd ask me."

"As I was honored when Riley's parents asked me to care for him. They were good friends of mine and respected members of the town council. They died up on Tamarack... fell off a cliff while surveying the area for some silly expansion plan of Dunderbeck's. Only Dunderbeck returned, though." The old woman took her hands from Riley's ears, placed a soft kiss upon his forehead, and wiped his tears away with her shawl.

Manchester looked to Tamarack, ever looming over Willow Prairie. "Tamarack," he whispered. "There seems to be a lot of tragedy surrounding that big gopher hill."

The people began to gather. Slowly, one at a time they came. They clasped their hands, their trembling hands, and looked up to Manchester. They had that same look Manchester had seen earlier in the day when Bugbear drew aside the curtains. They had that look of faith. And it was a look that turned Manchester's stomach... because it was faith in him.

"Ah, good day to you, Sire," one man said as he took a few steps forward on Mother Twitchett's lawn. "And what beautiful days

Willow Prairie has to look forward to when you return to us all that has been lost!"

Manchester smiled in a nervous twitching way.

"Oh, your Highness! Your Highness!" a woman cried out, her voice ringing like a church bell. "Please return my little Elijah soon!"

"And there'll be plenty of cheese and milk and beef for the royal pantry when you find my cattle, m'Lord!" a man shouted from the back.

The pleading came from everywhere. *"Find my wife." "Fetch my son." "Return my sweetheart." "Get my horse."* It seemed endless. Manchester nodded here and there, hoping to assure them that he was at least listening. He even looked to Mother Twitchett, but she concerned herself only with Riley and offered no help. Manchester's heart thrummed in his chest, his legs trembled, his head throbbed. He had to get away from them.

He set off of the porch with a frantic pace, his knobby knee legs twisting and bending with awkward resolve. They followed, some of them, shouting both their adulation and their anguish. Soon Manchester began jumping fences, cutting across yards, and slipping into alleys. A few straggled on with their yells and pleas. But even the most tenacious of these stopped near the outskirts of town as Manchester tumbled to the ground before the rusty gates of a junkyard.

"Ah, now there's the place to start looking!" one of the townsfolk said. "Plenty of places that folks could have got caught and trapped!"

The others muttered their agreement.

"Good luck with it, Sire!" someone piped. And the crowd dispersed with all sorts of agreeable chatter about how well their new king seemed to be working out.

Manchester sat in the dust. A slight wind sent the old iron gates creaking. Ravens circled overhead, their darting black shadows skimming across the barrels, bottles, cans, and castoffs. And there was a sound, a rummaging sound. Glass was broken, crates were toppled, a curse was hissed.

Manchester pulled himself into a crouch. Perhaps he had stumbled upon the missing townsfolk after all.

"Who's there?" he asked, his voice trembling like a schoolboy's during spring recital.

No answer. In fact, the noises stopped all together. With caution in his step, Manchester approached the junkyard. "Hello?" he said as he pushed one of the gates open. The rust rotted hinges gave way with an utter snap. Manchester jerked back to avoid the falling gate. After a few moments of deep breaths, racing heartbeats, and nervous fidgeting, he continued forward. "Rats," he whispered to himself. "I must've heard rats. Rats are common enough in junkyards." A dirt trail twisted through the mounds of trash. Manchester stepped along, avoiding the shards of glass and the jagged pieces of metal. Again came the clanging and clamoring. "Rats," he whispered. "Nothing more."

Manchester tracked the sounds to a certain pile of refuse. He summoned up as much courage as his shivering body could hold, and kicked a can into the mound. A rat scurried out, ducking into another pile of garbage almost before it could be seen. "Rats," Manchester chuckled.

There was a yell... a long, dreadful yell. A short, gray figure sprang from the top of the trash pile, sending cans and crates and bottles spilling and tumbling and flying. The creature landed upon Manchester, hands about his neck as it forced him to the ground.

"I warned you before, human," it hissed. "I warned you not to follow this path. And now I shall have to kill you."

Manchester tingled with fear. His limbs felt tired and helpless. His lungs strained to pull in air, but the grip was too tight. He could not even see what creature assailed him, for the sun was to its back, placing it in dark silhouette. All he could make out were pointed ears and a stunted body. "Bugbear," he gasped.

The thick little fingers tightened about Manchester's neck. "No," the creature said. "Do not compare me to that insect. I am much more. I serve a dark power. I serve the future."

Manchester smelled something odd upon the creature's breath... something rancid, like the deep mud of a rotting bog. This smell he found more unbearable than the hands at his throat. He twisted and turned to get away from the stench. He wormed and squirmed. He wiggled and writhed.

The monster gave a low moan. Smoke billowed from its hands. And there was a sizzling sound, as though something burned. The creature sprang away, releasing Manchester from its deadly grip. "Foul humans with your foul trinkets!" it bellowed.

Manchester sputtered in a few breaths of air and felt about his neck. The coin. The flattened coin he had turned into a necklace. Somehow it had hurt the monster.

"Whatever meaning that charm holds for you will be for naught when the master comes," the creature hissed. "Your kingdom shall not last." And as it held its smoldering hands, it scurried out the gates and into the shadows.

Heavy, labored breaths. Painful. Such strength. Surely the creature would have crushed Manchester's windpipe. If not for the charm. Something about the charm. But what? It was just a coin flattened by a train. But it saved his life. The creature had said, *"Whatever meaning that charm holds for you..."* Perhaps Manchester himself had given it the power to ward off such evil.

Perhaps his own belief in its perfection made it the bane of imperfect things.

Bugbear would know. Manchester closed his eyes, attempting to muster the strength to stand. He rolled about in the dirt a few moments, like an overturned turtle trying to right itself. Finally he creaked, cracked, and clambered to a stance.

A clang and clatter came from the distance. Manchester jerked like a tangled marionette. He squeezed the charm in his hand, placed his other hand about his sore neck, and staggered from the junkyard.

"Bugbear will know," he whispered, a trickle of despair tickling the back of his throat.

CHAPTER 13
TRANSLATIONS, PREPARATIONS, AND EXASPERATIONS

There is a saying amongst goblins: *"The pen travels where the foot dares not."* And as Bugbear labored over the mysterious mock-Latin scroll in Willow Prairie's library, he began to understand the wisdom behind this saying. His eyes darted in and out, around and about, up and down, swimming through the complex symbols and words, venturing into a scholarly landscape filled with pits, mountains, ledges, and quicksand. Bugbear had made quite a bit of progress in his studies of the various human written languages. Days ago he had mastered both French and English. And recently he had learned enough German and Arabic to decipher some interesting limericks. But the words on the ancient scroll still eluded him. Sundry snippets. Infrequent fragments. Teasing tidbits. But nothing more. Truly, the pen which wrote these lines trod worlds which would burn Bugbear's feet, and mind, to cinders.

"You seem upset, little man," Mother Twitchett said as she placed a wrinkled hand on Bugbear's shoulder.

"Not so much upset as frustrated," Bugbear sighed, leaning back in his chair and staring at the scroll with resignation.

"And why is that?" the old woman said as she took up a stool and sat beside him.

"This scroll," Bugbear said, waving at it with contempt. "Every time I think I've translated a word, I look again and the word is gone! It's like it has a mind of its own... and a very cruel, sadistic mind at that!"

Mother Twitchett smiled. She looked at the scroll, her gray head cocked with interest. "I've seen that kind of writing before."

Bugbear arched a brow and looked to the old woman. "Are you familiar with this maddening scrawl?"

"Yes. I do recall reading something very much like this years ago. Given time I could perhaps translate it."

Bugbear's stubby fingers crinkled the ancient parchment as he pulled it close to his chest. "Perhaps," he said with a suspicious drawl. "But why would you do that for me?"

"Who's to say I would do it for you?" the old woman replied. "Who's to say I wouldn't be doing it for my own sinister purposes of world domination."

Bugbear pulled back, his eyes widened with alarm.

Mother Twitchett laughed again. "I was teasing you, little man. When I say that I could translate your scroll, I am only being helpful. That is my way, understand. And after all, isn't it in the best interest of everyone if you find out how and why our two worlds have been brought together?"

Bugbear pulled back further, falling out of his chair, rolling about on the floor, and finally popping back up to hide behind the desk. "How do you know of such things?"

"One good eye sees more than many blind eyes," she replied. "I have been here in Willow Prairie for many years. I have been watching and waiting... even helping when I could." Mother Twitchett walked past Bugbear and stood by the window. She gazed outside, a soft, sentimental look smoothing over her wrinkled face.

Bugbear peered from behind the desk, craning to see that which the old woman saw. He noticed young Riley, sitting on the front steps of the library, his head cradled in his hands.

"There you see my greatest work, Mister Bugbear," Mother Twitchett said. "Whatever I've accomplished in my time here on these worlds, Riley is the pinnacle. That beautiful little boy, with his perfect, untarnished soul. I've looked after him since his parents died five years ago. I sometimes think I shall weep for the pure joy of knowing that I have raised such a fine boy. And it breaks my heart to see him so distraught. He loves that dog and cat. They are his best friends." The old woman turned about to look at Bugbear. "Have you ever had a best friend, Mister Bugbear?"

Bugbear fought the urge to duck back behind the desk. Instead he stood, letting his grip relax on the scroll. "Yes," he said, clearing his throat. "My gardener. His name was Duergar. Fine chap. When we were young gobletts we played Noggle Stones every afternoon after our lessons."

As Bugbear approached the window he noticed an eerie, haunting tune. Riley had taken up a fife, his fingers trembling over the holes as he puffed his tear-streamed cheeks.

"He keeps playing that song," Mother Twitchett sighed. "Hoping it will bring back Buckshot and Scratch. The poor dear."

Bugbear shook free the sentiment that had begun to collect in his head. He gritted his teeth and waddled back to his desk. "He really shouldn't be playing that dirge so close to a library, you know. Makes it entirely impossible to study."

Mother Twitchett turned to Bugbear. She seemed to glare at him for a second... just long enough for Bugbear to notice... just long enough to make Bugbear feel like an insect under a magnifying glass on a hot, sunny day.

The goblin turned back to the scroll, pretending to re-read its unwieldy words. "I... I hope he finds them."

"As do I," Mother Twitchett said softly. "I sometimes feel as if they are almost a part of him. It must be horrible to lose a part of oneself."

Bugbear nodded. He looked over the frustrating parchment once more. Then he looked to Mother Twitchett. "I suppose you already have your hands full with the boy," he started, a shudder of shame in his voice, "but if you could find time..." He held out the scroll.

Mother Twitchett slowly accepted the scroll. "I promise to be careful with it," she said. "But I must ask a favor of you now."

Bugbear's eyes went dark and hazy, as if they were the window on some violent storm. "Oh really?"

"If anything should ever happen to me, I want you to promise you shall watch out for my beloved Riley."

Bugbear shrugged. "I suppose I could do that. He seems an agreeable enough child. When he isn't moping over his lost pets, that is." He turned back to the books, flipping through the pages, letting himself get lost in the words... for fear of getting lost in the emotions Mother Twitchett's visit had invoked.

"I shall leave you to your studies, Master Bugbear," Mother Twitchett said with a bow.

"You are an unsettling woman, Mother Twitchett," Bugbear said almost without realizing it. "You cook stone potatoes. You see through clever disguises without realizing it. And you risk your life for imperfect strangers. Why is this?"

Mother Twitchett paused by the door. Her entire face wrinkled into a smile. "My dear Mister Bugbear, we are all lines written on the world's parchment. I simply do as the quill demands." And she left.

Bugbear snorted. "Self-important witch," he whispered. "But if she can decipher that maddening scroll, it's worth putting up with her cryptic tripe."

The mournful tune Riley had been playing came to an end. Despite his best efforts to keep his pug nose pressed to the books, Bugbear found his attention drawn to the window. He slowly walked over to the sill, brushing aside the curtain and gazing down upon

Mother Twitchett and Riley. The old woman put her arm around the boy and helped him to his feet. She rubbed his sun-bleached head as he buried his face in her embrace, the low, trembling sobs smothered by her body. Together they slowly shuffled down the street, their heads cradled into each other, their arms twined about each other's waists, and their voices humming back and forth in low murmurs.

Bugbear's gaze followed them a few moments longer, his eyes glazing over with envy. To have such a relationship. To know such love. To experience such tenderness and support. The goblin's loneliness suddenly became starker and more intense in contrast. Like the plodding droplets of a heavy, gray rain, a soft misery settled into the corners of Bugbear's mind.

He turned about and sat at the desk. His eyes lightly skimmed over the books piled at his elbows. He reflected upon his discoveries... how Sir Reginald and Whittlegrip had fought a great battle against some unknown foe upon the peak of nearby Tamarack... how the world was divided in half, humans on one side and the rest of the races on the other... how Sir Reginald founded the town of Willow Prairie, setting up antiquated principles that were followed by its citizens for centuries... how Whittlegrip founded the school of Non-Logical Thought... how everything seemed to be such a convoluted contrivance.

"Bugbear," Manchester said in a hoarse whisper as he came upon the little man. "Thank goodness. Tudmire told me I would find you here. I need your help."

Bugbear ducked his head into his shoulders, gritting his teeth and clenching his fists. "More visitors! How am I to ever finish my studies?" The goblin sighed, shaking his head and closing his eyes. "Be quick about it, Manchester!"

"I was attacked," the king shuddered. "By the same creature that attacked me in the forest."

Bugbear continued glancing over his books, addressing his apprentice with disinterest. "Details!" he barked.

"It leapt out at me in a junkyard outside of town. It tried to strangle me, but stopped when it felt this." Manchester held up the flattened coin charm.

The goblin turned about to look at Manchester. "What is that?" he asked, gently taking the charm into his palm and examining it.

"It's a coin that I placed on the railroad tracks. I turned it into a lucky charm."

"And the creature fled when it felt the charm?"

"Yes."

Bugbear released the charm and suddenly erupted into a rich, vibrant laugh. "Manchester, you empty-headed fool!"

Manchester stepped back a few more paces. "Excuse me?"

"Without realizing it, you have created a Non-Logical talisman!" Bugbear chortled. "Very impressive! Even I haven't done such a thing! But then again, I have no use for such trinkets seeing as how I seek to become a living battery for Non-Logical energy!"

"But if my charm is Non-Logical and it hurt the creature that attacked me, does that mean that the creature was *Logical?*"

"Not Logical in and of itself," Bugbear said. "It must have been *Negative Logical.*"

"'Negative Logical?'"

"Yes. It embraces all of the most negative and evil of Logical principles... the laws that tell us we can't do this, can't do that, can't dream, can't live forever... *can't, can't, can't.* Your charm, however, is Positive Non-Logical, meaning that you have invested some great significance in it, some foolish fancy that curdles the cream of logic."

Bugbear's eyes went round and wide, as if twin explosions had suddenly spread within them. "Of course!" The goblin paced as the inspirations free-floating in his head settled side by side in brilliant illumination. "That blasted scroll is a Non-Logical talisman as well! Perhaps created by Whittlegrip himself when the worlds were divided! That's why I was unable to decipher it! I was approaching it in a logical manner! I broke the four basic precepts of Non-Logical Thought, which can never be repeated enough! *Number one: Reality is Thought. Number two: Logic restricts Thought and thus restricts Reality. Number three: Abandon Logic, abandon restriction. And number four: Unrestricted Thought equals unrestricted Reality!* But now that I am armed with this vital knowledge, I shall unleash the scroll's secrets!" Bugbear raced to the desk, rummaging about the books and papers. "Drat! Drat! Drat! I gave it to that meddling matriarch! I must retrieve it!" The goblin bolted from the desk, almost bowling Manchester over as he made way towards the door.

"But what about the creature?" Manchester asked, following with a hesitant, gangly gait. "What was it? Why does it keep attacking me?"

"When one begins moving events, Manchester, one comes to the attention of others moving events. There is a good chance that the events we are moving here in Willow Prairie are in opposition to the events being moved by someone else somewhere else."

"But what events? And by whom?" Manchester asked.

"I'd wager all the animal and people disappearances are the events. As for whom, that I don't know," Bugbear said with a shrug and a stop. "But what I do know is that I'm on the verge of discovering the secret of that blasted scroll! And I have you to thank for it, Manchester! You and your silly belief in that silly charm! Perhaps there is some magnificence about you after all!"

"But I don't feel so magnificent. I just seem to keep stumbling into all of these discoveries by accident."

Bugbear laughed again, a shrill, grating, maniacal laugh. Then abruptly he stopped, staring at Manchester with wide, bloodshot eyes. "And thus is the nature of Non-Logical Thought... coincidence married with consistency!" And he took up his titter once more as he danced out the door, down the steps, and into the street.

CHAPTER 14
THE DRAGON BRIDE'S PROMISE

Maga felt eyes upon her. Eyes filled with dark and loathsome things. Eyes that accused. Eyes that hated. Eyes that never blinked. She tried to ignore them as she walked through the town square of Willow Prairie. Yet while the eyes fell upon her back, the gallows loomed before her, reminding her of a fate that might yet come to pass.

The people of Willow Prairie did not like her. Their stares and glares were an endless warning of this. She cursed herself for her hasty promise to the king... to Martin. If not for him, she would not suffer these hypocrites. She would leave for less hostile lands. But she was bound to him and his kingdom by honor now...and by something else she did not quite understand.

She paused near the old altar where the king had removed his quill the previous night. Her hands met the cold stone, running along the designs and runes carved deep upon the surface. It reminded her of a monument in the forest near where she was raised. She would go there often after her lessons. Her sisters had told her it was a remnant of their long departed human ancestors. She had found it comforting to sit by it... to imagine what it might be like to meet humans... to connect with that ancient and unknown piece of her ancestry. She would pretend that she was visiting some grand court, feasting with lords and ladies, boasting of her victories in battle and singing songs of Allherahiah and Sir Reginald.

Yet now that she had found such a court, her boasts dried in her throat, and the songs were stifled by hate. She longed for those days when her child's imagination granted herself and humanity far more dignity than reality allowed.

"You seemed awfully down for a girl who just escaped the gallows," a gentle voice reached out from behind Maga.

Maga turned to see Mother Twitchett and her young charge, Riley. She allowed a smile to break her pensive mood. "I may have escaped the gallows, but not the hatred which would place me there."

Mother Twitchett placed a hand upon Maga's shoulder. "You have friends here, dearie. Me and Riley. And of course the king. We'll see that everyone else comes around."

Maga touched Mother Twitchett's hand, finding her skin as cool and comforting as the stone altar. "The king," she sighed. "I'm afraid I may have upset him."

Mother Twitchett laughed. "He seems to think that he upset you!" she blurted. "Poor, poor children. Your heads and hearts are so unsettled that you'll never find your way." The old woman held out her hand to Maga, her good eye brimming with cheer. "Unless I help you, that is."

"You gonna help her dress up for the party tonight?" Riley asked as he tugged at Mother Twitchett's apron.

"It's a coronation, dear boy," Mother Twitchett said, looking down to Riley and rubbing his head. "And yes, I'd like to help her..." She turned back to Maga. "If she'll let me."

Maga smiled. A genuine, true, heartfelt smile that bubbled up from the center of her soul and spread out across her entire face. "Yes," she said softly as she took Mother Twitchett's hand and stood. "I would greatly appreciate your help."

"You can wear one of my momma's dresses," Riley said, grabbing Mother Twitchett's other hand. "She... she's gone," he added as grief washed away his cheer.

Maga reached out to stroke Riley's cheek. "My mother is gone too," she whispered. "Perhaps they have met up in Heaven."

Riley nodded and smiled. "You're probably right." He then broke away from the women and skipped down the street, playing his fife and twirling like a leaf in an updraft.

Mother Twitchett squeezed Maga's hand. "He's a sweet boy," she whispered. "Caring for him has been the culmination of my life's work." The old woman looked to Maga, her good eye welling with tears. "I know you don't come from these parts, and I know you don't owe me a thing... but should anything ever happen to me, would you look after the boy for me?"

Maga placed a hand to her lips and gasped. "I... I don't... That is..." She paused and looked to the boy as he pranced down the street, music following him. Even the hateful people of Willow Prairie turned their glares away from her and joyfully watched Riley's antics. "I owe you my life, Mother Twitchett. If you think me a fit guardian, I shall care for Riley as if he was my own son. But no harm shall befall you all the same. I shall see to it."

Mother Twitchett laughed as she hugged Maga. Maga wrapped herself in the warm, soft hug as though it was a blanket on a cold night.

"God bless you," Mother Twitchett sighed.

"He already has," Maga whispered.

"Do you know any good dog and cat songs?" Riley asked as he suddenly skipped back to Maga's side.

"Dog and cat songs?" Maga chuckled. "I'm afraid not."

"Oh," Riley said, his head hung low and his fife dangling from his hand.

"The poor boy has been looking everywhere for that cat and dog," Mother Twitchett sighed. "He's been playing songs, hoping to bring them home."

"Ah!" Maga said, her voice suddenly heavy with inspiration. "Well, in that case, I might be able to help."

Riley beamed with excitement. "Really? You know a song?"

"Yes," Maga said, stroking the boy's hair. "But I'll need your help. Try to keep up with me now."

Riley nodded enthusiastically as he put the fife to his lips.

Maga cleared her throat and looked up to the sky even as her feet began to lightly dance over the cobblestones.

Where has my heart gone
Where has my soul fled
Where is that sweet song
Full of words not said

Where is the grand court
Where is the Lady fair
Where is the sweet scent
Of jasmine on the air

Where is that child's dream
Where is that child's joy
Where is that laughter sweet
In which we all must join

Here it is, a song upon our lips
Here it is, a dance within our hips
Here it is, a prayer inside our souls
Here it is, for all the world to behold

Where is that great field
In which we all play

When Winter's sting yields
To Spring's gentle reign

Where is that soft dew
Upon the morning grass
Where is the world we knew
From endless ages past

Where is that wise king
To lead us down the slope
Where is that great queen
To sing our song of hope

Here they are, a song upon our lips
Here they are, a dance within our hips
Here they are, a prayer inside our souls
Here they are, for all the world to behold
Here we are, for all the world to behold.

Maga's song and dance wound all the way through the streets of Willow Prairie, twining around the square, through the marketplace, down the sidewalks, through the alleys, and across backyards. Riley and Mother Twitchett followed, keeping time and singing along with her. Even the townsfolk stopped their sour glares long enough to watch in amazement.

"She may be a witch," one old man observed, "but she sure can dance!"

"A beautiful song," a woman said. "Too bad a more respectable lady wasn't performing it."

"I've never seen Mother Twitchett dance like that before," a young girl remarked. "Bet that witch put a spell on her. Sure could use her at the next town social!"

The song even continued as Maga, Mother Twitchett, and Riley entered the boarding house, hoofing their ways upstairs where Mother Twitchett helped Maga into a variety of different gowns, did up her hair, and put on her make-up. By the time the song had played itself out, Maga stood before a full length mirror, admiring the rich red gown with its intricate embroidery and bead work. Her hair was pulled up into a silky raven tower, a silver barrette holding it in place. Her eyes were accented in blue eye shadow and her lips painted a light red. She smiled, seeing now before her the grand lady she had imagined holding court with the kings and queens of humankind.

"Thank you," she sighed, turning about to embrace Mother Twitchett. "You've turned a witch into a lady."

"Oh, pishaw!" Mother Twitchett said. "I've only let out the beauty that was already there. Beauty that the king already sees in you."

Maga pulled away and looked to the ground, the smile replaced by a pout. "I should apologize to him," she sighed.

"Pishaw again!" Mother Twitchett laughed. "A lady never apologizes. Even when she's wrong. Because nine times out of ten it's a man who forced her into being wrong in the first place!" Mother Twitchett smiled and smoothed out some of the wrinkles in the dress. "Be gracious and be gentle when you see him next. It is the king who shall apologize to you. Accept it and talk of it no more. A man's pride is brittle. The past can do a great deal of damage to it if it's not let go."

"You look real pretty, Miss Maga," Riley said as he smiled up to her. "Don't know how anyone could ever mistake you for a witch."

Maga bent down and kissed Riley on the cheek.

"Aw!" the boy spat. "Why'd you have to go and do that?"

"Compliments are dangerous things, young Master Riley," Maga laughed. "Use them sparingly. Especially around women who aren't used to them."

"I'll remember that," Riley said, wiping the lipstick from his cheek. "But someone had better go warn that poor king."

CHAPTER 15
THE CORONATION

After signing the papers, Manchester's first duty as king was to pass a temporary law forbidding the citizens of Willow Prairie from leaving the town limits. He had felt a bit totalitarian in imposing such a rule, but after consulting with Bugbear, he felt it was the only way to stem the tide of disappearances, as well as to prolong any accidental discoveries of ogres, dwarves, pixies, and the like.

His next duty was to attend the coronation ceremony. Manchester felt even more uncomfortable about this, seeing as how the town was in the midst of a tragedy. But Bugbear had assured him that a good party was just what everyone needed to take their minds off of their problems.

"But don't you think we should be planning what to do about the disappearances?" Manchester asked as he suffered under various barbers, tailors, and valets in Mother Twitchett's parlor.

"Manchester," Bugbear started, gazing at himself in a full-length mirror as he held the lapels of his cleanly pressed coat and admired his shiny new shoe buckles and red silk bow tie, "you should know by now that I am always planning. At this very moment I am working on a plan so cunning, so devious, and so complex that it would turn a fox blue with envy!"

"*Green*," Manchester corrected.

"Pardon?"

"One turns green with envy," Manchester said.

"As well one should!" Bugbear exclaimed. "After all, it's not everyone who can come up with such cunning plans!"

Manchester groaned as the tailor pulled in a tad too tight on his trousers. "And what is this plan?"

"We shall wait."

"Wait? That's your brilliant plan? To wait?"

"But of course," Bugbear said. "Have you learned nothing, my pupil? Even as we move events, there are events being moved against us. If we wait, then these events, as well as their movers, shall be revealed to us!"

"But if we wait too long, then won't these events have moved right over us?"

"True," Bugbear conceded. "But we shall wait just long enough. No more. No less."

"And how will we know how long is *just long enough*?"

"When *just long enough* comes *just in time*."

"I'm confused," Manchester sighed, finally having enough of the valets, barbers, and tailors, and shooing them away.

"Then all is going as planned," Bugbear snickered, rubbing his hands together with scheming glee.

Tudmire rushed through the front door, huffing and puffing. He stopped near Bugbear, bending over and placing his palms upon his knees as he attempted to regain his breath and his composure.

"What news, cousin?" Bugbear said, slapping Tudmire on the back.

Tudmire swallowed and breathed a few more heavy, labored gasps. "No good."

"You didn't find her?" Bugbear said, his face growing dark and angry.

"No," Tudmire said with a cower. "But I did find this." Tudmire held up a sheet of paper, covered with vibrant colors and rich calligraphy.

Bugbear snatched it away, looking it over with hungry, darting eyes. "Bah!" he said, wadding it up and tossing it over his shoulder. "An advertisement for the coronation! What good does this do me?"

"It promises an original coronation song," Tudmire stammered. "Written by you."

Bugbear stared at Tudmire with an arched brow. "I forgot!" he blurted. "Blather and bother! I forgot all about the blasted song! I must go compose! Keep an eye out for that meddlesome Mother Twitchett for me! I must have that scroll!" With that, the goblin scholar scurried up the stairs.

Manchester watched after him, then turned to the full length mirror to look over his new attire. "He's always in such a rush."

"Yes," Tudmire agreed as he sat upon the sofa and sighed. "That is my cousin. Rushing here, rushing there… but never really getting anywhere."

Manchester smiled, admiring the rich, purple velvet of his breeches, the fine, gold stitching of his coat, the intricate patterns on his ermine lined cloak, and the shine of his black, leather boots. "Well, I hope he's able to come up with a good song. Not that my ego needs it, but I'd hate for him to be embarrassed."

"No need to worry. Cousin Bugbear thrives under pressure. Some of his best compositions have been created on the spur of the moment. *The Ballad of Cheese No More. The Song of Silent Flatulence. The Lament of the Shattered Tea Cup.* Classics all in the lexicon of goblin ditties."

"I'm sure they are," Manchester chuckled as he turned away from the mirror. "So, you're the one who organized this dreadful torture. When does it commence?"

"Whenever," Tudmire said, stretching out on the sofa with a lazy yawn. "There's no rush. Keep the people waiting and you keep the people wanting, that's what I always say."

"Don't press your luck, that's what I always say," Manchester retorted. He moved to the window and gazed outside. The night fell dark and heavy across the sky. The stars flickered in haphazard rhythm, dancing around the sliver moon. "Have you seen Maga today?"

"Yes," Tudmire said. "But you must understand, goblins and dragon brides don't get on very well. I stayed my distance and merely observed. She was organizing the royal guard... what there is of them. I must say, this town certainly is lacking in the warrior department. Scrawny, ragtag bunch, they were. Not very well armed either. I suppose that's my department, though. I'll have to look into buying them some decent weapons. With your Highness' permission, of course."

"Yes," Manchester said. "They will need weapons. Rifles, pistols, swords. And uniforms. I hate to waste the town's money, but royal guards really should have uniforms."

"And a fancy name," Tudmire added.

"I suppose so," Manchester said, stroking his neatly trimmed beard. "How about 'Reginald's Elite?' Might as well give old Sir Reginald a nod, seeing as how he founded the town and stuck that silly quill there for me to find."

"I think that is very appropriate, m'Lord," Tudmire said. "Bugbear would readily agree, I'm sure."

The awkward, strained notes of an unpracticed brass band began to weave through the air. Manchester shuddered, bracing himself against the painful noise. From the window he could see them, a group of ten or so men and women, dressed in a haphazard array of military uniforms, marching with unswerving intent, and playing their instruments with unbelievable incompetence.

"For good or ill, it seems the coronation celebration has started," Manchester noted.

"It's for ill if you ask me!" Tudmire yelped, covering his ears, and curling up on the sofa.

"Come along, seneschal!" Manchester ordered as he walked over to the sofa and playfully nudged the goblin. "You're the one who arranged this torture. It's only fair you should be suffering through it with me."

Tudmire grumbled as he straightened up and slid off the sofa.

The band stopped at the steps of Mother Twitchett's porch as a crowd of townsfolk gathered about them. They continued their pathetic performance, the notes reaching out in a painful attempt to escape those who treated them in such a shameless manner.

Manchester and Tudmire stepped out onto the porch. The band stopped as Manchester raised his hand in salute. The people shouted praises, promises, and prayers. Manchester found the whole thing rather silly. But at least the band had stopped.

"Greetings, good people of Willow Prairie," the king said, his face breaking into a politician's smile. "You honor me with your songs and praises. But I shan't delay the celebrations any longer with my bloated, hot wind! Let us adjourn to the town square where my seneschal, Tudmire, has no doubt prepared a great feast!"

The crowd erupted with a series of 'Hoorays,' 'Hurrahs,' and 'Huzzahs!' The band then struck up with another tone-deaf offering, mutilating their notes with ruthless, if unintentional, savagery.

"Great Lady Luck," Tudmire whispered to the king. "I've been to slaughterhouses that had more musical appeal."

Manchester suppressed a laugh as he walked down the porch steps. Tudmire followed, with the band and crowd close behind.

Soon the king was leading a long, winding procession down the streets of Willow Prairie. People poked their heads out of windows and doors to watch the impromptu parade. Many rushed into the streets to join the celebration. Others merely stood in their yards, watching with awe, admiration, and exultation. Some more rambunctious observers even fired their pistols into the air. And a few less-than-enthusiastic bystanders sat on their porches, eyes glazed over with disinterest and apathy.

The town square was thrumming and humming with life. Streamers hung overhead as the purveyors of souvenirs and food vendors hawked their wares, barking like mad dogs.

The royal procession wound its way into the middle of the square. The sea of people parted as Manchester fought his way to the stone monument that had held the quill. Tudmire had made arrangements for a fine, oaken throne to be placed there. The king stood before this throne for a few moments, looking out over the crowds of people. His people. It made his mind roll over and spin like a runaway top. He almost fell over from the burden of it all... all those people filling the streets to honor him. What to do? What to say? What would fill these people with the kind of pride and hope they so desperately needed?

"Hello," Manchester said, for it was the only word that came to his derailed mind. "Well, let's start!" And those were the second, third, and fourth words that came to his mind. "Pathetic," he whispered to himself, the fifth word that came to his mind.

The lack of glory and eloquence in these words did not seem to matter much to the people. They danced and pranced and sang. The band stopped for they had no room to puff, pump, or bang.

Manchester took his seat on the throne, Tudmire struggled through the throng of celebrants to stand at his side.

"Quite a sight, isn't it?" the goblin said.

"Quite," Manchester said, shaking his head. "I just wonder when the reverence will be replaced by revolution."

"Why do you say that?"

"Bugbear says we should wait," Manchester said as he watched the people mingle and make merry. "But I've heard these folks. I've heard their pleas, their wants, their desperation. We must stop these disappearances. It's why they have put so much faith in me. Because they expect me to help them."

Tudmire nodded, his face grim and contemplative. "A dangerous proposition, m'boy. Dangerous indeed."

There was sudden shouting, grumbling, and rumbling from the front of the crowd. Bugbear pushed his way into view, mounting the steps up to the throne as he looked back upon the crowd with distaste.

"Clinging vermin!" he spat. "I believe your next royal act should be to provide a bodyguard for your advisor, Manchester!"

"You've written your song already?" Manchester marveled.

"Yes! Yes! Of course!" Bugbear snarled. "It was a simple matter for one of my genius. The real chore was suffering through that sea of idiots!"

"Really, cousin," Tudmire cautioned with a finger placed to his lips, "you shouldn't go on like that. They might hear you."

"Bah! They don't even realize what's truly happened to their world, let alone what I think about them! Imagine, two halves of a long separated world finally reunited and all they can yammer about is missing cattle and erstwhile loved ones they barely acknowledged when they had them!"

"What do you suggest then?" Manchester said as he looked upon Bugbear with disapproval. "Should I tell them the entire story? Should I tell them that somehow the worlds of fey and humanity have been thrust together?"

"Are you daft?" Bugbear hissed. "As it is we are fortunate that most of them believe Tudmire and I are merely ugly, little humans. If they were to know the entire scope of the past few days' events, there would be mass hysteria! Your first duty as king is to keep the people happy. And to keep the people happy, you must keep the people ignorant."

"Uhm," Tudmire interrupted in a conflict-diffusing tone, "I don't imagine we'll be able to keep it from them for too much longer. When I was scurrying about looking for Mother Twitchett, I heard some of the locals talking about some rather large tracks on the outskirts of town. And some folks even claimed to have spotted large, hulking creatures lumbering about."

"Ogres?" Manchester gulped.

"Perhaps," Bugbear replied. "But whether the people discover the truth eventually or not is irrelevant. We must find that interfering crone and that scroll!"

"There she is!" Manchester blurted.

"Mother Twitchett?" Bugbear erupted. "Where?"

"Not Mother Twitchett," Manchester said, his eyes turning moist and dewy as he looked out over the crowd. "Maga."

"Oh bother!" Bugbear snorted. "I haven't seen such a disgusting display since you went on that butter-roasted sleel eating binge, Tudmire!"

"No doubt about it," Tudmire said as he looked at Manchester with a smile, "the boy's in love."

Manchester ignored both goblins, raising his hand and waving it in Maga's direction.

Maga smiled as she began moving through the crowd. The people parted, seemingly frightened of her. Many even shot her accusing and bitter glances. But Maga kept her gaze on Manchester, moving forward with a small, crooked grin pulling at her lips. She found her way to Manchester and knelt before him. "My king."

"Please," Manchester said, holding out his hand to her. "Don't kneel. It makes me very uncomfortable."

"I know," Maga said, letting the grin come to a full smile. She then rose, giving a nod to Tudmire and Bugbear. "I see you are still in the company of goblins."

"Yes," Manchester started.

"What of it?" Bugbear interrupted, taking a step towards Maga. "He is king! If he sees fit to take the advice goblins, then that is his business!"

"He would be better off taking the advice of slugg mulpers!" Maga replied.

"Would a slugg mulper have reminded him of his power to pardon condemned prisoners?" Bugbear said. "You owe your life to me as much as Manchester! And having dragon brides kneel doesn't make me uncomfortable at all!"

Manchester placed his arm between Maga and Bugbear, attempting to dispel the tension. "Let's not quibble. This is supposed to be a celebration."

"I might be more inclined to celebrate if there wasn't talk of dismantling the gallows," Bugbear spat bitterly as he waddled back into the crowd.

Maga glared after the little man. "If not for your attachment to the creature, my lord, I'd be sheathing my sword in his gullet."

"Uhm," Tudmire started, "I believe I'll see to the preparation of the feast." He cowered and ducked away from the others, melting into the crowd like a fat pat of butter into a hot pile of peas.

"You've frightened my friends," Manchester said.

"I apologize," Maga sighed. "But you must understand, they are goblins. I know their tricks, where you have had little experience with their kind."

"Perhaps," Manchester said, leaning back on the throne. "But I have had experience with prejudice."

Maga looked at the king with an arched brow. She smiled again. "Truly, these people are wiser than I thought if they have embraced a king such as you. Your point is well taken. I shall treat your goblins with respect if they do the same for me."

"I'm fairly certain I can talk Tudmire into agreeing to that, as he seems quite fond of his skin," Manchester chuckled. "But Bugbear may be a problem. He is stubborn. But fortunately he is also obsessed with that scroll... and tea... and Non-Logical Thought. That should keep him busy enough that he'll stay out of your way."

There was an uneasy silence... the kind that slips in and stands around like a drunk waiting for the bar to open. Manchester looked at Maga, his eyes darting over her, taking greater notice of her rich, red gown, beaded with brilliant stones and stitched with intricate designs and patterns. However, she yet wore her sword, strapped to her waist by a belt of leather with silver studs.

"That's a nice dress," Manchester whispered.

"Thank you," Maga said. "Mother Twitchett gave it to me."

"Then you had a chance to speak with her?" Manchester said, trying to hide his anxiousness, but doing a poor job of it as he crossed and uncrossed his legs, rested his chin on his hand, then placed both hands on the arms of the throne.

"Yes," Maga said, her eyes sparkling. "She told me..."

The shrill call of a trumpet punched through the air, drawing all eyes and ears to the gallows, yet standing in the midst of the crowd. Bugbear stood upon the platform, holding up his hands, Tudmire beside him, blasting away with the trumpet.

"Attention! Attention!" Bugbear called, trying to shout over the din of the trumpet. Finally Bugbear turned to smack Tudmire aside the head, ending the trumpeting tirade. "Attention! Welcome one and all to the coronation of King Martin the First! As his advisor and royal minstrel, it is my pleasure to present a special song I have composed in his honor!"

A series of low murmurs rumbled through the crowd. Some seemed to voice interest and anticipation. Others seemed somewhat less enthusiastic. But all paid attention as Bugbear motioned for the crowd to move back. He then placed a small music box on the stage, wound the key, and the strands of music commenced.

Like light, airy wisps of smoke, the music danced through the air, tangling and twining into the ears of the audience. The band members hung their heads in shame, as if each climbing note brought further dishonor to their own pathetic performance.

Bugbear stood upon the stage, bouncing up and down in wide-smiling enthusiasm, and waving his arms back and forth in rhythmic excitement. And then he started his song.

When gentle hearts are filled with song
All the world sings along.

When brutal minds are plotting war
The world weeps and sings no more.

So take ye now the hand of fate

And walk with him through Heaven's gate

For all that comes from God's good will
Was brought to pass when king took quill.

Even the best king can't do it alone.
Even the best king needs a helping hand.
Even the best king can't do it alone.
Only the best king is bound to the land.

Cast aside your fears and doubts
And exercise your cheers and shouts.

And raise your cups in proud homage
To your new king's great entourage.

The past is gone, the future's here;
The word is writ, the writing's clear.

You have your king, a noble sort.
Now do your part to help his court

Even the best king can't do it alone.
Even the best king needs a helping hand.
Even the best king can't do it alone.
Only the best king is bound to the land.

My song is almost...

There was a gunshot. Like a hollow, echoing crack of thunder it broke through the night, ending Bugbear's song. And then the screams began... wailing, mournful cries that twisted the minds and hearts of the townsfolk, causing them to both wince and gasp all at once.

Manchester sprang from the throne, not exactly certain what he was doing, but doing it nonetheless. He ran through the stunned crowd, Maga close behind with her sword drawn.

"What's all this then?" Bugbear grumbled as he watched on with shock and disdain. "Someone has the gall to get shot in the middle of my opus?"

Tudmire stumbled from the platform, shooting Bugbear a crooked glance as he followed Manchester and Maga. The rest of the crowd soon flowed in behind them, mumbling, muttering, and carrying on as curious crowds typically do.

She was lying on the ground. Manchester quickened his pace. God, not her. Anyone but her. He forced his legs to move faster. The flickering street light illuminated her fallen form. It was her. It was. Manchester felt a pit open in his stomach, deep, swirling, and nauseating. He reached her and knelt at her side.

"Mother Twitchett..."

She looked up to him, her one good eye growing dim. "The king. Oh, dear boy. You made me a promise. You said you'd look after my Riley. Pawe has taken him. And he's taken your friend's scroll."

"Get me a doctor!" Manchester yelled back to the crowd.

"Too late for that," Mother Twitchett gasped. "But not too late for my dear Riley. Find him."

"I shall," Manchester whispered. "But please don't die."

"The quill has finished my story, dear king. Now it writes for you." She chuckled, gasped, and rattled out her last breath.

Maga placed a hand upon Manchester's shoulder. "She is gone," the dragon bride said softly.

It was then that a great curtain of grief fell across the townsfolk. Every heart—old, young, man, woman, romantic, or realist—trembled, quaked, and shattered as Mother Twitchett died. The misery seeped into every nook and cranny of their humanity. No one was immune. No one was untouched. No one said a word.

That is, almost no one.

"There she is!" Bugbear blurted as he shoved his way through the mourners. "Where's my scroll?"

"She's dead," Manchester whispered.

Bugbear blinked. He looked at the still form. Then he looked to Manchester. "Did she say what she'd done with my scroll?"

Manchester frowned. He stood up and glared at the little goblin. "Yes," he hissed. "It was taken by Pawe when he shot her and kidnapped Riley."

Bugbear cocked his head. "The boy has been kidnapped?"

"Yes," Manchester said. "And I don't intend to wait around while someone else continues to move events! I shall personally lead the expedition to find them!"

Maga stood up and took Manchester's hand in hers. "And where my king goes, I go."

Bugbear waddled in place a few moments, looking from Mother Twitchett's still body to Manchester and Maga, and then back again. "I shall go as well. I need that scroll." Bugbear seemed to become aware of several sharp, severe stares. He *hemmed, hawed,* and *harrumphed.* "And the boy. The boy must be saved, of course."

"Tudmire," Manchester said to his seneschal, "you shall stay behind and look after the kingdom while we're gone."

The fat goblin stood to attention, wiping the tears from his baggy eyes. "I shall do my best, m'Lord."

"Not to upset your Majesty during this delicate moment," a thin, rasping voice slithered forth, "but I believe the nature of succession calls for the regent to take the reigns of power."

"Dunderbeck," Manchester growled as he spotted the oily scarecrow at the front of the crowd. "Very well. But Tudmire shall keep a close eye on you. If anything untoward occurs in my absence, there shall be two funerals in Willow Prairie!"

"I understand," Dunderbeck said with a nod and a slink back into the crowd.

Manchester felt power pulsing through him. There, under the soft glow of the streetlight, the townspeople gathering about him, he suddenly felt as if he was in control. He suddenly felt the voice of authority echoing through his heart. He suddenly felt that a great, yet unknown path spread before him.

"Gather supplies," he ordered. "We set out tonight."

CHAPTER 16
RUINS

"Are you certain she knows what she's doing?" Bugbear sighed.

Maga turned back to give the goblin a stern glare, then she continued studying the woodland trail by lantern light.

"Please, Bugbear," Manchester said. "Don't cause any trouble. Maga assures me that she is an expert tracker. But even an expert can have a hard time of it in the middle of the night."

"Then why don't we wait until tomorrow morning when there is proper light?" Bugbear said.

"Because I'm tired of waiting," Manchester replied. "And there is a boy out there who needs our help. I promised Mother Twitchett."

Bugbear recalled his own promise to Mother Twitchett. But that was when she had promised to translate the scroll. And the scroll was gone now. As was Riley. Thus, would it not be reasonable for Bugbear to assume the agreement null? Of course! But there was Manchester. His bargain with the king was still in effect. So, he was bound to join the frivolous excursion.

"Might I at least recommend we work on a plan of action before confronting Pawe?" Bugbear said.

Maga looked up from the trail. "He does have a point. Better to have a strategy rather than walking blindly into a trap."

"Wonder of wonders!" Bugbear gasped. "The witch of Willow Prairie actually agrees with a goblin's advice!"

"Good grief!" Manchester exclaimed. "I'll send you both back to town and do this myself if either one of you utters so much as another syllable against the other!"

Bugbear and Maga glared at each other just a few moments longer before looking to Manchester.

"Fair enough," Bugbear said. "It only makes sense that we should attempt a truce. It is the boy and the scroll that matter now." Bugbear tried to suppress the frothing foam of resentment building inside. Imagine, being told what to do by his own apprentice! It was almost as if Manchester was actually believing all this king nonsense. Bugbear cursed himself for doing too thorough a job in his king-making endeavors. He reached into his coat-of-many-pockets and removed a map. "First I suggest we find our exact location."

Maga and Manchester gathered around, illuminating the map with their lanterns. Bugbear found their proximity stifling, but he tolerated their heavy breathing, blotting shadows, and stale odors for the sake of avoiding another argument.

"Here," Bugbear said, pointing to a spot on the map. "This is where we are, a few miles outside of town. From what Maga has been able to discover from the tracks, it seems Pawe is moving west. That could bring him into the rumored location of Eglwys Cacynen!"

"'Rumored location?'" Maga said, a hint of skepticism in her voice.

"Yes. Rumored. I was planning on performing an archeological survey of the area to prove or disprove its validity. But then of course I got all tangled up in this merged worlds mess."

"Well, you might just get your chance after all," Manchester said as he pulled up his lantern and gazed off into the night-cloaked forest.

"Pawe doesn't even know about your goblin monasteries," Maga said. "There's no reason to believe that he is going to Eglwys Cacynen. He may have simply picked west as a random direction."

"And he may have simply stolen my scroll for toilet paper," Bugbear replied as he rolled up the map and tucked it inside his pocket. "We'll never know until we find him. Which brings me to my next point. What do we do when we find him? He is armed with a gun. What do we have?"

Maga patted her sword hilt. "My blade. And my arrows."

Manchester looked to Bugbear and shrugged. "The townsfolk provided me with a hunting knife and a pistol. But I'm not exactly sure how to use the pistol."

"Then it seems the most effective weapon we have is my keen intellect," Bugbear said. "With that in mind, I suggest you do your best to keep me alive!"

Manchester and Maga sighed, shrugged and set out on the trail. Bugbear waddled behind, snickering softly to himself, for some reason finding humor in the frustration of his companions.

Quite suddenly and brutally reality shattered and fell away before his eyes. Bugbear knew that a vision was about to start. His flesh tingled and his mind crumbled. A bright, white landscape unfolded before him. Then he saw goblins... thousands of them, toiling in fields that stretched on to the horizon and beyond. He saw a great shadow falling over these fields and these goblins, blotting out the white light, plunging the world into darkness.

Then there was nothing. For the longest, most dreadful, most torturous time, there was nothing. Finally, the world came into view again. It was Willow Prairie, smoldering and ruined. The townsfolk sprawled in the streets dead and dying. Savage animal-like creatures hunched over them, doing unspeakable, carnivorous acts. The shadow fell over them, once again creating darkness. Eternal, unbearable, unrelenting darkness.

"Merciful madness! Someone stop the darkness!" Bugbear shouted.

Manchester and Maga stopped and turned about to stare at Bugbear.

"It's night. There's not much we can do about darkness," Manchester said with a glower.

Bugbear blinked as the real world came into view once more. "It was a vision," he croaked, wiping the sweat from his brow.

"Another one?" Manchester said. "What was it this time?" The king moved to Bugbear's side, placing a hand on his shoulder. "Are you okay? Do you need to rest?"

"Stop fussing, Manchester!" Bugbear said as he swatted Manchester's hand from his shoulder. "I'll be fine. It was darkness. I saw darkness. And suffering. And death."

"He speaks to the dead?" Maga said, her fingers wrapping about her sword hilt as she gazed at the goblin with a new brand of distrust.

"They are visions," Manchester said quickly, as if attempting to defuse another potential conflict. "He used to take medicine for them, but he ran out."

Maga stared at the goblin a moment longer, eyes narrow and wary, then turned back to the trail.

This particular vision had not weakened Bugbear as much as his previous attacks. Still, Manchester had to steady him from time to time as they followed the twisting woodland trail. And every flitting shadow, every orphan sound, every wretched sensation, sent Bugbear spinning, bobbing, and jerking in terror. His nerves skittered and crawled with a life of their own, sending great tremors through his little body. And dark thoughts weighed his head down into his shoulders, hunching his body so that he seemed like some frightened turtle with no shell in which to hide.

"The trail breaks up here," Maga said. "There are other tracks meeting with Pawe's. Almost like animal tracks."

"Could he have been hunting for food?" Manchester asked.

"Not likely," Maga replied. "We would have heard some gunshots. Besides, these tracks are intermingling with Pawe's and Riley's. Then they go off together."

"Could Pawe have been running from them?"

"No," Maga said, running her hands along the tracks, her eyes scanning every facet of their landscape. "These are like the animals I fought a few days ago. The man-beasts. There is no sign of struggle and no sign of pursuit. It's as if Pawe was with them."

"Not surprising," Manchester said. "He was probably behind their attack on you to begin with. But where did these creatures come from? And how did Pawe gain such influence over them?"

"Perhaps it is they who have the influence over him," Bugbear said, the potential mystery nudging him out of his stupor. "Or perhaps both are influenced by the same master."

"Dunderbeck?"

"A likely suspect," Bugbear agreed. "But too likely. Too logical. I prefer to imagine a grander threat. An opponent worthy of my genius."

"Well, someone is feeling better," Maga said.

"Not really," Bugbear said. "But I'm feeling well enough to offer you the benefit of my wisdom."

"Then please benefit us with an explanation of that." Manchester pointed to a spot in the distance, just a mile or so into the forest. The moon sat in a stark crescent, huddled behind a series of tall, stone spires. Birds (or some other kinds of winged creatures) swarmed about these spires, dipping, darting, and diving in a daring aerodynamic display.

It was a surreal moment. Truly. Bugbear could only stare in abject wonder, pondering the oddity upon which he now gazed. This uncanny structure that dominated the sky like some primordial monolith stabbed his mind with an electrical excitement, a jubilant realization.

"Eglwys Cacynen," he whispered. "I was right. But I never realized it would be so complete. The legends said that it had been destroyed during a mysterious raid. But there it is."

"And that's where the tracks go," Maga said.

"Then that's where we go!" Bugbear jumped up and ran into the brush, a mad giggle bubbling from his mouth.

"Get back here, you little maniac!" Maga spat.

Bugbear did not listen to her. He was too busy surrendering to the moment. Cursed visions! Torturing him with their cryptic images! But Bugbear would not let them sour this moment. He would embrace this discovery, accepting it as the obvious reward for his patience, reverence, and persistence in keeping Whittlegrip's legacy alive. At last! The lost monastery!

Gnashing, yellow teeth. Slashing, gnarled claws. Flashing, green eyes. It leapt upon Bugbear, emerging from the forest in a whirl of movement and sound. Its pig-like snout glistened with spittle. Its coarse brown fur bristled as an enraged cat's. And its grasping claws reached for Bugbear, undulating and twisting like gnarled branches in an autumn wind.

"Away, foul creature!" Bugbear shouted.

Shining silver blade. Shimmering scaled mail. Shattering animal bone. Maga was upon the beast, her sword rending the creature with one savage, scarlet stroke after another cruel, crimson cut. Bugbear fell back into a patch of ferns, looking upon the carnage with a mix of fear, disgust, and awe.

The creature collapsed into a pool of its own blood, rolling and writhing, spitting and sputtering, and finally, mercifully, dying.

"What the devil was that thing?" Manchester said, rushing upon the scene.

"A tragedy," Bugbear said, getting to his feet and looking down at the corpse. He cautiously bent closer, daring to poke at the dead thing with a stick, examining its snout, teeth, and other features. "Porcine for the most part. Yet I also detect some canine attributes. Possibly wolf. And there is definitely a considerable amount of human in its make-up. It may well be related to the creatures that attacked you, Maga." Bugbear's mind reeled with a sudden recognition. This creature before him was much like the animal-men he had seen in his visions. The ones warring with humans. The ones who decimated Willow Prairie.

"Good Lord!" Manchester blurted.

Both Bugbear and Maga shushed their king and waved him down.

"Good Lord," Manchester repeated in more subdued volume. "Missing animals? Missing people? Could it be that somehow this," he motioned to the deformed corpse, "is what has become of them? Twisted into inhuman patchworks?"

"An interesting hypothesis," Bugbear mused as he dropped the stick and looked off to the spire. "And an interesting name for what may well be a new species. *Patchworks.*"

"I don't like being out in the open like this," Maga said. "We've made a lot of noise. We should move aside and make a strategy."

"Agreed," Bugbear said. "Pawe will most likely be expecting company. We won't be able to simply waltz right in." The goblin recognized his own recent foolishness in rushing ahead without thinking. The shame pulled his gaze to the ground and caused him to grumble and mutter. "I apologize for being so rash. Not very good form for a royal advisor."

Maga looked at Bugbear with something akin to shock. "I... I don't know what to say," she gasped. "I honestly have never known a goblin to apologize in such a way before."

"Well, don't get used to it," Bugbear snapped as he suddenly realized he did not like being in such an inferior position. "My mistakes are as rare as a dragon bride's thoughts."

Manchester raised his hand to halt Maga's retort. "Apology accepted, and we'll leave it at that. Now, let's commence our strategy."

"Indeed," a silky woman's voice purred from behind them.

The trio spun about, startled, bewildered, and stunned. A pale woman stood upon a small ridge, gazing down upon them with piercing red eyes. She wore a red cloak, red bodice, and red pantaloons. Her arms were draped in gold bracelets, her fingers covered in gold rings, her ears heavy with gold earrings. And her white hair flowed down her shoulders like snow caressing the side of a mountain. Around her gathered all manner of patchwork creatures, gibbering, growling, and clinging to her legs like devoted children.

"*A coranieid?*" Bugbear said, his voice smothered by disbelief. "But the coranieid are extinct! Wiped out by the Mumblers' curse!"

"So our enemies would like to believe," the otherworldly woman said. "Yet I survive, the last of my doomed race."

"It seems you've made some friends, however," Bugbear noted as he motioned to the menagerie at her feet. "Emphasis on the word '*made.*'"

The woman's red eyes flashed as she laughed. She looked down upon Bugbear, regarding him with a cruel smile. "Ever astute, you goblins. Indeed, I have created this small army, using the same alchemy which I perfected to counteract the Mumblers' curse."

"Well, you are to be congratulated," Bugbear nodded curtly. "Now if you'll excuse us, we are on the trail of a dangerous felon and have no time for orphaned alchemists and their patchwork pets."

The goblin turned to waddle away, but a cocking pistol and a gruff voice froze him in place.

"Stay put, short stuff," Pawe said.

Bugbear turned about to see the erstwhile constable moving forward through the parting patchworks. He leveled his pistol at the threesome. "I have to admit, you greenhorns got yourself some spunk. Didn't expect anyone to follow me out here."

"Where's the boy?" Manchester growled as he rushed forward. Maga and Bugbear were barely able to keep him contained and out of range of the gnashing patchwork jaws.

"The boy is no longer your concern," the coranieid woman said.

"And what exactly is our concern?" Bugbear asked, looking to the woman with a mixture of mistrust and distaste.

"To become loyal servants to my master," she replied.

"And your master would be?" Bugbear asked.

The woman merely smiled, her lips drawing a harsh, crooked, red line across her porcelain face. "Take them," she said with a grand, sweeping motion to her carnivorous cronies.

The patchworks were upon them, slavering and clambering over them like maggots thronging upon an animal carcass.

Bugbear felt and smelled the hot, rancid breath of a dozen hungry predators. He anticipated the dull pinch of their fangs driving into his flesh. But they only gripped him with their clawed hands, and tugged, pulled, and dragged him off into the deep, dark night.

CHAPTER 17
DINNER WITH A TEMPTRESS

Manchester had been hurried away from Bugbear and Maga... shuffled off into the more serviceable chambers of Eglwys Cacynen while his companions were carried down into the deep, dark sub-levels. The king had maintained his silence for the most part, biding his time and hoping that he might learn the whereabouts of young Riley.

The patchworks escorted him into a round, stone-cobbled room, decorated with intricate tapestries, delicate vases, and delicately carved wooden furniture. They motioned him towards a long table set with fine china and spotless silverware. Manchester sat down at the head upon a throne-like chair. His bulky escorts then took their places by the doorway. Shortly various patchwork servants commenced bringing in huge, silver trays overflowing with meats, cheeses, breads, and fruits. Manchester took special note of these patchworks, for they seemed different than the others he had seen... smaller, more docile. They appeared to be stitched together with such creatures as weasels, stoats, hedgehogs, and moles. The larger patchworks would often shove them and bark at them, as though disgusted by their inferior make-up. The small patchworks finished their subservient duties and slunk out the door, cowering before the harsh glares of their brutish brothers.

Manchester stared at the steaming platters. He wondered what manner of meat these beasts had served him. He looked to the guards who stared back, smacking their lips, seeming to find their guest more appetizing than the food. Manchester quickly turned away, recalling school lessons concerning eye contact and dominance. He had no intention of provoking these monsters. He quickly grabbed a pear and bit into it, using a napkin to dab the juice from his chin. For some reason he felt the need to behave more civilized than usual, perhaps to remind him of his own humanity amongst these inhuman creatures.

"Excellent," the coranieid woman said as she strode into the room, her heels clickety-clacking on the stone floor. "Keep eating. We want you nice and plump for the feast tomorrow!"

Manchester spat the chewed pear portion from his mouth and looked up to his captor with wide eyes.

She laughed. "Merely a jest, dear king," she said as she sat down opposite him at the table. "I have no intention of consuming such a magnificent specimen. As delicious as you may be." Her red lips curved into a playful smile, and her red eyes flashed with something deep, sinister, and wholly frightening.

"I wish to see the boy," Manchester said in strong, even tones. Hang this dominance alpha male nonsense! He would not allow this foolishness. Let these beasts tear him to shreds! He would sooner be dead than fail to fulfill his promise to dear Mother Twitchett!

"I told you," the pale woman purred, "the boy is no longer your concern. In fact, he is no longer anyone's concern. But, if it will put your mind at ease, your friends are with him right now."

"And where is that? What have you done with them?"

"They are guests in the dungeon," she answered as she poured a splash of red liquid into a golden goblet. "All three are very much alive, I assure you. And they shall remain that way... as long as you cooperate."

"How cliché!" Manchester spat. He then paused for a moment, looking down in self reflection. That sounded exactly like something Bugbear might say. What a disturbing realization.

"Oh, really?" the coranieid woman said, a hint of offense in her voice. "I am so dreadfully sorry I could not provide you with a more original challenge! Perhaps if I were to have them butchered and served for dinner, that would be more acceptable."

The thought of such a sickening sin contorted Manchester's face. He looked to the steaming meat with renewed distrust and hesitance. "No. The dungeon is good enough for now."

The pale mistress' harsh expression softened as she passed the goblet to Manchester. "Excellent! Then I can see we shall get along famously!"

Manchester received the goblet and sniffed at it suspiciously.

"Red wine," his hostess said. "An aes dana vintage. The aes dana produce superb wine, you know."

"Aes dana?" Manchester said as he sipped the wine, finding it surprisingly palatable.

"I believe you human folk call them elves. Or fairies. Or Tuatha de Dannan. Goodness! Your people have so many names for so few things! I swear, you're worse than dwarves!"

"Dwarves," Manchester snickered. "Now that's a familiar word." He raised his glass and offered the coranieid a smile, much to his own disbelief.

She returned his toast and smile. "I am Ollamh Cron."

"Not a familiar word," Manchester slurred.

"Oh, but it shall be, my dear little king. For I am one of the elite. One of the few divinely inspired visionaries who has seen the future!"

Manchester shook his head. The wine seemed to have had an instant effect on him, sending his thoughts and perceptions into a slanted, funhouse spiral. He wobbled in his chair as a sudden curiosity wormed its way into his stupor. "Bugbear called you 'a coranieid.' Said something about you being extinct. May I ask what he meant?"

For a moment Ollamh Cron seemed to battle a fire inside herself. Then she set her smoldering eyes on Manchester and let out something between a hiss and a sigh. "The coranieid were one of the original six races. Goblins, aes dana, dwarves, ogres, humans, and us. But where the other races fell under the influence of the dragons, we served a different, subtler power. Because this power advocated a philosophy of conquest, the dragons led the other races against it... and us. The Mumblers, ancient human wise men who knew the Divine Names of all things, weaved a curse about the coranieid, making all reality poison to us. Within days the entire Coranieid Empire was destroyed. Save for me, as I had found the alchemical formula to counteract the curse, although too late to save my doomed brothers and sisters."

"Good for you!" Manchester piped as he took another snort of wine. "You must feel great about yourself!"

"Yes. But not nearly as great as I feel by serving another survivor of that ancient conflict. There is no greater destiny than serving him."

"Him?"

"Him."

"Who's him?" Manchester asked.

"He is the one who was one, who then was two, but who is one once more."

The words danced through Manchester's head. Their meanings tumbled and stumbled and jumbled into the alcoholic soup stewing in his brain. He stared at Ollamh Cron, blank-faced and blinking. "That's just swell. Really. I'm so happy for you and him. And him. Great."

"You do not understand."

The king released a wide smile. "No. I don't." He gulped down more of the aes dana wine. "But neither do you, apparently."

"What do you mean by that?" Ollamh Cron asked.

"I'm not certain," Manchester replied as he poured another goblet of wine. "But I imagine it has a lot to do with the fact that I'm rather drunk." He laughed, a long, snorting, uncontrolled laugh.

"You should not laugh," she said. "Cysgod Gof shall usher in a new, golden age for this world!"

Manchester's laugh grew to a fevered pitch. "Amazing!" he sputtered as he regained his composure. "That's exactly what the people in Willow Prairie say about me! Poor Cysgod Gof! I know exactly how he must feel. Such pressure." He drained another goblet and reached for the wine bottle.

The coranieid temptress snatched the bottle away from him. "Enough," she seethed. "We have important matters to discuss. I offer an alliance. Join me in my cause. Join me in the service of Cysgod Gof. Add the might of your kingdom to his armies and we shall conquer this new world. All humans, goblins, dwarves, ogres, aes dana, dragon brides... everything that walks, crawls, swims, and flies... everything that talks, squawks, buzzes, and sings... every living creature shall bow before us. We shall be the masters of a new age!"

Manchester looked to her, his head wobbling on his neck like a sandbag balancing atop a twig. "I have enough problems ruling one town. I wouldn't even begin to know what to do with a world."

"So your answer is no?"

"So my answer is no."

She glared at him, nostrils flaring and chest heaving with deep, angry breaths. "Then you shall be destroyed like all the others who have opposed me!"

"Wouldn't Cysgod Gof have to approve of that?" Manchester said. "He is your master after all."

"He's not here yet."

"He's not here yet?" Manchester said with an arched brow. "Interesting. Where is he then?"

"Beneath our feet. Waiting."

The king lifted his foot and looked at the bottom of his shoe. "What's he waiting for? To be scraped off?"

"Outrage!" Ollamh Cron shrieked. The patchwork guards growled and move towards Manchester.

Manchester took up a knife from beside his plate. How foolish of them, he thought, to so graciously provide him with a weapon. He stood up, weak-kneed from the wine, and brandished the blade. Drunk as he was, he found a great vigor rushing through him. Courage filled him as well. And inspiration. He remembered Bugbear's lessons. As he glared at the patchworks, then to Ollamh Cron, then around the room to the torches, a plan came to him.

He leapt upon the table, dashing across it, upsetting the plates, trays, goblets, and glasses. As the patchworks came full upon him, he took up the bottle of wine and sprang into the air, landing some distance from them, near the torches lining the wall.

"What are you doing?" Ollamh Cron screeched.

"Moving events," Manchester laughed. He threw the open bottle at the approaching patchworks, letting the wine splatter over them. The bottle then burst as it hit the floor behind them, further spreading the red liquid. Then he let fly with a torch, igniting the fuel in a crimson flash.

The flames skittered up the bodies of the animal men, embracing them in wild, red rage. They howled, rolled, and ran, spreading the fire through the chamber. Little licks of red and yellow devoured the ornate tapestries and wall hangings.

Ollamh Cron leapt up in a furious flurry. She raged and screamed against Manchester. "Fool! What have you done?"

Manchester shook his head as a man waking from a dream. "I... I'm not sure," he muttered.

Now he was trapped. The flames were between him and his enemies... but also between him and the doorway. He slid back to the wall, inching along as he watched the raging patchworks falling over themselves.

Ollamh Cron made quick her own escape, bolting the door behind her in an attempt to keep the flaming animal men from spreading the fire. "I could have made you more than a king!" she cried from behind the door. "I could have made you a god!"

"No thanks!" Manchester called back defiantly. "I already have a God!" As his hands moved along the smooth stones, he met with cool, night air. There was an open window behind him. Escape! He whirled about and peered down. A very treacherous escape! He had not realized how high the keep was until he gazed down those walls. They stretched down, down, down in spiraling vertigo. A small ledge offered some hope. His only hope. With a caution that sent every muscle fiber taut and trembling, he stepped outside. The stonework seemed sturdy enough, although a few pebbles and shards skittered before his nervous foot shuffles.

Manchester heard the patchworks howling and screeching inside while Ollamh Cron bellowed out her commands. And the flames grew higher, like the red fingers of fallen angels reaching towards the heavens. The top levels of the keep were now entirely devoured by the hungry blaze. It seemed that aes dana wine was as potent a fuel as it was a drink.

The tongues were tasting after Manchester, pushing him frantically along the ledge. And there was not much more ledge to be had.

The wine must have been making a return assault on his senses, as the king then witnessed the most black and unsettling form moving towards him. Certainly it was a hallucination. No one but himself could be foolish enough to be shuffling about on this treacherous ledge!

"Your death," the shape hissed. "A glorious thing it shall be. Like an artist, I shall sculpt it. Like a minstrel, I shall sing it. Like a love, I shall cherish it. All in his name."

It was the shadow creature. The horrible, hideous, harrowing shadow creature. Manchester held up his coin charm to keep the fiend at bay. But the movement unbalanced him and sent him flailing and floundering from his perch, gracelessly clawing at the night air. Twelve feet later he met with a stone balcony. The impact jarred every bone and organ in his body, numbing and paralyzing him. Still, he praised his luck in avoiding a more serious and terminal introduction to the raging river some seventy-five feet beyond the balcony, where the charm now spiraled, disappearing into the churning, rushing waters.

The shadow creature had a less difficult time of it. It crawled down the wall, defying the laws of physics, its movements quick and skittering like a spider's.

Manchester tried to get up... tried to escape... but he was frozen, both with pain and fear.

The creature moved upon him in eerie, menacing strides. It raised the shovel high and prepared to strike.

CHAPTER 18
WHAT HAPPENED TO RILEY?

"A recent addition," Bugbear said as he tested the bars of his cell. "Sturdy dwarven metal, I'd wager."

"I never did like dwarves," Maga said as she strained at her own prison.

"Just because they smelt lasting iron is no reason to dislike an entire race," Bugbear replied as he manipulated two slender rat rib bones into the lock on his prison. The bones soon snapped under the stress of the endeavor. "Their clever locks however, merit a deluge of hatred and contempt!"

"What do you suppose they've done with Martin?" Maga asked.

"Who?" Bugbear said, peering about the dungeon, taking in the what details were available in the dim lighting.

"The king!"

"Oh! Manchester? I suppose they're attempting to win him over to their cause. A typical coranieid tactic. Woo with flattery and false promises. Conquer with kindness. Then destroy. There's actually quite a bit to admire about the coranieid."

Maga snorted and sat down in the pile of straw that passed for her bed.

Bugbear continued his observations. Torch light ebbed and flowed through the room like a yellow-orange tide, sometimes exposing disturbing details... ancient, rusted torture devices... piles of rags and refuse that might once have been living creatures... very bad murals depicting great events in coranieid mythology. There were other cells here as well... stark, empty tombs decorated with the crisscrossed shadows of iron bars. Only one of the prisons held a small pile of rubbish in a far corner. Perhaps a rat nest, or the remains of a guest... or both.

Two patchworks stood guard at the doorway where winding stone steps led to the upper levels. One of the beastlings seemed part wolf and part lynx. The other was cobbled together with nastiest pieces of bull and mustang. Both stamped and snorted and paced in place, clearly uncomfortable with such cramped, stuffy surroundings. Once again Bugbear was reminded of his haunting visions of such patchwork creatures rampaging through the streets of Willow Prairie. He shuddered, closed his eyes, and turned away to observe less disturbing things.

The stonework, despite its great age, still seemed as sturdy as the day Whittlegrip laid it. Bugbear could even make out a few faded goblin runes carved into the stones. *"With blood and tears we lay these stones, to stand as long as martyrs' bones,"* he whispered, reading one of the legendary lines.

Then, with a head heavy in gloom, he turned to look at Maga as she reclined on the loose straw, her eyes closed and lips pursed as if awaiting the kiss of some bold savior.

"Hopeless," Bugbear said.

"What was that?" Maga said, rousing from her trance.

"That's the word for this moment," Bugbear said. "For I see no escape. No plan of action. No weaknesses in our prisons. The word is *hopeless.* Unless you happen to be a coranieid. Then I suppose the word would be, *'Bwhahahahahahaha!'"*

Maga shook her head and sighed, pulling herself out of the straw. "What about that little religion you're always going on about? Can that get us out of this mess?"

"By 'little religion' I assume you refer to Non-Logical Thought?" Bugbear said, his brow furrowed at the dragon bride's thinly veiled insult. "It might be of use. But I must find just the right event to move. For as the bee carefully rotates its wings in miraculous flight, I must carefully rotate my mind in miraculous postulations! One stray thought might bring the entire monastery down upon our heads!"

Maga shook her head and snorted. "Admit it. It's just another scheme, like all goblin endeavors."

Bugbear gripped the bars of his cell, pressing his pug face against the cold iron and glaring at Maga. "There is no scheme in Non-Logical Thought!" he yelled. "It is the purest of pursuits! A lyrical voyage through the undiscovered truths of unreality! As a matter of..."

The pile of rags in the other cell moved. Only slightly at first, but enough that Maga noticed, and waved a hand in Bugbear's direction to alert him. They both watched in silence as the rags trembled slightly, heaving and bulging, undulating and pulsating, shivering and shaking. And then music. A fife. Soft, quiet strands. Flitting through the gloom like fireflies at dusk.

The guards snarled and snorted, scuffling from their posts towards the derelict sounds. The bull/mustang tapped a hoof-hand against the bars of the rag-thing's cell. "No music!"

Still the tune fumbled forth, groping its way through the empty heart of the stone keep.

"There's something familiar about that tune," Bugbear whispered to himself.

"No music!" the wolf/lynx growled, reaching through the bars and swiping at the rags cowering in the corner.

But the song grew stronger, punching its way through the eerie quiet, dashing itself against the harsh pall of fear, breaking through the melancholy shadows.

The patchwork guards hastily took the keys from the peg, fumbled with them, shoved one into the lock, turned it, and flung open the door. *"No music!"*

The song would not die. It filled the room, a thin but powerful tune, tumbling and spinning through the air like one of Bugbear's precious bees.

"I know that song!" Bugbear exclaimed.

The guards lumbered over to the pile of rags, the bull/mustang leaning closer, its wet muzzle steaming and puffing with anger. "We said, no..."

The rags erupted as though launched from a canon. A lean creature of black and white fur leapt upon the bull/mustang, his savage fangs biting deep into the throat. The guard let out a bone-rumbling bellow as it fell back upon the stone floor, the black and white creature clinging to its neck in tenacious frenzy.

"It's Riley!" Bugbear shouted. "By Whittlegrip's wisdom, it's Riley!"

Eyes round with terror, the wolf/lynx backed against the bars of the neighboring cage, where Maga snatched the keys from its loosened grip, and wrapped her arm about its neck, pulling it into the bars and choking it there as it clawed and kicked and gurgled.

The black and white beast rose from his conquest, wiping the spittle and blood from his muzzle. "They thought we were weak," he growled. "Malformed and useless. Locking us up and hoping to feed us to their troops. We prove them wrong." Turquoise cat eyes narrowed, looking to Maga and then to Bugbear. "We are one, and one is stronger than many."

"Riley," Bugbear gasped. "Dear boy. I'm so sorry." And Bugbear had seldom spoken so honestly from his heart. There was no bombast to relay his shock. No eloquence to voice his outrage. No philosophical ponderings to dismiss his guilt. There was only the deep, dark, unrelenting echo of sorrow, and the bitter sting of barely suppressed tears. "I promised her. I promised her..."

As Maga dropped the unconscious wolf/lynx to the ground, she looked to the black and white dog/cat. A lump of misery entered her voice as she choked: "That's Riley?"

The creature cocked his head and looked to Bugbear and Maga in the certain way dogs do when hearing their names. "Yes," he said, padding forward in cat-like caution. "Riley is here. Riley, Buckshot, and Scratch... all together again."

"By the Great Drake!" Maga cursed. "I'll drive my sword into that witch's black heart!"

The hackles rose on Riley's back and neck. He cowered and crept to the open door of his cell. "We sense you are upset. Fear. Sadness. Anger. Why do you feel these things?"

Maga reached around through the bars and unlocked her cell. She watched the young patchwork as she crossed over to Bugbear's cell. "Does he realize what's happened to him?" she whispered to the goblin as she worked the lock.

Bugbear looked at the creature, observing his animal-like behaviors. Sniffing. Crouching. Whining. Growling. Then he saw the fife gripped in his clawed hand. "I believe he does realize it," Bugbear whispered in reply. "But he... *they* don't care. It's what they want."

"What?" Maga gasped with disbelief as she opened the door.

"No time to explain now," Bugbear said as he brushed past the dragon bride. "We must find the king."

"The king!" Riley blurted as in a burst of sudden excitement he ran in circles about Bugbear and Maga. "We shall find his scent for you! Yes! Very useful we shall be in finding the king!" And then he bolted up the stairs ahead of them.

"What are we going to do with him?" Maga asked, for the first time since she'd met him, looking to Bugbear for an answer.

Bugbear closed his eyes. "I don't know," he replied. His head was now thick with doubtful dirt, sorry soot, and guilty grit. All his posturing and self-importance. All his egotistical bluster. All his empty concerns. All came back upon him in a dark, cloud of dust, crashing through his mind with billows of black and shards of silver.

"I promised her," he whispered.

CHAPTER 19
FURIES IN THE FLAMES

The shovel blade bit deep into Manchester's heel, piercing his boot and the flesh it should have protected. The cold, unearthly metal chilled him to the marrow, tendrils of pain skittering along raw, throbbing nerves.

"A king's wound," the shadow-beast hissed. "You should be proud."

Manchester gritted his teeth, forcing himself to crawl along the rampart. The loose shards of stone scraped his hands and jabbed at him through his clothing. Behind him the shadow creature laughed and the flames danced.

"I'm not finished yet," he gasped, turning onto his back and facing the gloating creature.

"You are finished," the creature said. "But like all great works of art, your death must wait a time before it can be fully appreciated."

The creature smiled. Beneath the shadows which hid its features, Manchester could see the yellow teeth. And then it faded back, slithering into the flames to disappear.

It stung. It stung like the devil. A deep, ringing, echoing pain that screamed through every fiber of Manchester's being. He gripped the afflicted heel with his hand, which only made the pain worse. He pulled his hand away and made to draw a handkerchief from his pocket. Then he saw. There was no blood on his hand from where it had touched the wound. There was only a dry, gray powder, like soot. In the light of the flames, he saw the same powder on his heel. No blood. Only powder.

The flames. While he had been concerned about his wound, he had ignored their advance. They were nearly upon him now, only feet away. He inched further along the rampart. Soon he would be at the edge, and he would join his Non-Logical charm, carried away by the merciless river below.

The surface of the rampart changed as Manchester scuttled along his back. The shards of broken stone seemed to give way to a less harsh material... something akin to...

"... *Wooooooooooooooooooood!*" Manchester exclaimed, realizing what it was just as it decided to give way beneath him. Once again he found himself falling, not quite as far as when he fell from the ledge to the rampart, but far enough that he cursed his life and all the high places it seemed to fancy. He came to a thudding end some ten feet from where he started, splinters and chunks of wood landing about and upon him. When he could bring himself to open his eyes again, he saw that he had fallen through a trap door... a handy way for troops to access the rampart... and an even handier way for foolish magician-kings to stumble out of very messy deaths.

Then came the sniffing. Followed by the slobbering.

Puh-tack! Puh-tack!

"Ogres!" Manchester exclaimed. Once more he scurried and scampered, this time regaining his uncertain feet, and putting his fists up in an offensive posture.

"We found the king, as we promised!" a scruffy black and white dog-thing said as it pranced and danced before him.

"What in the name of Chung Ling Soo?" Manchester blurted.

"Manchester, you conduct yourself with all the grace and subtlety of a staph infection!" came a shrill voice from the shadowed hall behind the creature.

"Bugbear?" Manchester said.

"Indeed," the goblin said as he stepped into view, followed closely by Maga. "And the poor soul you so rudely addressed is young Riley, an unfortunate victim of our coranieid host's mad experiments!"

Manchester backed to the wall, and slid down until he sat, looking to the furry creature with wide, disbelieving eyes. "Riley?" he gasped.

"Yes, king?" the creature replied, cocking his head and letting a long tongue loll out the side of his mouth.

"This is too far," Manchester said. "Too much. Too evil."

"Yes, yes," Bugbear said, waddling up to Manchester and tugging at his arm. "*Far too much evil.* We're all impressed with your moral outrage. Now, let's be on our way."

Manchester began to follow Bugbear's pull, but winced and floundered back to the floor as his wound reminded him of its presence.

"You've been injured," Maga said, her voice trembling with concern as she brushed past Bugbear and reached out to Manchester.

"The shadow-beast," Manchester gasped, leaning into Maga's arms. "He stabbed me in the ankle. But I think I can manage."

"You'd best manage," Bugbear said as he pointed up through the shattered wooden trapdoor to the flames which licked its edges. "Apparently someone's started a fire!"

With Maga's support, Manchester pulled himself to his feet. "That would have been me. I was moving events. This coranieid—her name is Ollamh Cron, by the way—tried to recruit me. Something about a hidden master buried in the earth, or some such nonsense. I don't remember too much. I was drunk at the time. Still a bit tipsy."

Bugbear looked to Manchester, his eyes wide and unblinking. "You," he gasped, "moved an event?"

"I think," Manchester said, as Maga continued helping him walk forward. "Does anyone know how to get out of here?"

Bugbear waddled forth to catch up with Maga and Manchester, Riley prancing around them, excitedly wagging his tail. "Legend has it there are aqueducts fed by the river in the sub-levels below. If we can avoid your *event* and the patchworks, then that would be our best chance to escape."

"We can smell water, we can!" Riley blurted. "We shall lead! We shall find!"

And the patchwork padded off into the darkness ahead.

Manchester's mind mirrored that darkness. His thoughts bumped and fumbled into unseen obstacles, searching for words to frame his sorrow. Riley, dear Riley. That golden boy. That precious innocent. That inspired youth. His perfection had now been ripped from him. His childhood destroyed. His purity obliterated. And in the wreckage... in the ruin... in the rubble... a stark, soul-shattering tragedy remained.

As they navigated the narrow, musty halls of the goblin keep, strange fantasies navigated Manchester's emotions. Vengeance. Anger. Outrage. They piled into his thoughts, squeezing out civilized concerns. He imagined Ollamh Cron's pale face stretched into a scream as she lay beneath the fallen stones of Eglwys Cacynen. *Death. Death. Death.* The word echoed through Manchester's head. *Death. Death. Death.* The word promised a release of the dark thoughts that plagued him. *Death. Death. Death.* The word eased him and frightened him all at once.

They turned a corner, mounting a series of steps that led down into darker, more obscure areas of the monastery. Manchester's mind turned another corner, leading to light. Death was not the answer. Neither was vengeance. *I am a king now,* he thought. *I am not allowed such luxuries. Justice, not vengeance. Patience, not impulse. Wisdom, not rage.*

Once more he looked to the prancing black and white beast-boy scouting before them, and he recalled the little rhyme Tudmire had told him:

> *White, Gray, and Black Stones*
> *Scattered 'Cross the Board.*
> *Now You Must Unite Them*
> *To Become The Noggle Lord!*

Manchester allowed himself to smile as a comfort silently met his thoughts. Riley, Buckshot, and Scratch... like three white Noggle Stones, joined together against the shadows.

The darkness left his mind, gasping like a dying October wind. Light reigned now. And it gave the king strength. It filled him with peace. It reminded him of responsibilities.

If only it had reminded him of his wound and the last step on the stairs.

"Martin!" Maga shouted as she watched him stumble from her steadying arms and collapse.

Manchester looked up from the cold stone floor. "Sorry about that. Things got mixed up somewhere between my heel and my head."

Riley padded up to the fallen monarch, sniffing and panting. "The wound is bad. We can smell infection already."

"We really should treat it," Maga said, carefully lifting the heel to examine it.

Manchester winced and drew back. "Not now," he said. "We need to get out of here."

"At least let me put some bandages on it," Maga said. "Bugbear, would you lend a hand?"

They turned about peering into the darkness, seeking the familiar form of the stunted, frazzled goblin.

"Bugbear? Where are you?"

CHAPTER 20
THE TREASURES OF EGLWYS CACYNEN

Few times in Bugbear's life had he been unable to find his tongue. Even on the day he was born he possessed the faculties to utter a few words to commemorate the grand event:

Unclean world, cluttered with filth,
Find your worth in one grand birth

And there are those who would argue that the goblin had been talking non-stop since.

However, as he and his companions wound through the ancient passageways of Eglwys Cacynen he caught a glimpse... one of those glimpses that at first seems unreal... too good to be true... but then as it settles into ones mind and pinches the fatty arms of doubt, it stands full and bold. And so, this glimpse took a hold of Bugbear's eyes and mind, until it was a glimpse no longer, but instead a revelation... a revelation that made Bugbear's brain water with sentient salivation.

A room stood off of the main corridor, its oaken door open as if in invitation. Inside, flickering torch light revealed bookcases overflowing with all manner of tome, parchment, book, and journal. And this is when Bugbear lost his tongue. His ears went next as he barely heard his companions rambling on about wounds and bandages. He thought he heard his name mentioned, but by then he had entered the room and left behind all concerns save the exploration of this newly discovered scholar-scape.

The famed library of Eglwys Cacynen! The musty scent of ancient parchment tickled Bugbear's nose in that old and comforting way. His bulging eyes jumped from shelf to shelf, frantically seeking nothing in particular and everything at once. His feet shuffled along the dusty stone floor, scuffing and scraping in a steady, hypnotic rhythm. And the air caressed him with cool whispers and soothing hisses.

To most the room would seem a disorganized, disheveled, and disturbing display. But to Bugbear every yellowing page, every weathered binding, every fading letter was a new world waiting for discovery. Here amongst these mighty oaken bookcases and crinkled parchment landscapes he could find a peace of sorts... a refuge from the nagging, distracting, maddening voices of reality... and the torturous, relentless, disastrous visions of unreality.

Bugbear reached out, with both hand and mind, seeking the perfect printed partner for his scholarly excursions. Recipes for resurrection. Formulas for fabrication. Instructions for invention. Such tempting academic aromas wafted before his mind's nostrils. But they watered not his mental mouth. For his appetite was set upon that rarest of intellectual delicacies... the lost writings of Whittlegrip!

They were here... buried beneath the lesser scholarship of unsuccessful successors... floundering under the pretentious ponderings of pathetic impostors... hidden behind the worthless words of undeserving disciples. They were here... calling out in thin whispers of inspiration... taunting in haunting melodies of illumination... beckoning with bitter breaths of wisdom. They were here. They were here. They were here.

And something else. Something familiar. Something desirable. Something smelling of musty memories and faded fantasies. It was strong and bold, grabbing Bugbear's nostrils and pulling him forth like a trained dog.

He stopped at a desk, coated in gray dust and spotted with mildew, save for one place where a silver box sat in a sliver of moonlight cast from the narrow window above. The box was goblinish in make, adorned with the traditional pictorial decorations associated with the silversmiths of Caer Galwch. Twistroot, the legendary goblin trickster, stole immortality from the underworld. Bulworm, the legendary goblin huntsman, freed the Swan-Maiden from her ancient curse. Dumful, the legendary goblin idiot, traded places with a noble on the eve of Owain's Feast. And there was a lot of other boring rot which Bugbear found not nearly as interesting as the specter which beckoned him from beneath the glimmering lid.

Hands trembling with drumming dread, mouth smacking with dry despair, eyes wide with delirious dismay, he laid his fingers upon the ornate lid... and opened it.

It spread out within the opulent confines of the box, like a lover awaiting the return of her warrior-husband. Savory. Seductive. Sinful. The gray granules glistened like a tiny sea of pearls, each one seeming to call out in a small, whispering voice.

"We have been waiting."

"I am here," Bugbear replied, lifting the box and gazing upon its contents with a fanatical affection typically reserved by madmen for their madness. "My precious banderberry root tea."

"Bugbear!" barked a voice from behind, its intent sheathed in parental anger.

The scholar jumped, fumbling the box in his hands and batting it back and forth until finally maintaining a firm grip.

"What?" Bugbear spat as he turned about to glare at Maga.

"Do not wander off on your own!" she said, returning his glare. "Martin is wounded and we need your help!"

"Yes, of course," Bugbear said, carefully closing and latching the lid and placing the box inside of his coat. "I was in here looking for..." He looked about, eyes and head darting in different directions, seeking out a prop to support his canopy of lies. A few scraps of cloth dangled from one of the nearby shelves. He quickly snatched them as if they had always been in his thoughts. "Bandages! Bandages for his wound!"

But suddenly Bugbear became aware of words on these cloths... not written... but spoken. He heard them... the ancient words of Whittlegrip himself, inscribed upon these cloths in the lost language of Non-Logical Thought!

"There are four basic precepts of Non-Logical Thought, which can never be repeated enough," the cloth said. *"Number one: Reality is Thought. Number two: Logic restricts Thought and thus restricts Reality. Number three: Abandon Logic, abandon restriction. And number four: Unrestricted Thought equals unrestricted Reality."*

"Well," Maga said, not hearing the words of the cloth, "hand them over!"

"No," Bugbear whispered, pulling them close. "These are valuable beyond measure. They contain an intellect and wisdom! A lost voice that can alter the existence of all who hear it!" He unbuttoned his plaid vest, tore it from his body with a violent display, and threw it at Maga's feet. "Use this to bandage Manchester's wound!"

Maga glared at the goblin as she picked up the discarded garment. "You tempt a terrible fate, little man. I tolerate your eccentric mood swings by Martin's will. But when you begin to hold your studies in higher regard than his well-being, my tolerance reaches its limits."

Bugbear ignored the dragon bride's threat, stuffing the cloth treasures into his jacket pocket. "A shame we don't have time to search for that unusual scroll Mother Twitchett lost." And with a scowl, a growl, and several severe stomps he brushed past Maga into the dim hallway.

"You play with fire," Maga hissed after him.

CHAPTER 21
INTO THE UNDERWORLD

Manchester found the screams the most disturbing part. The old stone hallways amplified and distorted the howls and screeches, twisting them into something that would dispirit a nightmare. And the shadows... half-human shapes contorting and flickering against the walls, the flames feeding their evil undulations. These sights danced before Manchester's haunted eyes, reminding him that the greatest tragedies of the world were often writ by a careless king's hand.

"I did this," he gasped as Maga helped him hobble through the corridor. "I set this terror loose."

Maga pulled him closer, as a mother would her child. She said nothing... at least nothing that could be heard... only what could be felt.

"The Patchworker took the worst of them, King Munchausen," Riley said, breaking away momentarily from his tracking. "Thieves. Bandits. Ruffians. The greedy and small and devious. These were what she needed for her army. Do not mourn their deaths. They would have killed you for table scraps."

"And for a scrap of compassion, they might have spared me," Manchester replied.

Riley cocked his head, looked to the king, and perked his ears. "We are not certain if you are foolish or if you are wise. Perhaps there is something worthwhile in being both."

And the animal-boy returned to his tracking, padding forward as Manchester, Maga, and Bugbear followed.

Manchester looked to Bugbear in an attempt to distract himself from the terror around them. The goblin had found something when he went in search of bandages... writings on patches of cloth, from which he now read in mad, rustling whispers.

"In time Whittlegrip took to the wilderness where he conversed with the bees, learning from them many an ensorcelled secret!"

The way Bugbear read from the passages, sputtering, gibbering, foam flaking from his lips... Manchester almost found himself longing for the tragic spectacle of the dying patchworks. And yet he knew these were important documents, for between Bugbear's frantic whispers he could hear them telling him so. As unsettling as that was.

The pain battled its way back to Manchester's thoughts, throbbing in his heel like an angry thug battering at a door. Manchester acknowledged it, wincing and staggering, leaning on Maga for more support.

"I'm sorry," he gasped. "It seems I've become quite the burden."

"Hardly," Maga replied. "There are no burdens for those who serve kings."

Manchester mustered a smile and a nod. But the pain would not allow any words of gratitude, as it filled his mouth with gasps and moans.

"We smell the water," Riley said. "It is close now. Down this hall."

The beast-boy led his companions through a narrow, moss-matted hallway. The floor sloped downward, at some points rather steeply, and the moist ground made for treacherous going. Manchester found himself leaning more heavily on Maga, which in turn seemed to slow the dragon bride's progress. Bugbear had the least difficulty, for so enraptured was he in his studies that even his feet appeared to ignore the obstacles of reality.

And Riley, while far more graceful and sure-footed than his companions, simply gave into the slippery passage, allowing the slime-slathered slope to carry him half-howling and half-laughing on a wild slide down into the darksome depths.

It was a queer spectacle, seeing all three playful personas of boy, cat, and dog frolicking together in a whirl of whimsy.

Soon Manchester and Maga found themselves joining the festive fall as they finally lost their collective footing. When Manchester was a child, on those days his illness didn't keep him in bed, his father would take him tobogganing on Pokagon Hill. This ride down the muck-encrusted corridors of Eglwys Cacynen reminded him of those days. Except it wasn't as cold. And he had no toboggan. And Maga smelled nicer than his father.

The darkness broke as the slope opened up into a wide aqueduct. The water ran approximately fifty yards to an opening into the river proper. Manchester had less than three seconds to realize all of this before he found himself flung into the air and dropped into the water. The water filled his world, and he felt a sudden weakness... an inability to move his arms and legs in any kind of usable manner. He thrashed a bit, attempting to pull his way to the surface. But he may as well have been clawing at air in an attempt to fly.

Arms reached about his waist and pulled him up. Maga. As always, Maga. He broke to the surface, gasping for air, and she pulled him to the water's edge where together they found handholds on the ancient stone walkway. Downstream, Riley dog paddled towards the same goal, his mutterings falling between disgust and delight... cat and dog conflicting over whether to have fury or fun with this new environment.

Manchester looked about as he spat and sputtered. The moon cast a dull but usable light into the aqueduct through the river opening.

"Where's Bugbear?" he asked, as the goblin was not in sight.

"Martin," Maga said, "you are getting weaker by the moment. I need to treat your wound. Bugbear can find his own way. It's an annoying trait goblins have."

"I will not leave him," Manchester said, almost growling.

"He would leave you," Maga replied.

The words trickled through his mind, as the water trickled down his face. It was a disturbing possibility, yet a possibility all the same. Bugbear wouldn't abandon them out of malice or cowardice, but he might out of distraction or disinterest. The goblin's mind worked in ways alien and bewildering... considerably more now that he had found those unusual documents.

The disturbing possibility dissolved as Bugbear appeared, strolling along the pathway beside the aqueduct, dry as a Noggle Stone, and still lost in the whispering wisdom of the arcane cloths.

"How did he get here?" Maga asked as she watched the goblin waddle past on his oblivious way. "And without a spot of slime or water on him?"

"There are four basic precepts of Non-Logical Thought, which can never be repeated enough," Manchester said as he watched Bugbear with admiration and disbelief. "*Number one: Reality is Thought. Number two: Logic restricts Thought and thus restricts Reality. Number three: Abandon Logic, abandon restriction. And number four: Unrestricted Thought equals unrestricted Reality.*"

Maga looked to Manchester, her silver eyes flashing with reflected moonlight. "Somehow, coming from you it almost sounds interesting." She smiled and eased him along the edge of the aqueduct, towards the river.

Manchester forgot the pain in his heel. He forgot the guilt he felt over the fire. He forgot his duties and responsibilities as king of Willow Prairie. He almost forgot how to breathe. For his head was filled with words now, bumping and crashing into one another in an attempt to form a sentence... a sentence Manchester could not muster the courage to utter. So when the words settled into place, they simply stayed in his head, waiting for a moment that might never come.

And these words were simple, but powerful. They could take Manchester's life in a magnificent new direction... or send him spiraling into a magnificent new despair. Men had faced these words for centuries, challenging them and embracing them. They were words that sometimes started wars, and sometimes ended them.

Manchester would keep the words in his head for now, until his heart felt they should be free.

And those hidden words were: *"I love you."*

CHAPTER 22
WORDS

There were things going on around Bugbear. And he was aware of several of these things. For example, he knew that he, Manchester, Maga, and Riley were in a clearing in the woods. He knew he sat before a campfire with a boiling teapot. He knew Riley was scavenging for game in the surrounding brush. And he knew Maga sat by the river, dressing the king's wound. He knew all of these things.

But most of all he knew the writings of Whittlegrip. The Non-Logical prose had captured him, holding him in a world of words, a landscape of language, a nation of narrative. It was an unusual yet satisfying existence, partly waking and partly dreaming. And he found it nearly impossible to leave, as each word was a strand in a rope that tied Bugbear to the tales on the cloths.

He learned of Whittlegrip and his early studies in Non-Logical Thought. And there was the monk's first meeting with the valiant Sir Reginald during a great war between humans and goblins. Bugbear felt the thunder of history rumbling through his bones. The lightning of creation flashing through his mind. And the winds of inspiration sweeping through his soul. Seldom had he known such completion, such fulfillment. Everything he had suffered for, fought for, sought for, and yearned for lay out before him, like a great endless horizon where the sun never set.

"We have brought supper," came a voice, finding Bugbear's ear and working its way through the wordish wanderings.

The ropes went slack and Bugbear looked up from his studies. Riley stood before him, tail wagging, and a rat clutched in his clawed hand.

Bugbear smiled. This deathless and divine document could wait a moment. After all, one could stare into the center of Non-Logic for only so long before one's mind went numb with wonder. Now Bugbear would take his mind and heart for a walk. And he could think of no better companion on such an excursion than Riley.

"Riley Ratcatcher!" Bugbear laughed.

The beast-boy cocked his head to the side, his ears perking up and his nose twitching. "'*Ratcatcher?*'" he said. "We like that name. May we have it?"

"Certainly," Bugbear said. "And you may have the rat as well. I have packed some cheese and bread for myself. And I imagine Maga and Manchester are too preoccupied to think of food."

"Will the king make it official?" Riley Ratcatcher asked.

"What?" Bugbear said as he reached into his coat for a bundle of cheese and bread wrapped in cloth. "His sickening infatuation with Maga? Bah! He has other concerns he must address first. The threat of that coranieid witch and her hidden master, for one. And then there's..."

"No," Riley said as he dropped the squirming rat, letting it scurry back into the brush. "Our name. Will he make our name official? Will we be known as the *ratcatcher?* As you are known as the *advisor?*"

Bugbear chuckled as he nibbled on his meager meal. "Yes! Yes, I believe that would be a most suitable title for you! And an honor for the king to have you serving him in such a post! I'll speak with Tudmire about writing up the official documents when we return to town."

Riley's tail thumped against the ground, and his throat rumbled with a satisfied purr. "We would like that. We think Mother Twitchett will be proud of us. We hope to see her soon."

A lump of cheese and bread stopped halfway in Bugbear's throat, forcing him to swallow with an extra bit of effort. "Riley, my dear boy. Mother Twitchett is dead. Constable Pawe shot her."

Riley looked to the ground. Then the fire. Then the stars. "No," he said. "Mother Twitchett does not die. We can still feel her. Near to us. Near to you. Near to the king. Mother Twitchett does not die. We will all see her again."

Bugbear frowned and grumbled. He wrapped his food back into the bundle and placed it back in his coat pocket. "Sentimental drivel," he spat. "You have accepted your current situation with grace and maturity. Now you must accept another tragedy. Grieve for Mother Twitchett. Then move on to more productive endeavors."

"Is that productive?" Riley said, pointing to an ornate tin lying on the log next to Bugbear.

Bugbear looked to Riley, his eyes suddenly narrow and bitter. He took up the tin and held it to his chest. "This is my medicine. None of your concern."

"Yes," Riley said, turning away. "Mother Twitchett has told us as much."

Bugbear watched the beast-boy stalk back to the brush to continue his sniffing and prowling.

The teapot whistled, drawing Bugbear's attention back to the tin and the treasure it held. From his coat-of-many-pockets, he removed a delicate bone china cup and saucer. Then he opened the tin, digging out a heaping spoonful and dumping it into the cup. He took up the pot with cautious control and poured the steaming water into the cup. After replacing the lid on the tin, setting the pot on the ground, and stirring the grains of tea into the water, Bugbear lifted the cup to his nose, inhaling the steam and gasping with delight.

"Ah, sweet seduction! Too long have we been parted! Too long have my lips hungered for your pharmaceutical affections! Too long has my holistic hunger been denied!"

The cloths stirred at Bugbear's feet. Weak whispers wafted up to his ears. "*Remember... remember... remember... Whittlegrip's call... Whittlegrip's words... Whittlegrip's truth.*"

Bugbear tensed and trembled, as if suddenly being stretched on a rack. Darksome worries stirred in his head. Frayed notions twisted and turned. Wild winds wound through empty tunnels of thought. Then suddenly he was lost, desperately empty of opinion and cognition. Only the tea and the cloths existed, each pulling at him, teasing and tugging with different promises and different pleasures.

"*There is a chill in the air,*" the steaming cup seemed to hiss. "*Warm your bones. Drink. Drink. Drink.*"

"*There is an evil on the rise,*" the yellowed cloths seemed to whisper. "*Fill your head. Read. Read. Read.*"

"There is an evil on the rise. Fill your head. Read. Read. Read."

What madness had assailed him that he would suddenly be torn by two such trivial and divergent urges? Why did the pursuit of one pleasure seem to exclude the pursuit of the other? Had he not sipped tea while perusing manuscripts countless times in the past? Why now, here in this clearing, did he suddenly feel as if the wrong choice would forever doom him and the right choice would forever redeem him?

As he searched his sluggish mind and tattered heart, his eyes wandered in the lazy manner eyes are wont when the brain has no pressing duties for them. In a shower of moonlight he spied Maga and Manchester at the riverside. They spoke in hushed tones, occasionally looking back to Bugbear. In between they would laugh and giggle like schoolchildren.

"Conspiracy," Bugbear spat. It was a notion that nestled comfortably inside the empty spaces of his mind. "They seek to undermine my authority! To upset my delicate plans! By Nullsnit's worrywarts! I should have taken the crown for myself and let that witch hang!"

With no further thought and no further temptation, Bugbear gulped down the steaming tea. It burned his tongue, blistered his throat, and boiled his stomach. He closed his eyes and embraced the sensations. A bubbling numbness washed through his body. A nervous power raged through his veins. A tingling madness skittered through his spine.

The cloths were silent as Bugbear rolled them up and tucked them into his pocket. There was nothing now but a gentle silence. A tender peace. All the voices were gone. The dread and paranoia had faded. The edge was dulled and the flame extinguished.

Bugbear poured himself another cup of tea.

CHAPTER 23
THE MONKEY YEARS

"I can feel the sting of winter coming," Maga said as she dipped the bandage in the water at the river's edge.

Manchester winced when she placed the cold cloth to his heel. "Isn't autumn supposed to have a turn?"

Maga shrugged and continued dressing the wound. "Who knows what the seasons are supposed to do in these queer times?"

"True enough," Manchester replied. "How does it look? Any sign of infection like Riley said?"

"It is a strange wound, my king. There is no blood, yet it is deep. And try as I might, I cannot wash away this strange black powder."

"But it will be okay?"

Maga finished wrapping the wound. She looked down for a moment. "I need proper medicines and equipment. Perhaps when we get back to Willow Prairie..."

Manchester nodded and forced a slight smile. "The shadow-beast called it *a king's wound.* I hope it doesn't lead to *a king's death.*"

"You shall live forever!" Maga suddenly blurted, and then turned away with the embarrassment such outbursts often herald. "I mean... you shall live a long time. And even when you are gone, you shall be remembered. For you are such a man that songs shall be sung of your deeds and tales told of your valor."

Manchester laughed. "Sorry songs and tepid tales, I'm sure! There's nothing in this sad sack of suffering worthy of such honors."

Maga placed a fingertip to her king's lips. "I will hear no more self-slander. For ages we draig gwraig have served the dreams of the glorious dragon dynasty. For one of our order to stray from this narrow path, as I have for you, the cause must be of the greatest nobility and the purest worth. When you belittle yourself, you belittle my wisdom in following you."

Manchester gently took Maga's hand and removed her finger from his lips. He held the hand and stared at it for a time as he sought words to frame his fluttering emotions. "I'm sorry. I suppose I just felt the need to balance all of this royal fame with a bit of humility."

There was a silence. Not awkward, as was the silence they had shared before, but reflective. The partial moon cast its silver light down upon them, and the stars clustered about in swirling formations, glimmering as if they fought the blackness that held them.

"I have a song to sing, my king," Maga said, her eyes looking down to the water's edge. "It is about my mother and her lost love, Sir Reginald."

"I would very much like to hear it," Manchester said, pulling Maga's hand to his heart and smiling.

Maga closed her eyes as though seeking words long held in the center of her heart. She took a deep breath. And then she sang.

> *Across the seas,*
> *Past distant leagues*
> *There lies a tragic isle.*

> *And on its shores*
> *Stand ancient lords*
> *Weeping in denial.*

> *Our world is lost,*

And at what cost.
We're scattered in a storm.

While two worlds spin
Through ancient sin .
Our king is not yet born.

But here and now
I make my vow
Though we may part forever,

I give my heart
To your sweet art
Your grand and bold endeavor.

So when our kin
Meet ages hence
They'll embrace as we once did.

And though we're gone,
Our lover's song
Shall be heard upon their lips.

As Maga finished she lowered her eyes and slowly pulled her hand from Manchester's heart.

"You're beautiful," Manchester gasped. Then, of course, he hemmed and hawed, as he was apt to do when revealing more of his feelings than he wished. "That is, the song... it was beautiful. Thank you."

Maga smiled, as she was apt to do when Manchester revealed more of his feelings than he wished.

Manchester looked towards Bugbear and Riley, attempting to deflect attention away from his embarrassing emotional display. "I wonder what they're talking about," he mused.

Maga looked to the goblin and the patchwork. "I hope he's not filling the poor boy's head with foolishness."

"Please, Maga. Give Bugbear some credit. He is a good sort... deep down. And he's my mentor, after all."

Maga grumbled and folded her arms. "The only one of your decisions I've opposed, dear king. All the same, I imagine there's little harm he can do Riley." The dragon bride smiled as she watched the beast-boy trot into the brush and leap through the tall grass. "The boy is truly perfect. So playful and joyful." Maga placed her head upon Manchester's shoulder as she continued watching Riley frolic. "You called Allherahiah's song beautiful. But there... there in that cavorting youth... there is the greatest beauty God ever placed upon His creation."

"*The Monkey Years*," Manchester chortled.

"'*The Monkey Years*?'" Maga repeated.

"My Uncle Theodore called that time between infancy and adulthood, "*the Monkey Years*." You could be anybody. Do anything. Go anywhere. Like monkeys living free and wild. Old enough to know a few tricks, but young enough to keep them to yourself." Manchester leaned his head upon Maga's, watching Riley's antics. "I miss *the Monkey Years*."

CHAPTER 24
RETURN TO WILLOW PRAIRIE

At daybreak, the rescue party set out for Willow Prairie. There had been little time for sleep during the night's many violent and volatile events, yet Manchester insisted upon a quick pace. The town would have to be warned, after all. The time for Bugbear's secrets was over. Soon there would be war.

War. The word sat like a fat, unwanted dinner guest inside Bugbear's head. And it was smoking a pipe. And telling dreadfully boring stories about its holiday in Upper Gunglehaven. *War.* Bugbear recalled the vision he had had days ago. The great battle between patchworks and humans. Now it seemed this vision was prophecy after all. And that would mean the other visions would come true as well. Manchester would be overwhelmed by shadow. And then, Bugbear himself would fall. *War.*

"Can we stop for a spot of tea?" Bugbear asked, stopping to sit upon a rock as the companions continued their ways upon the forest trails.

"That would make the fifth tea break in as many miles," Maga said as she turned about, teeth and fists clenched firmly.

"You have no idea of the pressure I'm under, witch," Bugbear growled, rising from his seat to meet the dragon bride's challenge.

"*'Pressure?'*" Manchester broke in, turning about and leaning upon the makeshift crutch Maga had fashioned from a pair of sticks and twine. "*'Pressure?'*" With firm, steady steps that denied the existence of his wound, Manchester moved upon Bugbear, brushing Maga aside. "I am the king of Willow Prairie. And on the other side of that mountain," Manchester pointed to the grim, cloud-shrouded peak of Tamarack, "is a savage force that would overwhelm and destroy my people. If I don't organize a militia before Ollamh Cron can regroup from last night's fire, Sir Reginald's legacy will lay in ruins." Manchester leaned close into Bugbear's face, his expression contorted by a barely controlled rage. "That, my little advisor, is *pressure.*"

Bugbear fell back, tripping over the rock and floundering on the forest floor. The fire in Manchester's eyes. The venom in his voice. The strength of his wrath. They frightened Bugbear. He had seen such displays of dominance before, against the ogres and against Constable Pawe. But this was the first time such fearsome rage had been directed squarely at him. Small and petty sensations washed over Bugbear. His role in this mad play had suddenly become unclear, perhaps even unwritten. Manchester had taken the lead now.

Perhaps it was time for Bugbear to leave the stage altogether.

"My... my apologies," Bugbear stammered as he got to his feet. "I fear I have misplaced my priorities. Of course, we must continue." With a humble bow he motioned back to the trail.

Manchester's anger seemed to retreat back to the dark place from whence it came. "We're all on edge," he said softly, placing a gentle hand upon Bugbear's shoulder. "Ollamh Cron and her master are a threat to us all. But together..." Manchester reached out to Maga with his other hand. The dragon bride smiled and clasped the hand. "Together we can face any foe."

Part of Bugbear wanted to mock Manchester's cliché, sentimental nonsense that it was. But most of Bugbear merely wanted to appease Manchester for fear of rousing his rage once again.

"I bow to your superior wisdom, my king," Bugbear said. "Truly the student has become the master." Bugbear's own cliché did little to wash the bitter taste from his brain. But as Manchester seemed so fond of speaking clichés, Bugbear felt he might be pleased to hear them as well.

For several sickening moments the three stood together, holding one another's sweaty hands and exchanging false smiles. Well, perhaps Manchester's smile was true. Bugbear had no doubt that despite this newly found backbone, Manchester was and always would be honest. But Maga... her face was as false as Mister Overdale's beard. But then again, so was Bugbear's.

"Time's wasting," Riley snorted as his head poked through the hypocrite's huddle. "They gather on Tamarack. We sense evil things up there. The earth rumbles as if she's going to give birth... to something very, very mean."

Bugbear looked to the mountain. The gray clouds had become thicker than usual, and they swirled in a very peculiar fashion. "Smoke and steam," Bugbear observed. "They're excavating."

"What would they be excavating?" Maga wondered aloud.

"Cysgod Gof," Manchester gasped.

"What was that?" Bugbear said, the words hitting him like a dwarven smithy's hammer.

"Cysgod Gof," Manchester repeated. "That's the name of Ollamh Cron's hidden master. She said he was waiting *beneath our feet*."

"'*Cysgod Gof!*'" Bugbear said, shaking his precious parchments in Manchester's face. "Also called *the Shadow Smith!* This is the ancient threat faced by Whittlegrip and Sir Reginald!"

"How did they defeat him before?" Maga asked.

"I don't know. I haven't gotten that far."

"Well, get there," Manchester said, his face set in grim and unmoving stone.

Bugbear felt a tremble of shame. Of fear. Of anxiety. The cloths hung limp in his hand as he looked to them. They were silent and unresponsive. "I can't hear them anymore," he whimpered.

"Then read them," Manchester said, his voice thick with frustration.

Bugbear nodded and unrolled one of the clothes to read the words. "I shall try."

Manchester turned away, a grumble of disgust rumbling from his throat.

Maga lingered near Bugbear as Manchester and Riley continued forging along the trail. "Are you ill?" she asked, regarding Bugbear with a penetrating gaze.

Bugbear looked to her, his mind already pondering the same question. "No," he lied. "No concern of yours, in any case."

He quickly waddled past the dragon bride, shuffling through his cloth parchments, trying to decipher a scholarly path that had once been as clear to him as his overwhelming thirst for tea.

"Don't let Martin's temper upset you," Maga continued as she caught up to the struggling scholar. "Between his wound and the responsibilities of kingship..."

"And his growing infatuation with you," Bugbear added.

"Excuse me?" Maga said, hands on her hips, and irritation in her voice.

Bugbear continued walking and sorting through his parchments. "He loves you, you fluff-headed twit. Remember that when such affairs of the heart cause the loss of his head."

Maga stood in front of Bugbear, halting his haphazard advance. "I didn't want to hear that," she sighed.

"You feel the same, I take it?" Bugbear said, lowering the cloths and looking up to Maga.

"Yes," Maga breathed. "With every fiber of my being."

"Then your fates are sealed. And I'll have no part of it. I'll report to Manchester what I can find in these parchments, then I'll be taking my leave of this kingdom and its star-crossed idiots."

"You would leave him because of me?" Maga said with furrowed brow and bitter breath.

"No," Bugbear said, storming around Maga. "I would leave him because of me."

The remainder of the journey was silent. Oh, birds sang songs, and crisp leaves crunched beneath feet, and Riley barked and shouted at a few woodland creatures that happened across the trail. But no one spoke. Manchester struggled to keep up his determined pace. Maga struggled to keep her emotions in place. And Bugbear struggled to read the silent cloths.

When they finally came upon the outskirts of town, Manchester decided that Riley should wait in the brush until such time as he could explain the patchwork situation to the citizens. Riley readily agreed as there seemed to be a great many woodchucks, chipmunks, and field mice in the area to keep him preoccupied.

There was yelling in Willow Prairie this morning as Bugbear, Manchester, and Maga entered town. Curses. Exclamations. Gunshots. And it all seemed to center around the town square. The companions rushed to the sounds, as fast as Bugbear's stunted legs and Manchester's wound would allow.

The gallows. They had never been taken down. And now the entire town swarmed around them, shouting in excitement and in anger. The gallows were being used on this cold morning in Willow Prairie. They were being used... on Tudmire!

"Halt!" Manchester yelled as Tudmire's still body swayed on the end of the rope.

"The king?" someone blurted in surprise.

"Yes! The king!" Manchester shouted to the crowd as he pushed his way to the gallows steps. "Let him down this instant!"

Dunderbeck stood at the top of the stairs, looking upon Manchester with shock and disbelief. "You... you're alive?"

As the hangmen lowered Tudmire's deathly still body from the rope, Manchester hobbled up the steps to face Dunderbeck.

"Yes, alive," he hissed into Dunderbeck's recoiling face. With a swift and deft motion Manchester hooked the magistrate's leg with his crutch and flipped him onto his back. Dunderbeck fell with a most violent and satisfying thud, and Manchester knelt upon the scarecrow's chest, raising the crutch high, ready to strike the coward in his wincing, worried face. "Does he still live?" Manchester called to Bugbear and Maga.

Bugbear cradled Tudmire's head, listening for a heartbeat through his blubbery frame. He heard it, faint and hesitant, but it was there. As was his rasping, uncertain breath. Then Tudmire's eyes fluttered open. "*Eeeyyyuuggghhh*," he gasped. "When's the last time you brushed your teeth, cousin?"

"He'll live," Bugbear answered, dropping Tudmire's melon head to the ground as he stood. "At least as long as I don't have any say in it."

Manchester pressed the tip of his crutch to Dunderbeck's neck. "What treachery is this, Underspeck?"

"That's... that's *Dunderbeck*," Dunderbeck stammered.

"*Underspeck*!" Manchester shouted, pressing the crutch deeper into the magistrate's neck. "Explain this spectacle... *Underspeck*!"

"Someone saw... *creatures* outside of town yesterday," Dunderbeck gasped. "Huge, malformed things. Three of them."

"The ogres," Manchester and Bugbear both whispered as one.

"We questioned the goblin," Dunderbeck continued. "But he wouldn't tell us what he knew. Said something about *royal secrets*. When you didn't return, we assumed the goblin was part of some plot to assassinate you. Some of the townsfolk got upset. I tried to stop them, but they formed a lynch mob. I…"

Manchester pinched Dunderbeck's face, squeezing his mouth into a pucker. "You are a liar. I despise liars. Liars must be made an example."

The king got off of Dunderbeck's chest, standing over him and looking down with the kind of contempt saints hold for sinners. "Maga," he said with a wave of his hand. "Place this garbage in the jail."

Maga nodded and moved forward, drawing her blade as she approached the cowering Dunderbeck. The crowd began to stir in protest, defending Dunderbeck and once more calling for answers to their questions.

"The magistrate was the only one who'd listen to us!"
"Did you find any of the missing people?"
"What about those critters we seen?"
"Why were you gone so long?"
"What happened to your foot?"
"When are we going to get to hang someone?"

Maga paused and looked to Manchester.

Manchester glared out across the bewildered and agitated crowd. His eyes seemed to fall upon each face with the fury and speed of lightning. "I believe it's about time someone reminded you people that you're idiots!" he said, his voice rumbling as thunder to accompany the lightning.

The crowd gasped, recoiling in shock over the cross words from their beloved king.

Manchester continued his cruel and brutal assault on his subjects. "I am not only your king! I am your keeper of knowledge! And I decide when and if I shall share that knowledge!"

Bugbear suddenly felt that not only was he no longer in the play, but now he was in the audience... merely an observer... with bad seats... sitting behind a woman with a large, feather-festooned hat. And most vexing of all, despite the wretched view, Manchester was mesmerizing in the lead role.

The people parted, heads bowed and eyes lowered. Maga walked past them, holding out her hand to the yet stunned and prone Dunderbeck. Dunderbeck reached out to Maga, ready to take her hand.

Then the play took an unexpected turn.

Yelping, yelling, and yowling, Riley Ratcatcher rampaged through the crowd, pursuing a frightened opossum through fumbling feet and between trembling legs. Of course, the crowd erupted with shock, terror, and fury, as crowds are apt to do when weird beast-boys scurry about their feet.

"We're under attack!"

"Monsters!"

"Kill it!"

"No!" Manchester yelled. "If anyone lays a hand on that boy, I'll cut that hand off myself!"

But no one could hear the king. Their ears were too full of their own outrage.

'Round and about and under and through Riley went, nipping at the tail of his furry foe.

"Foul pouch-belly!" he growled. "We shall lay your carcass before good King Munchausen!"

Some of the townsfolk stumbled out of the patchwork's path. Others made wild, clumsy grabs at the diving and dodging creature. But all were hysterical with disbelief.

Finally, the opossum darted beneath the gallows. As Riley attempted to follow, he inadvertently tumbled into the barely conscious and unsteadily rising Tudmire. Patchwork and goblin fell to the ground in a squirming heap of fur and folly. As the townsfolk crept upon them and Tudmire shook the confusion from his melon-head, he looked to Riley with eyes wide in delirious disbelief and devastated discovery. And then when he was almost nose to nose with the patchwork, Riley shouted: "*Boo!*"

The goblin tumbled and scurried back, his body a jumble of nervous fear.

"They're in cahoots!" a citizen shouted.

"We don't even know how to get there!" Riley protested as someone plucked him up by the scruff of his neck. "So how could we be in *Cahoots?*"

"Put the boy down!" Manchester exclaimed, hobbling down the steps into the midst of the crowd. "He is under my protection!"

"You protect monsters?" an elderly woman gasped.

"This is no monster!" Manchester said. "It is young Riley, Mother Twitchett's dog son... I mean godson! He was captured by an alchemist on the other side of Tamarack! She has been performing perverse experiments on the missing townsfolk!"

"I don't believe you," said the man holding Riley.

"You owe us a quarter for mowing your lawn, Mister Sagramore," Riley said, looking up to the man with his soft, turquoise eyes. "Hard work. All the worse for having to trim around the still you have hidden in your backyard."

Mister Sagramore dropped Riley and fell back into the crowd. "This is witchcraft!" he blurted.

"Burn the witches! Hang the goblins! Dethrone the king!" an old woman shouted.

The rest of the crowd soon joined her protest, their angry voices ringing through the square like broken church bells.

"I can help him," Dunderbeck whispered to Bugbear as Maga moved away from them in defense of Manchester.

"Then by all means, do so," Bugbear replied with a dry lack of concern.

"I'll expect a pardon and a reinstatement as magistrate," Dunderbeck continued.

"Expect what you like. It's between you and the king."

"He scarcely makes a move without your say-so."

"So you say," Bugbear snorted. "He follows his own counsel of late. I am merely one more subject in *His Majesty's Tragic Kingdom.*"

Dunderbeck seemed to smile at this, and Bugbear felt he had perhaps revealed a bit more than he should have. And in that he suddenly felt weaker and more insignificant.

"However, I am not without my resources," he corrected, straightening his collar and standing a bit taller. "If you have any influence over this rabble, soothe their rage and turn their wrath. Do this and I shall tell Manchester of your assistance. Perhaps he shall take pity on you and do as you request."

"I need a guarantee."

"Don't we all," Bugbear said with a roll of his eyes.

Dunderbeck looked off to the snarling crowd as it swarmed about Tudmire, Riley, Manchester, and Maga. Bugbear's eyes followed, regarding the scene with something between concern and disdain.

"Is death guarantee enough?" Dunderbeck said.

"Do it and I promise Manchester shall reinstate you," Bugbear sighed, turning away from the crowd and Dunderbeck.

Bugbear did not need to see Dunderbeck to know he was smiling. A conniver and a deceiver would do no less when succeeding in his treacherous art. What Dunderbeck did not know, however, was that Bugbear cared little of the outcome of this twisted production. He simply wanted to leave.

"My dear friends," Dunderbeck said as he poised atop the gallows steps with outstretched arms, "do not let your fears eclipse your hearts. Has our king been gone so long that we have forgotten his wisdom and honor? If this creature is young Riley as he claims, let us rejoice! For the king has done as he has promised! He has recovered the boy! And he has discovered what has become of our missing loved ones! Now, more than ever, we must support him! We must take up arms against this new threat! We must prepare for war!"

That word again. *War.* It scraped the inside of Bugbear's skull like a rusty knife. He needed to leave before it scraped all the way through.

The townsfolk raised their fists in collective jubilation. "War!" they shouted. "For victory!" they yelled. "For King Martin!" they roared. They parted, allowing Riley, Tudmire, Maga, and Manchester to retreat back to the gallows steps.

"This changes nothing," Manchester whispered to Dunderbeck. "You're still going to jail."

"Your advisor assured me I'm not," Dunderbeck replied.

Manchester looked to Bugbear with a raised eyebrow. Bugbear felt his shoulders rise and his head sink. "I did," he said with rasping shame.

"It was not your place!" Manchester growled. "I am the king here, not you."

Maga placed a hand upon Manchester's shoulder. "Martin," she said. "He had no choice. Dunderbeck had them whipped into a frenzy to start with. Only he could have calmed them. For good or ill, you must abide by Bugbear's word. He is a part of your administration, after all."

Manchester sighed. It was a sigh Bugbear knew well. For it was the same sigh Bugbear himself had used when faced with the most annoying and confounding of idiots.

"So be it," Manchester said. "But you'll have no part in the war plans, Dunderbeck."

"Nor shall I," Bugbear hissed for only himself to hear.

And the crowd continued its chant. "*War! War! War!*"

CHAPTER 25
WAR FROM THE WINDOW

Their feet fell upon the cold cobble streets like hammer upon anvil. *Thoom! Thoom! Thoom!* And Tudmire's voice, shrill and demanding, pierced the morning air like needle through sackcloth. *"One, two, three! Hup! Hup! One, two, three! Hup! Hup! Step lively, lads!"*

"Does he know what he's doing?" Manchester asked, turning away from the window and hobbling back to sit at the edge of his bed.

"He can't do any damage," Maga said as she poured a pouch of herbs into a steaming cup of broth. "I tried working with them myself. Quite undisciplined and not terribly bright, I'm afraid."

"They're bright enough," Manchester replied, sprawling back on the bed and wincing as his heel throbbed against its bandages. "They're simply distracted. And who can blame them? They know the truth now... how the world has changed... become bigger and stranger than all their dreams and nightmares shoved into a leaky bucket. Goblins. Ogres. Patchworks. And the Shadow Smith."

"Drink this, my king," Maga said, pushing the cup to Manchester's lips. "It will soothe your pain and help you rest."

Manchester drank from the steaming cup and leaned back on his pillow. "I spent most of my childhood in a bed watching other children play outside my window," he said softly.

His eyes wandered to the window once again. *"Hup! Hup!"* Tudmire barked as he swatted one of the struggling young soldiers with a horse switch. *"Watch your step, lad! One, two, three! Hup! Hup!"*

"Now I fear I'll be watching children die outside my window."

Maga placed the cup on the night table. She lay a hand upon Manchester's forehead. "You are cold."

"Yes," he said, pulling the covers up to his chin. "I am cold. You were right. winter is coming. I saw frost on the window this morning."

Maga said nothing. She simply rubbed Manchester's hands in hers, warming them with her warmth, soothing them with her tenderness.

"Have you heard from Bugbear?" Manchester asked. "It's been three days since I've seen him."

"He is in his study," Maga replied. "He asked not to be disturbed. But I've seen to it that Miss Orland sets food outside his door."

Manchester turned and looked to the ceiling. This was Mother Twitchett's house. And this was the same room they had rented from her their first night in Willow Prairie. Tudmire and Bugbear had taken up different quarters since. But Manchester liked it here. The wallpaper. The furniture. The decorations. They reminded him of home. And home reminded him of dreams.

"I've been harsh to Bugbear," he said. "I'd forgotten how important he is. How much he's helped me."

Maga laughed a small laugh. "I have begun to realize his value myself. He sees the world in a way that is both frustrating and honest."

"Yes. Honest. I should be honest as well." Manchester pulled his hand from Maga's, bracing himself as he pulled himself upright. "Maga," he whispered, his eyes beginning to moisten with tears. "Every day I get weaker. Every day the wound bites deeper into my heel, and my spirit. I can feel myself... slipping away."

"Martin," Maga said, her own eyes beginning to well.

"When I go, I want you and Bugbear to rule Willow Prairie... together. I trust the two of you more than I trust myself. Please, do this for me. Please, put aside your differences and work together for the peace I wasn't able to give these dear, simple people."

Maga collapsed into a shower of sorrow, burying her raven-crowned head into Manchester's lap. "Martin," she sobbed. "My king. My love."

"*Love*," Manchester sighed as he stroked Maga's silky locks. "Yes. Love."

"Well," Bugbear said with all the abruptness of a crowing cock, "finally declared our undying devotion for one another, have we? About time!"

"Bugbear!" Manchester said, the uneasy sorrow giving way to a comfortable joy. "I've missed you, my advisor!"

"As well you should!" Bugbear piped, waddling into the room to warm himself by the fire. "For I have discovered vital information concerning your darksome opponent."

Maga pulled her face from Manchester, wiping away the tears as she regarded Bugbear. "The cloths? You were able to decipher them?"

"Yes. Although they did not speak to me as they had near the ruins of Eglwys Cacynen, I was able to pick through their words in the traditional scholarly way. You face a terrible evil, King Martin."

"The Shadow Smith," Manchester said. "How evil?"

"So evil that Whittlegrip and Sir Reginald split the world asunder to keep his shadows from overwhelming all. Thus the secret of that mysterious scroll. It was penned by Whittlegrip and Reginald themselves. It's a Non-Logical law dividing the world into Annwfn and Earth. It was the only way they could stop him, you see. After the worlds were sundered, Reginald took the quill that penned the words and placed it on the altar where you found it. And Whittlegrip took the scroll to Eglwys Cacynen, where it remained until it fell into ogre hands during a raid. And you already know how it came to us through Tudmire's Noggle Stones game."

"And how did the world's reunite?" Manchester asked. "And why now?"

Bugbear shrugged. "The right series of events. The proper people doing the improper things."

Bugbear turned about abruptly, throwing the cloths at the foot of Manchester's bed. "Me! Me! Me!" The goblin raged, his face orange and contorted. "It was my doing, Manchester! My pursuit of Non-Logical Thought! When I touched the scroll, I awakened it! I reminded it!"

"But this is the way things were meant to be," Manchester said, reaching out to his friend in an attempt to soothe and calm him. "The worlds need to be one."

"And when the worlds are one," Bugbear spat, "so is the Shadow Smith! Whittlegrip and Reginald had imprisoned the Shadow Smith within his keep atop Tamarack Mountain, sending it tumbling down upon him during a great siege! A great war that united goblin, human, dragon bride, ogre... every race in creation! And when they wrote their scroll, Tamarack was their starting point! The birthplace of their grand scheme! Like a great hammer, the scroll drove a Non-Logical spike down the center of the mountain, splitting not only the world in twain, but the Shadow Smith as well! His evil diluted, he could conquer no one! Destroy nothing! Rule nowhere! He could only sleep within the cold, dark earths, dreaming and waiting! Until now."

"Can... can you..." Maga looked to Manchester and lowered her eyes to the floor. "Can you split the world apart once more?"

"I can do nothing!" Bugbear screeched, sending both Maga and Manchester recoiling. The goblin rushed towards them. "My inspiration is spent! My intellect unraveled! I am defenseless and worthless!"

Manchester turned from Bugbear, not so much for the words as for the foul breath that accompanied them. He had smelled something like that before. Rotten and reeking. Musty and stinking.

"This war is yours," Bugbear said, suddenly calm as he turned away. "Nothing can defeat the Shadow Smith. Whittlegrip and Reginald knew that. If only they had destroyed the scroll before it fell into my cursed hands."

"Bugbear," Manchester said, reaching out once more to his friend. "It's not your fault. You didn't know."

"Yes," Bugbear hissed. "I didn't know. And therein lies my sin. I trifled with powers beyond my meager mentality. I plunged my insignificant intellect into the sacred well of Non-Logical Thought! I should never have set foot upon such a treacherous path!"

"But it was your dream," Manchester said.

"Not my dream!" Bugbear spat, turning about in circles like a confused cat. "Whittlegrip's! Whittlegrip's dream! Just as Willow Prairie is your dream!"

The goblin stopped his spinning and stumbled towards the doorway, bracing himself against the wall. "I'm tired of living in someone else's dream."

And Bugbear staggered out into the hallway, small sobs trailing behind him.

"Bugbear!" Manchester called, throwing away his covers and rolling to his feet. He fell, his heel instantly refusing to carry his weight.

Maga knelt beside him.

"Bugbear!" Manchester continued. "I need you! We all need you!"

Maga cradled the king in her arms.

"*Hup! Hup!*" Tudmire continued outside the window. "*Step lively, lads! Step lively! There's a war to be won! Hup! Hup!*"

CHAPTER 26
LEAVING THE DREAMS BEHIND

Bugbear stared at the scattered papers and disheveled books. Once they had been as dear to him as his own breath. But now they were strangers... silent and unmoving ghosts, cluttering a world he longed to leave.

He looked to the silver box sitting on the window sill. Only the tea mattered now. All the years of research and study withered to nothing in the glow of that precious obsession. He would take the banderberry root tea with him and nothing more. The books would remain here in his chambers in the Willow Prairie library for some other fool to stumble upon and waste precious years in delirious deceptions.

Bugbear carefully placed the box in his inner coat pocket. As he turned to walk out the door, he suddenly caught his reflection in a full length mirror. Usually he avoided such vain pastimes, but now he could not help but admire the way his three foot frame filled his olive garb. He seemed somehow fresher and younger now. He imagined it had something to do with the abandoning of his responsibilities. If only he had saved himself, and the world, so much anguish and shame by taking up a life of rudderless direction long ago.

"Come back here! Hup! Hup!"

It was Tudmire's voice, coming from downstairs.

"No more switching for you, Turdmore!" Riley snickered in reply.

Both were quickly thumping and fumbling their clumsy and intrusive ways up the stairs. Bugbear turned away from the mirror in anticipation of the unwelcome guests.

The beast-boy sprang into the room, Tudmire's horse switch clenched between his teeth. Tudmire soon followed, dressed in his ill-fitting uniform covered with frills, sashes, and jangling medals he had won from genuine soldiers in crooked games of Noggle Stones.

"Hide us, Booberg!" Riley said, spitting out the switch and scurrying behind Bugbear in an attempt to evade the furious Tudmire. "He grows mad with power!"

"Hand over the scalawag!" Tudmire demanded as he faced his cousin. "This is the king's business!"

"And this," Bugbear said, picking up the switch, "is the king's as well. And as my last official act as royal advisor, I shall claim it for myself, thus diffusing your little military action."

"Not fair!" Tudmire protested, poking his finger into Bugbear's chest. "How am I supposed to whip my troops into shape without a proper switch?" Then Tudmire's eyes went wide with realization. "Did you say your 'last' official act?"

"Indeed," Bugbear said, tapping the switch handle on Tudmire's chest of medals. "I'm giving it all up. The royal court. The studying. The Non-Logical Thought."

"'Non-Logical Thought?'" Tudmire balked. "You're giving up Non-Logical Thought? But it's your passion! Your dream!"

"That's the second time someone's told me that it's my dream," Bugbear chuckled as he brushed past Tudmire on his way to his desk. "I don't have my own dreams, cousin. That's what I'm leaving to find."

"But what about the war?" Tudmire asked.

"And the possums?" Riley added. "We can't be expected to kill them all ourselves!"

"I leave the war and the opossums to you, my friends."

"Then we must make haste!" Riley exclaimed, falling to all fours and darting out the door. "With every moment of inaction the foul pouch-bellies grow stronger and more organized!"

Bugbear smiled as he watched Riley scurry off. "Neither of us is needed here, Tudmire."

"Bah!" Tudmire snorted as he admired himself in the mirror. "Abandon your post if you wish, but don't besmirch my reputation with your cowardly accusations! I am an important part of the king's administration!"

"You have never been anything more than a clown," Bugbear said. "And now Riley has replaced you."

"But I'm training the army," Tudmire protested. "Without me…"

"Without you or with you they would remain as pathetic as they always shall be. Only Maga could turn them into any kind of effective fighting force. And she is too… distracted."

Bugbear waddled to his desk, spying one last remnant, one last relic of his old life. The bee jar.

"Cousin!" Tudmire continued, following his cousin, arms flailing in panic. "You can't leave! You can't give up all of this! Manchester needs you!"

"I need me more," Bugbear said, taking up the jar and gazing at the bee. "I'm through being trapped by the expectations of others." He carried the jar to the window. "It's time to be free." He opened the window, letting in the crisp, cool air. "It's time to fly." He removed the lid from the jar, letting the bee take flight. "It's time to be."

"You realize he'll die out there in the cold," Tudmire snorted.

"As if he was alive in here," Bugbear smirked, setting the empty jar on the sill as he closed the window. "Willow Prairie's future is nothing but battle cries and clichés, cousin. Best to leave before it gets too loud."

"But I've found dignity here! Honor! Responsibility!"

"And it fits you as awkwardly as that ridiculous uniform!" Bugbear laughed. "You will never belong here, Tudmire! You can ape respectability all you like, but you can't change what you are! A gambler! A schemer! A ne'er-do-well! A few medals and an air of self-importance won't cover the stench of your past, you poor, deluded dullard!"

Tudmire's face fell like a deflated balloon. His eyes closed and his shoulders slumped. "You're right. I don't deserve these medals. I don't belong here. I'm nothing but a charlatan."

Bugbear smiled, patting his cousin's shoulder. "Truth is liberating. I take it you'll be joining me then?"

"I have debts to settle," Tudmire said sadly as he pulled away. "I'll be traveling a different road than you."

"Good luck with that," Bugbear said with a shrug. "We'll meet again some day, I suppose. Perhaps at one of Grand Uncle Crick's fluggle roast?"

"Fluggles make me break out in hives," Tudmire said, walking out the door without another word nor another glance.

Bugbear chuckled. He found something gratifying about destroying Tudmire's dreams, forcing him to wake up to reality.

"Reality," he hissed to himself. "Reality is a dream worth following."

Then he patted the silver box inside his coat, took up the horse switch, and danced out the door.

CHAPTER 27
ABANDONED IN A BLIZZARD

As the bitter, winter wind carried the tattered night over
Willow Prairie, King Martin slept. It was a feverish sleep. Brain
frothing in a sea of midnight. Gray flecks of consciousness spattering
the edges of his thoughts. Horrible, contorting spasms wracking his
body. Yes, it was such a wretched night's sleep that only sentence
fragments could adequately relay the discomfort.

There was a moment though, when the dream became clear
and obvious. He stood upon a desert of ashes, great rolling gray
dunes rising and falling like melancholy waves. A black sun beat
down with cold, bone-numbing rays, and birds of black shadow
circled overhead. The sky was white and bleak, almost blinding in its
intensity.

In the distance upon the largest dune he saw a figure, small
and obscured by distance. Manchester held up his hand and shouted
to the stranger. But the words refused to exist. A silent pantomime
was all he could muster. He rushed towards the distant dune, but his
foot caught on a black root. He fell forward and found himself
suddenly kneeling before the mound, which was somehow not
nearly so huge nor so distance as it had seemed. It was but four feet
high, and inches from his face, and the figure upon it was no bigger
than his thumb. It was Bugbear, tiny and enraged, with all the color
washed away from his clothes and his face. He perched atop the
little mound of ash staring Manchester straight in the face.

"*I told you,*" he shouted in a tiny, tinny voice, "*I'm tired of
living in someone else's dreams!*"

Before Manchester could react, the tiny goblin took up a
black shovel and with two silent, lightning stabs, struck out the

king's eyes. Manchester recoiled, falling back with a noiseless scream as he clutched at his empty sockets. Blackness surrounded him, covering him in a cold and painful shroud. And the tiny, tinny voice of Bugbear filled his disordered head.

"*Now, you must live in my nightmares!*"

The king found his voice, shouting out with a shrill and noisome terror: "Bugbear! Why do you blind me and abandon me?"

The illusion shattered as Manchester bolted out of bed, throwing away his covers and screaming with rage and anguish. The faint light of a bedside lamp reminded him of reality and the world around him. The soft whispers of Maga, who roused from her vigil at his bedside, reminded him of his life and his responsibilities.

"Martin," Maga said, "what ails you?"

"A dream," he gasped. "A vision. A nightmare. I saw Bugbear. He blinded me with a black shovel."

"He's gone now, Martin," Maga soothed, pulling the covers back over his trembling form. "Forget about him. Rest and heal."

"He used to have dreams like these," Manchester shuddered. "I was his student. Has his madness spread to me now?"

"It's not madness," she said. "It's your illness. I'll fix you some more broth."

"Not hungry," he gasped. "Just frightened."

"Nothing shall harm you while I'm here, my king."

"I'm not frightened for me. I'm frightened for Bugbear. What if the nightmare was a premonition? What if he's stranded in a desert of ash? Small and alone."

Maga frowned and stood up. "He abandoned you," she said, walking to the window. "Any danger he faces now is his own responsibility."

"All the more frightening," Manchester said, removing the blankets and pulling himself upright. "All the more reason I must find him."

"There is movement on the streets," Maga said, her voice laced with alarm. "Torches. Voices. Marching."

"What? Could Tudmire be running the troops through some drills?"

"No. There are too many of them. This is a crowd. A mob. And they're coming this way."

"Then I shall greet them," Manchester said, pulling his boots to his bedside as he swung his feet over the edge.

"Let me deal with them," Maga said, turning about and patting the hilt of her sword. "You are still too weak to handle such stress."

"My top hat and coat, if you please," Manchester said, wincing as he slid the boot over his wounded heel.

She smiled to him and glided across the floor, reaching the coat rack and hat stand, where she took up the requested garments. "Speak with them if you must, but when I see the strain getting to you..."

"Strain I can handle," Manchester grunted as he got to his feet and took the hat and coat from Maga. "It's the dreadful anticipation preceding it that churns my brain."

By the time Manchester had donned his hat and buttoned his coat to its top button, the knock came at the door. Actually, it was much less a knock and much more a bang. And it was not so much a *May we come in?* kind of bang as it was a *We must come in!* kind of bang. This bang was followed by a lot of muttering and sputtering and general waiting about for an answer.

Manchester managed the steps down to the front door, sometimes with Maga's help, but mostly on his own. The heel still hurt, more than ever before. But Manchester found himself all the more determined to put the pain in its place. He held down the screams that longed to bolt from his throat, and he ignored the crippling impulses that told him to fall down and give up.

After summoning up all the bitter pride he could crowd into his gangly frame, he stood tall and steady, nodding to Maga as he flung open the door. He glared out upon the mumbling mob, suppressing a shudder as the cold wind blasted a cluster of snowflakes into his face. Snow. It drifted over the streets of Willow Prairie, dancing in streams of lamplight.

"What's all this then?" Manchester demanded as he shook the flakes from his beard.

Dunderbeck stepped forth, which did not surprise Manchester in the least, as arranging such disruptions seemed to be his calling in life. "Someone has absconded with a good portion of the town treasury," the magistrate answered.

This revelation was followed by a series of serious snorts and snuffles from the crowd.

"Were there any clues at the scene?" Manchester asked, taking on a very serious tone himself.

"We found him," Dunderbeck said, motioning back into the crowd.

The townsfolk parted as Dunderbeck pointed, revealing Mister Sagramore holding a leash with Riley uncomfortably straining at the end.

"We were tracking possums when we caught Turdmore's scent," Riley pleaded as he floundered within Tudmire's oversized military coat with its frills, sashes, and jangling medals. "We followed to the bank where we found his soldier's coat. That's when

Mister Sagramore snatched us in a grain sack! Such treachery can only mean he's in league with the pouch-bellies!"

"A *nosewitness*," Dunderbeck said. "He tracked your goblin friend to the bank where he found his favorite article of clothing. And now this Tudmire is nowhere to be found. And what of the other one? Your advisor? Where is he?"

"He left my service earlier today," Manchester said between teeth clenched in hesitance.

The muttering resumed, dancing from one pair of lips to the next as if it was living thing.

"As we suspected," Dunderbeck continued. "The goblins have deceived us all, stealing our money and betraying us to this Shadow Smith!"

"Nonsense!" Manchester growled. "Bugbear and Tudmire would do no such thing! More likely you are behind it, Dunderbeck! Framing my friends to secure your power base in Willow Prairie!"

"You never listen to us!" one of the townsfolk shouted.

"You always side with those creatures!" another yelled.

"Indeed!" Dunderbeck said. "Since he became king, we've lost Constable Pawe, Mother Twitchett, and," he motioned to the tethered Riley Ratcatcher, "he claims this beast is young Riley! Perhaps it is time we reconsider Willow Prairie's position on royalty!"

"Dunderbeck," Manchester hissed, grabbing the magistrate by his collar and pulling him close, "what is your game? Three days ago, you defended us and helped us retain the town's loyalty. Now you turn on us, instigating rebellion."

"Like the early winter, I go where the wind directs me," Dunderbeck whispered with a smile. "Now, I suggest you release me before my people grow angrier."

Manchester pushed Dunderbeck away. Some of the townsfolk caught him as he stumbled back and then sprang forward to grapple with Manchester. Like a cat unsheathing her claws, Maga poised her blade between the advancing crowd and her king.

"Dunderbeck," she said, her silver eyes flashing with reflected torch light, "call them off, or I swear I'll paint the streets with their blood!"

The townsfolk did not need Dunderbeck to tell them to stand down. They heard Maga's warning clearly enough, and they reacted accordingly, backing away.

"Release Riley as well," Manchester demanded as he hobbled forth.

Maga kept the folk away with the tip of her blade, waving it from one face to the next in warning. She followed Manchester's footsteps as he shambled up to Mister Sagramore. Sagramore bowed his head, looking to the snow-coated ground as though looking for his fallen pride. He said nothing as he handed the leash over to the king.

"You've turned your back on me, Willow Prairie," he said in a deep, commanding voice that shattered the night like rolling thunder. He undid the demeaning leash, setting the young patchwork free. "You've allied yourself with paranoia and mistrust. You cannot remain my subjects when subject to such false creeds."

"King Munchausen, no!" Riley blurted.

Manchester placed a calming hand upon Riley's head.

The crowd seemed equally unsettled by Manchester's words.

"Choose now," he commanded. "Choose between me and your hypocrisy. For a true king shall not compete with lies and shadows."

They looked to the ground. Their lips moved, but no sounds came forth. They fidgeted in place, feet stamping, heads bobbing, fingers dancing in sweaty palms.

"Willow Prairie has never needed a king!" Dunderbeck spat. "We are not some superstitious sheep to be herded by myths and fairy tales! We are a proud and strong community!"

"*Yes!*" someone shouted in agreement.

"*He's right! We don't need no king!*"

"*Get out of here!*"

"*And take that witch and freak with you!*"

Manchester looked out across the sea of rage, his brown eyes meeting the gaze of each of his detractors. He hobbled further into the crowd, defiant and steady, his jaw set firm and his fists clenched. They had turned on him. And a part of him was glad for it. A part of him was glad to be released from the burden of leadership and to suddenly be ordinary and unimportant again. And yet a higher, nobler part of him felt a crippling pain more severe than the throbbing wound in his heel. For he had hoped to turn Willow Prairie into something as pure and glorious as his childhood daydreams. He had imagined a land swimming in laughter, a kingdom drowning in joy, a realm saturated in peace. No anger. No prejudice. No strife. Bugbear would scold him for indulging in such sentimental fancies. But Manchester found a usefulness in these delusions. For like germs they could spread and infect others, until the world was sick with perfection.

But now it seemed Willow Prairie was immune.

"Come along," he whispered to Maga and Riley. "Before they remember that those gallows have yet to actually be used."

There were no more words, no more mumbles, no more shouts. The people of Willow Prairie simply watched as their erstwhile king limped down the street, the proud warrior and feral boy following in his imperfect footfalls.

"Good Lord!" Manchester gasped as he saw an orange glow on the other side of town. "They've set the library on fire! All of Bugbear's research! Lost!"

Maga rushed up and took Manchester's arm, urging him forth. "He had given up on his studies, remember?"

"But I might have picked up where he left off," Manchester grunted. "I was his apprentice, after all. A student of Non-Logical Thought."

At those words, Manchester suddenly smiled as if remembering where he had hidden some forgotten treasure. He reached into his vest pocket to make certain *it* was still there. It was, undisturbed since the night he claimed it.

The crowd followed several paces behind the exiles as they wound into the town square.

Now is the time to move my event, Manchester thought in devious secrecy. He stumbled as they neared the stone altar beside the gallows. Maga moved to steady her king (as Manchester knew she would), but he pulled her with him, landing against the altar as he grasped her hands. "Remember this," he whispered as he placed the sacred quill in her hand and guided it back to its ancient resting place in the inkwell.

Maga looked to Manchester with bewilderment. "What?"

"Reginald left it here for me," he said, pulling himself upright and her with him. "I leave it here for you. Remember."

She nodded, perhaps not quite understanding him, but trusting him all the same.

They continued their trek, the townsfolk and Dunderbeck unaware that the king's weapon had been returned to its sheath.

As Manchester struggled to maintain his footing in the snow, his thoughts turned to his parents. He hoped they were safe, far from such madness as lost kingdoms and risen tyrants. He smiled as he recalled how good they were... the kind of people he had hoped would fill Willow Prairie. Cheerful. Generous. Honest. He remembered the smell of his father's tobacco shop, pungent and sweet. And he remembered his mother's laugh, soft and gentle. He remembered bedtime stories and homemade pies and Christmas presents spilling out of a moth-eaten stocking. These were the warm and inspiring thoughts that filled his head as he was herded through the snow-shrouded streets by the traitors of Willow Prairie.

They came to the edge of town, where the railroad tracks scarred the earth in iron and wood stitches. Here Manchester paused, looking to the horizon where the tracks disappeared into the white snow and black night.

"Go," Dunderbeck said from behind. "Go and darken Willow Prairie no longer."

Manchester turned around, looking once again into the dimly lit faces of the townsfolk. Words formed in his mind, but they never met his tongue. For words counted for little now. Nothing he could say would change their tiny minds. That would come later. That would come from Maga. Somehow Manchester knew this, through a small prophecy that stirred in his heart.

Manchester turned away from Willow Prairie, and shambled through the snow into the skeletal black forest. Maga followed, pausing only to glare at her king's betrayers. Riley ran ahead of them both, snapping at the snowflakes and rolling in the drifts.

"We must find a river," Manchester said to Maga as she moved up to steady him.

"For water?" she asked.

"For fate," he replied.

CHAPTER 28
SACRED BONDS

"Bitter times," Bugbear snorted as he curled up in his makeshift shelter of logs and limbs propped against the tangled roots of an oak. He peered out between the black shapes of the wood to see the snow drifting down in delicate doom. Soon it would overwhelm his little haven, burying him in wet, white cold. He would most likely die here. Which would not have bothered him so terribly much if it did not mean he would have to part with his precious banderberry root tea.

He had tried to start a fire earlier, but he was terribly deficient in such woodcraft. He still nursed the blisters from his futile fumbling with rubbing sticks and striking stones. If only he had started a small flame long enough to heat a cup of tea. But, he would have to savor the grains raw and dry.

He pulled the silver box from his coat, opened the lid, and ran his fingertip gently through the fine powder. He closed his eyes, letting the seductive sensation warm his chilled body.

"Bitter times," he hissed between smiling lips. He removed a finger laden with tea and licked it with lip-smacking delight.

"*Tamarack calls*," the wind whispered in the dismal way of dying dreams.

Bugbear looked up. He gazed through the jumble of white and black shapes that polluted the midnight forest.

"Who's there?" he asked.

"*Tamarack calls*," the voice repeated.

"Hmph!" Bugbear grunted. "Strange times as well." He took up another finger of tea, letting the grains roll about in his mouth, slide over his tongue, and ease under his palate.

"*Tamarack calls,*" the voice returned.

"Tamarack annoys," Bugbear grunted. "And yet..." Through the slats of his shelter he could see the peak, looming but a mile or two away. It jutted through the center of the great storm as if it was a blade which had pierced the sky, with the snow raining down as Heaven's blood. He suddenly felt drawn to it... compelled to climb its summit and glare down upon the world beneath.

"*Tamarack calls.*"

"Yes," Bugbear hissed and nodded. "Yes. I hear it."

He pushed one of the limbs aside, opening the little shelter to the full brunt of the blizzard. The cold snow stung his face like pins of ice. The wind wrapped about his bones and smothered him in a cold misery. And yet, Tamarack called. And he would answer. Tamarack called. And he would follow. Tamarack called. And he would surrender.

Bugbear left his little refuge with a troublesome tumble and a slip and a stumble. As he ventured forth, defying the all-consuming storm, he found the snow was nearly to his hips. He trudged through it, plowing his path like a burrowing mole. The forest was bleak and stark like the landscape of a nightmare. No life. No color. No hope. There was only the sound of the wind, the sting of the cold, and the struggle of white snow against black night.

The goblin found himself thinking of Manchester. It was a sudden thought, although not entirely unwelcome, as Bugbear had felt some regret over leaving the king with such worrisome words at such crucial times. And so, he thought of the king. He thought of his bungling and his stammering. He thought of his slips and trips. He thought of his glorious conquests and frivolous romance. All brought a smile to his face.

"*Tamarack calls,*" the voice moaned once more.

"Yes! Yes! Yes!" Bugbear spat into the wild winds. "I'm moving as fast as short legs and tall drifts will allow!"

And then another voice came upon the wind, just ahead upon a trail now almost completely obscured by snow. Bugbear stopped for a moment to peer through the black and the white. In a stream of moonlight he saw a donkey and a cart and a driver.

"*Hup! Hup!*" the driver shouted as he cracked his whip. The donkey brayed and struggled forth through the deep snow. In the back of the cart large sacks were piled, heaped upon one another like the stones of a great monolith. And the squat, fat driver sat upon the heap, shouting his orders and cracking his whip. "*Hup! Hup!*"

"Tudmire?" Bugbear gasped to himself.

As the cart moved ahead, deeper still into the naked forest, Bugbear stepped out upon the trail. One of the sacks had fallen, its contents spilled to the ground in a mound of golden glitter. "Coins," Bugbear whispered. Yes, they were coins. And as Bugbear picked one up to examine in the moonlight he could see that they were marked with the seal of Willow Prairie. The goblin laughed. "Tudmire. You may be the only one to have actually come out of this war ahead."

And Tudmire drove on into the bitter night, never seeing Bugbear, only seen by Bugbear.

Bugbear left the fallen sack and moved on. He saw another smaller trail winding up through the slopes at the base of Tamarack. He set out upon this trod, noticing the snow seemed less hindering, and the path less hidden.

Strange things happened as Bugbear ascended Tamarack Mountain. Through his feet, up his shins, in his middle, and to the top of his head, Bugbear could feel a strange vibration. The ground hummed and shivered. And the air buzzed and quivered.

Unwelcome smells rode the air, part smoke and part acid. And the snow melted in the wake of these dreadful phenomenon, the darkness parted, and the world turned from black and white to all imaginable shades of gray.

Nothing seemed to live here any more. Oh, there were trees, and most even had leaves. Yet, these trees had no color and they did not wave and sway with the wind as trees were apt to do. They stood still and unmoving, dead as hope and empty as a pauper's purse.

The only place Bugbear saw movement was in the great clouds of smoke which billowed near Tamarack's peak. And soon even this stopped. As did the humming. And the buzzing. Only the smells remained. And a new sound of muttering, mumbling, and meddling.

Bugbear reached the plateau on Tamarack's peak, peering from a hiding place behind a ragged hedge of brush and grass. And there he saw. He witnessed. He feared.

A great mob of patchworks stood before a great hole in the earth. Beside them hissed recently worked steam engines... mighty machines designed for excavation. And at the edge of the hole stood Ollamh Cron, staring down into the chasm with eyes wide, smile wider, and arms opened.

Bugbear felt something cold and hard smash against the back of his head. It wasn't something he wanted to feel there. No, not at all. Yet there it was. And it was followed by something he didn't want to hear.

"Don't move an inch, or I'll take your misbegotten head."

Oh, he didn't want to hear that at all. He hated the word *"misbegotten."* Almost as much as he hated the rank, swampish breath that accompanied it.

"I shan't move an inch, but I shall talk a mile," Bugbear answered his unseen captor. "Who are you? What do you want of me? And why is everyone so interested in that big hole?"

"Move forward," the unseen menace said from behind as he pushed the cold, hard thing more aggressively against Bugbear's skull. "Ollamh Cron shall answer your questions."

And Bugbear did move forward, as he most certainly did not want to hear that word again.

Ollamh Cron and her patchwork slaves turned to see Bugbear as he waddled towards them from the brush. The coranieid witch's smile grew wider still, if that was truly possible. The unseen captor shoved the cold, hard thing to Bugbear's head, sending him to the ground at Ollamh Cron's feet.

"Get used to being on your knees, little man," she purred. "You'll be spending a great deal of time there in the years to come."

"I assume you've excavated your hidden master then?" Bugbear said, pulling himself to his feet and dusting off his breeches.

"Indeed," Ollamh Cron said. "I have just recited the words to revive him from his slumber. You are about to bear witness to the greatest event of our time! The reawakening of a god!"

Bugbear yawned. "Reawakenings put me to sleep."

Bugbear felt the cold, hard thing hit the back of his legs, sending him to his knees once more.

"Most discourteous! I protest!"

Bugbear turned about to address his attacker more vigorously. And yet his words dried in his throat upon seeing the captor now completely.

It was a goblin... a sick goblin, with gray skin stretched over a skeletal frame, teeth sharpened to points, eyes black and lifeless, and a shovel gripped in black nailed hands.

"I know you," Bugbear gasped. "You're Duergar, my childhood friend."

"Yes," the goblin hissed. "I was known as Duergar once. And I was a gardener. So lowly and so downtrodden. But now, I serve a god."

"Behold!" Ollamh Cron exclaimed as she motioned to the pit.

Bugbear turned, as did everyone, for a thunder rumbled forth from the hole, and black light spilled out, and smoke and gas spat and sputtered. The coranieid and her animal hordes fell to their knees (those that had them.)

Duergar knelt beside Bugbear, glaring at him with his black, glassy eyes. Bugbear could hold the gaze but a moment before fear of what lay beyond those dead eyes drove him to look to the pit.

Another rumble of thunder and burst of black light met the night. Then, with the ease of a snake, a shadow slithered forth, reaching up into the sky, growing like a darksome oak, blotting out the glow of the moon. And from this shadow he emerged, walking out onto the plateau with a confident and easy gait. He seemed little more than a man, and a very ordinary man at that. Only his coal eyes and chalk skin marked him as anything different or unique. Even his clothing consisted of nothing more than a long robe and slippers.

"Well," he said with a stretch and a yawn, "what an ordeal that was! Thank you oh so much for all of your hard work while I was out!"

Ollamh Cron knelt lower still, her face almost buried into the earth. "'Twas our pleasure, master."

The Shadow Smith clapped his hands with delight. "Is this a coranieid I see?"

Ollamh Cron allowed herself the dignity of raising her head and meeting his eyes. "Yes, master. I am the last of my race, sworn to serve you ages ago and destined to serve you ages hence."

Bugbear laughed. He laughed long. He laughed hard. He laughed until he feared he would laugh himself wet.

Duergar raised his shovel to strike down the disrespectful goblin, but the Shadow Smith waved him off.

As Bugbear rolled upon the ground, filthy with his own silliness, the Shadow Smith approached him. "What do you find so amusing, little one?" he asked in a voice smooth, soft, and easy.

"You!" Bugbear managed to sputter betwixt mouthfuls of mirth. "You're even less imposing than Manchester!" And this was followed by even more laughter.

The patchworks stamped and snorted, clearly unhappy with this display of irreverence. Duergar again leveled the shovel near Bugbear's head. But the Shadow Smith simply smiled and knelt before Bugbear, placing a hand upon the goblin's shoulder.

"Yes," he said. "I am a rather silly sod. Not very tall. Rather plain in the face. Pale complexion. Slight build. And I prefer a nice robe and slippers to arms and armor."

Bugbear's great peels of laughter trickled to a few snickers and guffaws as the Smith stood, backed away, and looked down to him with smiling eyes.

"But I have never had to rely upon brute force to conquer," he said, his eyes suddenly turning flame red. "I have never had to clash with enemies steel to steel and flesh to flesh," he continued, his voice suddenly deepening to a growl. "I have never had to stain my hands with sweat and blood nor strain my heart with labor and love," he roared, his body growing as tall and long and black as an ancient spire against a blood red moon.

As Bugbear watched this horrifying transformation, black tendrils ripped from the earth, twining about his arms and legs, holding him fast and binding him taut. He struggled and strained, but all in vain. For these roots were deep, and their grip was on him before he had even set eyes upon the Shadow Smith.

"The humble banderberry root," the Shadow Smith said with a grin. "How it has served me well." The fiend shrank back to his previous stature.

"You?" Bugbear gasped. "Banderberry root?"

"Oh, yes!" the Shadow Smith said. "When one is split in half and buried in the earth, one takes on many projects to keep one's sanity. The banderberry root proved particularly effective in stamping out that bothersome Non-Logical cult Whittlegrip had started up. As goblins seemed the most adept in the Non-Logical disciplines, I targeted them specifically with my devious new drug. Duergar was quite helpful in encouraging its use. I believe he introduced you to its *medicinal* qualities, did he not?"

Bugbear turned to the side, still straining at his bonds. He saw Duerger, standing with shovel in hand, smiling with dull gray fangs.

"So, my abandonment of Non-Logical Thought..."

"Totally the influence of the drug. As was your abandonment of good King Martin. And the eventual loss of your visions. Oh, those visions would have proven to be a terrible impediment to my plans! Couldn't have you predicting every move I made before I made it! I'm so glad you were as opposed to them as I was!"

Bugbear trembled and shook. He strained at the roots with every shred of his tiny strength. "I was the heir of Whittlegrip! You robbed me of my destiny!"

"That's not the only thing of yours I've taken," the Shadow Smith hissed as he drew closer to Bugbear. "*Bwbach Coblyn*," he whispered for only Bugbear to hear.

Bugbear did not believe what he had just heard. He shook his head. He opened and closed his eyes. He sputtered, spat, and fumed. His mind reeled and his body stiffened.

"Yes," the Shadow Smith began, playfully rubbing Bugbear's tangled mop of hair. "Your Cysegredig Rhwym. So easy to read when you have fallen in with my tea. *Bwbach Coblyn.* Such a lyrical name. A shame you can't use it more openly. But rest assured, it shall remain our little secret."

The Shadow Smith waved his hand and the roots dropped Bugbear to the ground.

Bwbach Coblyn rolled there for a moment upon the dry gray earth. He cried, his tears mixing with the dust. His body bobbed and throbbed, jerked and jiggled. He was suddenly like a fish floundering on a dock, thoughtless and panicked with no concept of where he was. Wispy memories suddenly fled his mind... moments from a life reflected in a dirty mirror. Whittlegrip. Tudmire. Riley. Maga. Manchester. They were no longer people, but merely names.

"And now I have shown you what lies beyond my bright smile and my dark eyes," the Shadow Smith said. "What do you say?"

Bwbach Coblyn crawled up to the Shadow Smith's feet. He pulled himself to his knees. He looked down and he reined in his sobs. And in a gurgling whispered gasp he said: "Thank you, master."

CHAPTER 29
THE RIVER OF DREAMS

Dawn broke over the peak of Tamarack. The sun seemed weak and strained as it spread its thin rays over the valley. Everything was washed in gray this morning... dull and lifeless... looking much the way Manchester felt.

The tiny shack he, Maga, and Riley had discovered last night provided little shelter against the storm. Its roof was pocked with holes. Its walls were rotting and bowed. Its floor was frozen dirt. Snow piled in spots, and the wind entered and left through all manner of holes both obvious and unseen.

No one had lived here for some time. And Manchester doubted anyone could live here for very much longer all the same.

Maga was the only spot of color and warmth in all the cold world. Her soft bronze flesh, flashing silver eyes, and warm raven hair reminded Manchester that some beauty yet remained in this wasteland. As he roused in the dim dawn hours she crouched before a small fire in the decaying stone hearth. From his tiny cot he watched her, every movement a grand and graceful gift to his eyes. Her slender hands waved over the struggling flames, coaxing them to life. Her full lips mouthed strange words, blending sound with hope. The fire grew under her care, dragon bride *spellcraft* filling in for the lack of true fuel.

"I don't suppose you could talk up a nice hot cup of coffee?" he wheezed with breath as strained as the daylight.

Maga turned about, her smile breaking the gloom. "Did you sleep well?" she asked as she rose and walked towards him.

"I had dreams," Manchester said, turning away from her to look up at the battered and tattered ceiling.

Maga knelt beside him and placed her hand upon his upon his chest. "Like Bugbear's?" she asked.

"Yes," Manchester replied. "Prophecies. Visions. Warnings. Bugbear is dead. And soon I shall be as well."

"No!" Maga protested. "These were nightmares and nothing more! Do not believe them, my king!"

"It is the way of things. In the winter things die, only to be reborn in the spring."

Maga pulled away from Manchester. "You frighten me, Martin."

Manchester let out a short and weak laugh. "Nothing frightens you, Maga. You are simply confused. But you'll understand soon enough."

She looked to the ground, the cold, hard earth. "I should change your bandages," she said.

Manchester sighed. He could not cobble together the words to ease her troubled heart. Not without lying. And he could never lie to her. So he let his words stand... a hot iron in her breast, a poison barb in her mind.

He barely understood the visions himself, so bold and loud they were that they had nearly overwhelmed all thought. And yet he saw Bugbear's death. The black tendrils squeezed the life from his body, leaving only his shadow behind. And he saw shadows overwhelm himself as well. And he saw the war... the great, bloody war. Patchworks against humans. And he saw something more. A great armored figure towering over them all, wading through their frenzied ranks like a mighty steam ship breaking the waves of the sea. Its armor was black, gray, and white. And its blade was huge and marked with the notches of many great battles. It fought neither patchwork nor human. It simply walked through them, its glowing eyes set upon a foe at the horizon. Manchester feared this creature. He feared its two metal faces, one set atop the other. He feared its determined and steady pace. But most of all he feared its name... a name he could not bring himself now to recall.

"Oh, Martin!" Maga exclaimed as she looked to his naked heel. "The infection has spread up the entire leg!"

"Further than that, I fear," he replied as he opened his coat and shirt.

The gritty, gray stain covered his chest now, and part of his neck. Maga was aghast. She pulled back and went to the fireside where she took up her helmet.

"You need water," she said quickly, as if the words might somehow chase away her alarm. "I shall melt some snow in my helmet."

Manchester said nothing. He knew better. There was no *spellcraft* that could make dead things live again. The words of his life had been written. It was best to simply let others read what they would, and hope they skipped the boring parts.

As Maga went to the door, she was met by Riley. Actually, she was nearly bowled over by Riley. As it was, the rickety door took the brunt of the patchwork's frantic entrance, falling off entirely as he scrambled inside the shack.

"Magnet! Munchausen!" he gasped as he fell to the floor in an exhausted hunch. "We were hunting for breakfast when we saw them! Patchworks! A dozen of them! A war party! They did not see us! But they have picked up your scent! They track the king by the spore of his wound!"

"Riley!" Maga said, gripping the beast-boy by the shoulders. "You hide in the brush about twenty yards from the shack! I shall take to the top of the large oak just outside the door! Signal me when you see them approach!"

"No," Manchester said as he slid his naked foot into his leather boot. He fought the pain that shot up his heel and fragmented through every part of his body like white hot shrapnel. He stood, unsteady at first, but as he saw their concerned eyes upon him, he drew up more strength and stood taller and steadier. "You two shall return to Willow Prairie. Dunderbeck will have filled their heads with more lies. You shall have to empty their heads and fill them with truth."

"And you?" Maga said, her voice wavering with doubt and fear.

"I shall go to the river. That is where I shall lead the enemy. That is where I shall die."

Maga looked to Manchester, her eyes moist and unblinking. Her lips trembled. Her body shook. And then she threw herself to his feet. "Don't!" she cried, suddenly sobbing and convulsing. All warrior pride, all courtly grace, all ancient wisdom washed away in a tide of grief.

Manchester bent down to her, placing his hand beneath her chin and gazing into her tear-ringed eyes.

"I can bear the pain of a wound that will not heal. I can bear the rejection of a kingdom I dreamt to rule. I can even bear the burden of knowing the time and place of my own death. But I cannot bear the sight of a great warrior reduced to tears." He smiled to her as he wiped the drops away with his fingertips. "Let me see you one last time as the fierce beauty who rescued me from the shadows in the forest. Let me see the warrior who shall lead my people into battle against the Shadow Smith. Let me see Maga Ap Allherahiah, the woman I love."

Maga returned the smile and lowered her head. "I have never met a man like you. At once so awkward and uncertain, then again so brave and bold. You are like two men. And I love them both."

Manchester pulled her into a hug. He wrapped his arms about her and felt the warmth of her breath on his chest. He smelled the rose petals in her hair. He let the moment sit in his mind, melting into every nook of his memory.

"I must go," he whispered as he pulled away.

Maga darted towards him, grabbing his face and pressing her lips to his. It was a desperate and bitter kiss... the kind that was born of grief. And yet there was love in that kiss as well. Passion. Warmth. Life. Allherahiah and Reginald lived once more in that kiss.

Manchester broke the embrace and placed his hands on Maga's shoulders. "Now, you and Riley must go warn the people of Willow Prairie," he said. "Gather them for war. I'll distract the patchworks. They've caught my scent. It's my blood they're after, all the same."

Maga drew her sword and bent to one knee. "I obey your commands, my king. It is my duty. It is my honor."

Riley bent to one knee in imitation. "The rat-catcher obeys as well."

Manchester placed a hand on each of their shoulders. "This is all too sentimental," he suddenly laughed. "Poor old Bugbear would have a fit. Let's end it now before we dishonor his memory."

Out in the snow they finally parted. With his wooden crutch Manchester set out towards the deep woods, while Maga and Riley made way to the trail back to town.

"Maga!" Manchester shouted to her as he remembered a bit of advice. She turned about to listen, perhaps hoping that his suicidal plan had all been a ruse. "In my Monkey Years I would sneak out of my parents house at night to walk the country roads.

And to chase away my fear of the darkness, I would sing songs. Remember that. Remember that when you rally the people of Willow Prairie."

Maga nodded. As did Riley. The patchwork took up his fife and played a song now... the slow mournful strains of his favorite tune. This was the song that carried good King Martin into the forest. This was the song that marked the last moment Maga saw him, hobbling through the snow and disappearing into the dead, black trees.

Manchester fought back his own tears. He did not like the way fate seemed to be moving him without his permission. He did not like being thrust into martyrdom when he finally had so many reasons to live. Most of all he did not like leaving Maga and Riley.

He could hear the snarling and growling of the patchworks now. He quickened his pace. He knew he would need to make it to the river before they caught him. There he would make his stand... a final battle before falling into myth.

He thought of Bugbear now. Bugbear, who had already passed beyond, if the visions were to be believed. He remembered the Non-Logical lessons. He remembered the disjointed rants. He remembered. Bugbear. His best friend. His advisor. His mentor. At least there was a chance Manchester would see him once more. Assuming they were bound for the same afterlife, that is.

He could yet hear the faint notes of Riley's song. They lifted him and inspired his dying body to move on. Every inch was a mile of pain. Every step was a marathon of misery. Every breath was a burning torment. And yet the music kept his spirit from fleeing his tattered frame.

The patchworks were almost upon him now. He could hear their paws and hooves scraping against the frozen earth. He could see the steam from their breath breaking the cold air. He could feel their hatred.

Finally the river. It raged. It boiled. It bubbled. The bitter cold could not contain it. It lived as always, a reality unto itself. Here Manchester turned, holding up his crutch as a weapon, swinging it wildly at the pack of thirteen patchworks who held him at bay. The beast men snapped and snarled at him. A particularly nasty cobble of hawk and stag stepped forward ahead of the rest.

"The master calls for you!" it cawed. "You come! You serve him!"

Manchester lumbered forth, snarling and growling with savagery that made the patchworks cower. He shattered his crutch over the hawk/stag's snout, sending it scurrying back with a screech and a snort. "Your master is a fraud! Nothing but shadow! I shall bring the light that ends him!" The other patchworks stomped and wobbled, moving back and forth in place, as if trying to determine whether they faced prey or hunter. Manchester gave them no time to decide. He leapt upon the biggest of the pack, a bear/fox, taking what remained of his jagged crutch handle and driving it down the beast's throat. The wood splintered and shredded inside its mouth and down its gullet. It fell back, Manchester still atop it. The other twelve swarmed about, suddenly finding enough rage to smother their fear. Manchester sprang into their midst, clubbing at every horned head, scaled hide, and furry backside until his crutch shattered to naught. Several patchworks fell, and yet others fled. But a handful of the most savage remained. Their teeth bit, claws ripped, and horns gorged. But Manchester withstood their attack. He imagined Riley's song... heard it in his head. And he thought of Maga leading the reformed patriots of Willow Prairie into battle. Then his fist met the muzzle of a horse/bat. His foot met the stomach of a wolf/turtle. His head butted the noggin of a cock/raccoon. All the while, through all the battle, the song gave him strength and Maga gave him hope.

The beasts had fallen. Any who had dared attack the king of Willow Prairie huddled in the snow, bleeding and exhausted. Manchester swayed over them, amazed at the skill with which he had dispatched them. Non-Logical Thought. It was the only way he could have conducted himself in such an effective manner. All the same, the battle had taken the last of his strength.

Drenched in his own blood, weakened by his king's wound, Manchester turned towards the river and fell to his knees. He took one last look at this world. How fitting. This was the very spot where Maga had sung her song of Allherahiah and Reginald. He took a deep breath, smiled back to the patchworks. And he fell into the cold, flowing river.

As he sank beneath the waters he saw a glint in the riverbed. Something metal. Before all went black, he reached for the object... and felt the familiar form of his talisman pressed against his palm.

CHAPTER 30
THE TEA BOY

Bwbach Coblyn saw many things in the Shadow Smith's camp atop Tamarack Mountain. When he had been Bugbear, he might have taken more notice of such events. But such important happenings were too confusing for poor, soft-headed Bwbach Coblyn. Soldiers marching and generals planning and big siege machines being hauled here and there. What exciting times! But all too important for Bwbach Coblyn to pay much heed. He simply served tea. Tea for his master. Tea for the Shadow Smith.

He carried the ornate silver tea tray with as much grace as his stubby and nervous frame would allow. One hand up above his head, the other on his hip, he sauntered from the mess tent to the master's tent, dodging all manner of beastly patchworks and goblin soldiers.

The master sat in a large oaken chair outside his canopy, Mistress Cron at his side, as always. A strange machine sat upon a table beside them. Bwbach Coblyn dimly recalled seeing such a device when he was known as Bugbear. It was a human invention called a *phonograph*. It played music. Beautiful sounds. Elegant notes. Perfect melodies. Bwbach Coblyn stopped and watched the record turn 'round and 'round and 'round. And his pointed ears twitched at the sounds he heard. He was mesmerized. Bewitched. Unraveled.

It was Ollamh Cron who saved the tea from spilling all over the master. Bwbach Coblyn snapped out of his trance just in time to see her steady his tray. Only a few drops of precious tea had been lost. But the shame was great, all the same.

"Fool!" Cron spat. "You nearly dumped your tea all over the master!"

"Forgive me, master!" Bwbach Coblyn pleaded as he placed the tray upon the table. "I was undone by that music!"

The Shadow Smith chuckled. "Yes," he said. "That is a human composer, my little tea boy. His name is Mozart, I believe." He sighed, looking up to the sky in the wistful way of a dreamer. "I have missed so much while imprisoned. The advances in science and art have been most impressive. The humans in particular are inspiring. So prolific."

Yes. Bwbach Coblyn seemed to recall a human he found particularly inspiring... a gangly chap full of all sorts of surprises and wonders. But these memories were thick, like sap in a winter tree. He could not tap them. He could not read them. They oozed through his mind in muddled, muddied mystery, barely remembered and hardly missed, obscured by a wall of dead dreams.

"The spell has gathered nicely," the master continued, looking about the gray, colorless world. "When the worlds reformed my curse settled back into place as perfectly as the day I shaped it."

"It is a masterpiece of arcane engineering, master," Ollamh Cron cooed. "No color. No illumination. Nothing extraordinary or grand. Only a great expanse of gray shapes."

"It is my gift to creation... a great flood to erase all hope and all desire. For what is hope but the bait for a treacherous trap? What is desire but an endless road through a hostile wilderness? Without hope and desire, there is no disappointment. 'Tis better to be damned outright than to have but glimpsed God's sweet smile. 'Tis better to lurk in dark, Stygian depths than to stand in light before closed gates. 'Tis better to suffer in silence than to hear the distant melodies of a choir elite. Almost to Heaven is too close to Hell. Best, in the end, to just stay here on Earth."

Bwbach Coblyn listened to his master. He found the words interesting. Profound. Brilliant. A part of him wished to share his own observations. But that was hope and that was desire. He dare not offend the master by indulging in these intellectual fantasies. Such ambitions were beyond a mere tea boy.

Another thought stirred in Bwbach Coblyn's head as the wind stirred a scrap of paper held down by the corner of the phonograph. He remembered that paper. As the master and mistress conversed, his mind strained to recall the *hows*, *whens*, and *wheres* of it all. Its yellowed, tattered edges. Its strange, alien scrawls. Its faint, whispering voice. He remembered that he had tried to read it once, in a past life. It was something important that he had lost not so long ago. But the master had it now. So it no longer concerned him. The wind died down and the paper settled onto the table, never to move again.

Duergar approached, slapping his fist to his chest and bowing before the Shadow Smith. "Master, our hunting party has returned. They report that the king of Willow Prairie has fallen."

"Where is the body?" the Shadow Smith asked as he took a sip of tea.

"Swept away by the river," Duergar replied.

The master scowled. Bwbach Coblyn feared he had made the tea too bitter. But it soon became apparent that it was the news the Smith found so distasteful.

"Send out another patrol. I want to see the body."

Duergar bowed. "Yes, master."

"What of the dragon bride?" the master asked, as he nibbled on a pastry.

"She was spotted with a rogue beast-warrior heading towards Willow Prairie."

"I'd prefer that she was dead as well," the Smith grumbled.

Bwbach Coblyn spoke. He spoke words he hoped would please his master, even though he knew hope was forbidden. "But master, does she not travel an endless road through a hostile wilderness?"

The master looked to Bwbach Coblyn, his eyes narrow and searching. Bwbach Coblyn cowered, hunching his shoulders and lowering his head to avoid his master's penetrating gaze.

"The tea boy speaks the truth," the Shadow Smith said. "Dunderbeck yet holds sway in Willow Prairie. Even now he persuades the citizens to abandon their homes, in accordance with my instructions. The dragon bride shall find herself most unwelcome." The master patted Bwbach Coblyn on the head. "Duergar," he said, "take our tea boy to the fields. I would put him in charge of refreshing our goblin gardeners. And, seeing as he offers such brilliant insights, I believe a promotion is in order. From hence forth he shall be *Tea Boy First Class!*"

Bwbach Coblyn blinked his eyes several times. His mouth turned up at the corners into something he believed was called a *smile*. This was something one was expected to do when happy. And Bwbach Coblyn felt that he should be happy, although he was not. Yet to not be would disappoint the master. So he did the thing he believed was called a *smile* to please the master, and not because he was happy at all.

"Thank you, master," he said, groveling on the ground before the great leader in his great chair.

Duergar pulled him up by his coat collar. "Up, dog! The master has more vital things to consider than your sniveling gratitude!"

And with that, Bwbach Coblyn was taken from the presence of the greatest being on the face of the earth, and herded to the fields where a bucket of tea and a ladle were thrust into his hands.

"Feed the goblin laborers!" Duerger demanded. "But only a cup per mouth! Can you manage such a delicate task?"

"For the master I can accomplish anything!" Bwbach Coblyn piped as he raised his ladle in salute.

Duergar snorted his disdain and tramped off to attend to other tasks.

Many goblins tended the tea fields. A few of the more agriculturally inclined patchworks tilled the soil as well. Moles. Rabbits. Groundhogs. Badgers. They put hoe and shovel to work. They toiled here on Tamarack, where the summer remained in defiance of the winter that had settled in the valley below. They dug at the weeds that threatened the precious tea. They worked until their hands were gray with soil and their fingernails black with dirt. All worked for the Shadow Smith. All worked together to grow the tea that would break the spirit of the world. What a glorious destiny unfolded before them here under the dull rays of a pale sun.

Bwbach Coblyn went to each toiling goblin in turn and fed them a serving of the tea. They drank greedily, sometimes clawing for more. But the tea boy was firm in his denial. "One cup per laborer!" he snapped at the wretched beggars. And they would fall back to their labors, dejected and scornful.

A goblin sprawled on the ground, weak, thin, and wheezing. "Up!" Bwbach Coblyn demanded. "I bring you tea and the tea brings you strength!"

"I see light," the goblin gasped. "Bright light. Beyond the gray sky and into the next world."

"What do you blather about?" Bwbach Coblyn said with a scowl. "There is no world but this one! No light but the will of our master!"

"I have lived too long in this lie," the goblin whispered. "The tea has taken too much of my truth. And without truth we are dead."

His breath rattled for a final, long moment. And then he lived no more.

Bwbach Coblyn stared at the corpse. His mind seemed to recall that death was supposed to be regrettable. But as the other laborers took up the body and dumped it in a fertilizer wagon, he shook such silly notions from his head. From tea comes life. And from death comes tea. The circle was complete.

Bwbach Coblyn dipped his ladle into the tea bucket. There was one serving left. There seemed little need to waste it. The master himself had said what a fine job he had been doing. A reward was in order. And tea would do nicely.

There was a buzzing. It flitted past one of Bwbach Coblyn's ears. Then it flitted past the other. He swatted at the annoyance and continued to bring the ladle to his lips. But the buzzing continued. Flitting past one ear. Then the other. Then flitting once more. Bwbach Coblyn finally dropped his bucket and ladle and looked about. He saw only the tea fields and his fellow servants. He grumbled slightly, and looked to the spilt tea with remorse. The buzzing returned. With wild gestures and frantic flailings he attempted to banish the cursed sound, and yet it persisted, until finally stopping as a bee lit upon his pug nose.

"A bee?" Bwbach Coblyn said, his eyes crossed to observe the tiny intruder. "Bees are important," he whispered as a memory wormed its way through the thick sod of his mind. "There was a time when I studied bees. Something about the way they flew. Something about philosophy." Bwbach Coblyn looked deep into the insect's honeycomb eyes. He saw things there... reflections of a forgotten life. A gambling cousin. A trio of ogres. A proud warrior woman. A frolicking youth. And a noble king. "Manchester," he gasped. "They killed him."

The bee took flight once more as Bugbear fell to his knees, vomiting bitter, gray fluid onto the dusty earth. "They killed him. My apprentice. My king. My friend." His throat burned. His stomach churned. His heart yearned. An avalanche of moments fell upon him all at once.

He remembered when Manchester had pulled the quill from the inkwell... how the light that showered down upon him seemed to drape him in the mantle of God. He remembered Maga, dispatching the patchwork outside of Eglwys Cacynen... how her blade flashed like lightning and her face flushed red with righteous fury. He remembered Tudmire, squatting before the campfire cooking up his fragrant squiddle cakes. And he remembered Riley Ratcatcher, leaping through the fields, darting through the tall grass, dancing with the world to a song that only children could hear.

He knew then what he had been... what he yet was. He was Bugbear, the official keeper of goblin wisdom and culture. A scholar. A minstrel. A prophet. And a slave to no one.

Something thin and hard poked him in the ribs as he wiped the bile from his lips. It was Duergar, jabbing him with the handle of his shovel. "Why do you stop?" he demanded. "Are you ill?"

"No," Bugbear snarled. "I am healthy as a bee."

And with that, Bugbear stood up and threw a handful of dirt into Duergar's face. Then Bugbear ran, following the bee as it flew east, away from the camp and towards the sloping forests that led to the valley. Duergar wiped the dust from his face and pursued, raising his shovel high, and his voice higher.

"*Deserter! Deserter! The tea boy is a deserter! To arms! To arms! Capture the traitor!*"

Bugbear huffed and puffed, struggling to keep up with his airborne guide. The memories and emotions of his life were still settling into place, unbalancing him and distracting him. But the bee encouraged him, falling back and buzzing about his head when he dropped too far behind.

"To arms! To arms! Capture the traitor!"

"Tea boy!" he heard the Smith call out. "Return at once! Return to your master!"

Bugbear dared not turn around... dared not acknowledge the call. He closed his eyes and pretended he heard other words. "*Teach me magic!*" Manchester called through the mist of his memory.

"*How much do you suppose we could sell him for?*" Tudmire blurted. "*Will we be known as the rat-catcher?*" Riley asked. "*I never did like dwarves,*" Maga said.

Bugbear held each and every word in his mind, savoring the moments that birthed them, remembering the friends who uttered them. The Shadow Smith's commands faded behind him.

With Duerger and a pack of patchworks in pursuit, Bugbear stumbled into the back of a cart near the edge of an incline. But he was not alone in this cart. It was piled with banderberry root. And the sight and smell buffeted Bugbear's brain with panic.

"Not now!" he protested as he recoiled from the hated and beloved plant. "I can't be tempted! I mustn't fall back into slavery! I have to..."

"Die, traitorous worm!" Duergar shouted as he leapt into the cart, swinging his shovel wildly at Bugbear's head.

Bugbear dodged to the side, the shovel missing his head but splintering the edge of the cart. The violent movement jerked the cart forward, easing it over the precipice and setting it on a course down the wooded mountainside.

"Fool!" Bugbear shouted as he scrambled to the front of the cart. "We're doomed!"

"You're only half correct!" Duergar spat as he swung once more at Bugbear.

Bugbear turned away, this time letting the floor of the cart take the blow. The world passed them by in a blur of black, white, and gray as the cart continued its high-velocity suicide run down Tamarack Mountain.

Duergar raised his shovel to strike again. Desperate and weaponless, Bugbear crab-walked back across the pile of banderberry roots, his hands falling upon the gritty, cold plants. His back to the wall of the wagon, he took up some of the roots and pelted his attacker. Duergar stumbled back, dropping his shovel off the back of the wagon.

"Ha!" Bugbear laughed. "How will you kill me without your silly shovel?"

Duergar roared as he leapt upon Bugbear, fingers grasping for revenge. Bugbear fell back, struggling to pry the fiend's hands from his throat. But the other goblin's strength was greater, fueled by an insane devotion to the Shadow Smith... a devotion Bugbear himself had shared but minutes before.

And the cart continued its careening course. It had reached the snowy slopes of the valley by now. And it had found its way into a particularly thick part of the forest. It was here that the cart met with an oak, splintering into kindling and sending banderberry roots and goblins soaring through the air.

Bugbear landed a good ten feet from the wreckage, sliding to a stop near a cliff edge. Duergar fell only a few feet from Bugbear, lodging into a snow bank. Shaking the confusion from his head, Bugbear struggled to his feet. Duerger did the same, with the added chore of brushing the snow from his head and torso.

Duergar advanced on Bugbear, his hands knotted into fists and his fangs clenched into jagged rage. Bugbear stepped back, looking between Duergar and the cliff edge. He had never been a good combatant. He remembered childhood wrestling matches with Duergar in which his friend always bettered him. But this was no childhood game. Duergar intended to kill him. And there was nowhere to run.

"Duergar," Bugbear gasped, holding out his hands as he stopped just at the edge. "Please, don't do this. You were my friend once. A peaceful gardener. You can be that again if you just forget the Shadow Smith and his lies."

"He has my Cysegredig Rhwym," Duergar hissed.

"He has mine as well. But that means nothing. I see that now. We goblins put so much stock in our true names, that we ignored our true selves! Whatever we are has more power than whatever we are called!"

"The master has shown me greatness," Duergar snarled, continuing his menacing advance. "You would have me turn back into a simple, lowly gardener? A joke? A speck? A clown? Then you are no friend of mine!"

The bee buzzed past Bugbear's ear, flying into the thin air beyond the cliff edge. Bugbear spun about and looked at the insect as it hovered in the air before him. And he understood. He turned to smile at Duergar.

"Then be a soldier," Bugbear said. "And I shall be a bee."

And then he leapt from the cliff.

CHAPTER 31
WAR SONG

Wrapped in cloaks, two spies entered Willow Prairie. They kept to the shadows, darting down alleyways, scaling walls, leaping across rooftops... the time-honored ways of the thief. Their cloaks were as gray as the world about them, letting them blend into the background. And both were nimble and wise in their craft, avoiding the eyes of the citizens while observing all happenings in the small town.

"They are leaving," Maga whispered to Riley as they crouched atop the highest point on Mother Twitchett's roof.

Indeed, every citizen loaded carts, wagons, skids, and carriages with their belongings. Mister Sagramore had even dismantled his still. And Missus Yassberry had carefully folded each and every one of her handmade quilts and placed them in her steam trunk. Houses were emptied and stores were closed. The streets thickened with refugees, as horse hooves and wagon wheels fought for room on the stone cobbles.

"Blunderdeck's doing?" Riley whispered.

"No doubt. And they aren't likely to stop on our account. We risk much being here."

"King Munchausen believed in us," Riley said as he held up his fife. "We shall play. You shall sing. Willow Prairie shall follow."

Maga smiled to the young patchwork and nodded. There was so much wisdom behind those turquoise cat eyes. So much worth beneath that mottled dog fur. So much wonder within those brief child's years.

Maga removed her cloak and dropped from the roof down into the teeming streets. As though splintered by a spike, the townsfolk scattered from her, their voices raised in alarm and disdain and their heads turned to avoid her warm color and glow. Yet Maga remained calm. She let her soul fill with song. And she stepped through the bewildered crowd, surrendering her feet to the mystical power of the Dragon Dance. From somewhere unseen, Riley played his fife, as Maga took in a deep breath and released sweet words onto the bitter wind.

> *The shadows grow*
> *'Cross pristine snow,*
> *And threaten to bury our faith;*
>
> *Yet the valiant few*
> *Who stand with you*
> *Are ready to harry the hate.*
>
> *The traitor spins*
> *A web of sins*
> *To part us from our land;*
>
> *Yet we're too wise*
> *To heed his lies,*
> *Instead we'll make our stand.*
>
> *We take up arms,*
> *And sound alarms*
> *For we shall take no more;*
>
> *There is no wrath*
> *Can block our path*
> *When we march off to war.*

So stand ye fast
Against the past
That's come back to haunt us all.

And gird thy swords,
For bitter war
In Tamarack's looming pall.

As her song stopped, so did Maga, kneeling before the stone altar which held the quill in the inkwell. The people had followed her, as Riley had predicted. Every single pair of hands had stopped packing long enough to take up a musical instrument. Every single pair of feet had stopped walking long enough to step in time with Maga's song. And every single pair of lips had stopped talking long enough to smile with the simple joy of living. They waited behind her now, silent and solemn. The words and the melody seemed to wend from person to person, filling each with inspiration and purpose.

Dunderbeck broke through the crowd. "The witch!" he screeched, pointing at Maga with trembling hand. "Seize her!"

The townsfolk looked to Maga. Some moved forward, but not enthusiastically. Others simply lowered their eyes, as if their heads were suddenly weighed down with guilt. For the first time since being among these people, she pitied them. She finally saw that they had been little more than pawns... pieces in a game started by Sir Reginald and Whittlegrip and concluded by the Shadow Smith and Dunderbeck. But even pawns could be moved too often, lose their power, and become worn with use. Maga did not draw her sword as she would have in the past. She simply smiled.

"Take her!" Dunderbeck demanded again.

"Yes," she said as she walked into their midst. They parted... not in fear, but in uncertainty. "Take me. Take me as one of your own. Take me as a citizen of Willow Prairie. For King Martin saw something in you. A power to dream and a power to hope. Those are great gifts. And you are a great people. I wish to be part of that greatness."

"Bah!" Dunderbeck spat. "You think we are foolish enough to accept a witch into our community?"

"I am no witch," Maga said, still smiling to the people. "I am a lost child who found a home. I am a shattered heart who found a great love. I am a shamed warrior who has found a cause worth defending. As I offered my blade to your king, I now offer it to you."

Many of the townsfolk seemed swayed by Maga's words. Some moved forward with warm smiles. Others looked back to Dunderbeck with stern glares.

"Do not listen to her prattle," he bellowed as he mounted the steps to the gallows. "She is a great deceiver sent by the enemy to distract us while they marshal their forces! We must flee this poisoned place! Its purpose has been lost amidst the lies and perversions of King Martin. Let the winter take this little village. Let the wind reign over this ghost town. There are better things out there for us!"

The people stirred, milling about in dumb indecision. Dunderbeck stood atop the gallows, looking out over the townsfolk, his face drawn into his salesman's smile and his arms open in false friendship. The people looked up to him, mostly afraid and uncertain, but also trusting and obedient. "Far from this cursed soil we shall build anew. A city of hope and stability. We shall embrace science and logic. We shall foster brotherhood and charity. And we shall..."

"You shall deceive the world!" Maga concluded, drawing attention back to her. "Look at what Dunderbeck has given you! An empty wasteland! An empty throne! An empty future! Has it been so long that you've forgotten!" Maga strode back to the altar where the quill rested in the inkwell. She waited, letting each pair of eyes fall upon her. And then with a scowl she removed the quill and held it aloft. The sun broke through the clouds, showering down upon her and melting away the gray gloom.

"I come to remind you!" she shouted, her head lifted towards the Heavens. "To remind you of your allegiance to King Martin!"

And then, with the color of life filling Willow Prairie once again, the people cried out, their faces masks of joy and their voices horns of triumph.

Dunderbeck fumed. He paced back and forth upon the gallows, shouting down at the liberated townsfolk. "Will you let a song rule your hearts?" he balked. "Will you let pretty words and a pretty face distract you from preserving your own lives? This place is tainted! It is cursed! Willow Prairie is an abomination!"

From a rooftop someone threw a rock. The rock hit the lever on the gallows, opening the trapdoors and letting Dunderbeck fall through the platform. The magistrate of Willow Prairie barely had the time to utter a gasp of surprise. A muffled thud followed.

"Do not speak that way about our town!" Riley Ratcatcher howled from the top of the church. He was trembling with grief, tears falling down his muzzle as he hugged the grand cross atop the steeple. "Our parents died for Willow Prairie! Mother Twitchett tells us this! Tells us of your betrayal! Tells us what you found up there! Tells us what you serve!" Riley raised his head to the sun-streaked sky. "Mother Twitchett! We have found our justice!"

Their hearts stopped upon seeing the boy and hearing his words. Some cried. Others fell to their knees in prayer.

"Mother Twitchett," someone sobbed. "How could we forget all you taught us?"

A group of townsfolk ascended the gallows steps, Mister Sagramore at their lead. As he gazed wide-eyed and disgusted down into the trapdoor, he took a breath and delivered the news. "Dunderbeck is dead. Broken neck."

The people muttered and whispered with concern and shock. Maga looked about, trying to read as many of their faces as she could. She saw relief... release... regret. At last the shadows had lifted from Willow Prairie, and the wise, gracious, and just people for whom Martin had dreamed and died, had awoken.

"I trace my bloodline back to the Nagonene," Sagramore finally said to Maga. "The very same Nagonene who accepted Reginald as their blood brother. The very same Nagonene who welcomed the white man to Willow Prairie and shared with them Reginald's dream. If not for you, we would have lost that dream today. On behalf of our ancestors and on behalf of our dream, I ask you to help us fight on."

Maga nodded. "Gather what weapons you have. We march on Tamarack at dawn."

CHAPTER 32
THE NON-LOGICAL NOOK

The sound of lapping water reminded him of his grandparents' cottage on the Little Lake of the Woods. What summers he had spent there in his Monkey Years! The moist air had been good for his allergies, and he had thrived there. Swimming. Fishing. Climbing trees. Could it be he had returned? Could this be his reward for all the pain, all the disappointment, all the torment he had endured?

Manchester raised his head and opened his eyes. He sprawled on a river bank, sand in his beard and weeds in his hair. A trout had even found its way into his vest. He removed it and released it back into the river. In his hand he still gripped the round, coin charm. His talisman. But where had it brought him?

His head swung back and forth, like a pendulum. He took in what details his still groggy mind would allow. Obviously, the river flowed behind him. And before him was a rolling green meadow, filled with sunlight and brilliant butterflies. To the other side of the river, he saw misty gray shapes, undefined and obscure.

"The blurry side is where I came from, I'd wager," he muttered to himself. "But what is this meadow? Heaven? If so, what are butterflies doing here? I hate butterflies."

Manchester heard a scream, faint at first, but getting louder. It was a familiar scream. Very abrasive and shrill. It grew louder. And closer. Until finally it ended when a short figure plummeted into the earth beside him.

The figure groaned and pulled itself from the sandy bank. "Most unsatisfactory," the creature said as he spat sand from his mouth.

"Bugbear?" Manchester said, not believing his tired eyes.

"Manchester?" Bugbear said, not believing his ringing ears.

"I thought you were dead!" they both exclaimed in unison.

They laughed as they embraced, forgetting any bitter words they may have exchanged or any regretful things they may have done.

"Do you have any idea where we are?" Manchester asked as they parted.

Bugbear arched his brow and shrugged as he looked about. "Perhaps we are dead. But it can't be Heaven with all of those dreadful butterflies."

The bee buzzed past, circling the companions several times as if coaxing them to follow.

"Is that your bee?" Manchester asked.

"Indeed," Bugbear replied. "I believe he's the one who brought me here."

Manchester held up his charm. "I think this is what brought me."

Bugbear laughed. "It seems our events are now moving us, my dear apprentice! Shall we follow my bee?"

"Might as well," Manchester said with a shrug.

Bugbear and Manchester followed the bee, through the field of butterflies and over the rolling hills. Along the way, they informed each other of their adventures. Manchester told of his exile and his battle with the patchworks, while Bugbear told of his enslavement and his conflict with Duergar. There was a certain sorrow to their tales... a distinct regret that they had not been able to help one another through these dire events. And there was a unspoken pledge that such challenges would not be faced alone in the future. It was as if all of the suffering and all of the torment had somehow cleared any and all animosity that existed between the friends. Through their ordeals they had been cleansed of concern, unburdened of weakness, and shed of petty problems. Oh, neither of them had changed overly much. Bugbear still seemed his sarcastic and abrasive self. And Manchester retained much of his muddling and ordinary ways. But a barrier had been removed... an invisible wall that had always kept them from understanding and accepting one another completely.

Manchester stopped for a moment as they crested another hill. He lifted his foot and cradled it.

"Your wound?" Bugbear asked.

Manchester smirked. "What wound? It's gone. Funny. I've been walking all this time and just realized it."

Bugbear let out an abrupt laugh as he rummaged through his vest pocket. He removed the ornate silver box that held his banderberry root tea.

Manchester's eyes widened. "You aren't..."

Bugbear's own eyes widened in response. He opened the lid... and promptly dumped the gray grains onto the ground. "A little something for the butterflies," he chortled.

"So, it seems we're both cured of our ills," Manchester observed as he stroked his beard.

"Yes, and while I'm not certain of the *who, how,* and *why,* I do believe I know *where* we can find out." Bugbear pointed downhill in a small valley where a small cottage sat in a spot of sunlight beneath a rainbow.

"Butterflies and rainbows," Manchester grumbled. "This is definitely not Heaven."

A short walk later and the pair stood at the doorstep.

"Go ahead and knock," Bugbear said.

"You knock," Manchester said with a furrowed brow.

"You're the bloody king," Bugbear protested.

"Well, you're the advisor," Manchester replied.

"And I'm advising you to knock!"

"And I'm ordering you to knock!"

"Order me, will you?"

"Yes, I will!"

The door flung open and Mother Twitchett glared at Bugbear and Manchester.

"I will not have you two arguing here of all places!" she chastised.

"Mother Twitchett?" Manchester blurted.

"Then we must be dead!" Bugbear gasped.

"Not yet you aren't! But you'll wish you were if you don't settle down and join me for a glass of lemonade!"

The matron smiled and winked.

Manchester looked to Bugbear. "Should we?"

The bee flew past them through the open door.

"The bee seems to think so," Bugbear said.

They sat at a large wooden table as Mother Twitchett placed a tray with three glasses and a pitcher of lemonade before them. The inside of the cottage was plain. It seemed to be a single room with rough wooden beams and walls, a potbelly stove in the corner, and a few cupboards. The only other furnishings were the simple wooden chairs upon which they sat and the large oak table. And beside the doorway, covered with a tarp, stood a tall thing... which seemed to make Manchester nervous.

"Please, help yourselves," Mother Twitchett said as she motioned to the pitcher.

Bugbear reached for a glass and poured himself a spot. "Forgive my lack of social graces," he said as he took a sip, "but we would much prefer answers to refreshments."

"Yes," Mother Twitchett chuckled. "Of course you would. What answers do you seek?"

"Where are we?" Manchester asked.

"A Non-Logical nook," Mother Twitchett answered. "A place of refuge written into the scroll Whittlegrip and Reginald created."

"Ah!" Bugbear said, almost spitting out his lemonade. "Brilliant! That explains what we are doing here! We both were in contact with Non-Logical talismans while near death! You with your charm and me with my bee! Thus, rather than dying, we were whisked off to this realm! How insightful of Whittlegrip and Reginald!"

"And what of you, Mother Twitchett?" Manchester said, picking up his empty glass and rolling it over in his hands. "Who exactly are you? What is your role in all of this?"

"Like this nook, I am but a line written on the scroll," she replied. "A guardian. A guide. A source of comfort. Since the sundering of the worlds I have been a part of Willow Prairie... the spirit of community and cooperation."

"So you aren't even a real person?" Manchester said with disbelief.

"A rather crude observation," Mother Twitchett said, her face sagging with offense.

"She's as real as you or me, Manchester," Bugbear broke in. "Remember Twistroot's writings? How goblins are crafted from words? No doubt Whittlegrip took inspiration from this and gave our dear Mother Twitchett life in the same way." He finished off his glass and poured himself another, taking a sip and smiling as another thought settled into the ironic places of his mind. "Besides, there's nothing in Twistroot's writings to suggest that humans and the other races weren't made with words as well. Goblins were simply made using *special* words."

"We don't have time for philosophy, Bugbear," Manchester said, giving little heed to Bugbear's musings. "We need to find a way to defeat the Shadow Smith."

"You can't," she answered.

Manchester looked down to his empty glass. "Then he'll cover the world in darkness."

"No," Mother Twitchett said. "I said *you* can't defeat him. But there is another who can."

Manchester shuddered as he looked to the tall thing covered in the tarp.

"You know of whom I speak, Martin," she continued. "You dreamt of him. And you dread him."

"What's she blathering about, Manchester?" Bugbear asked, a sudden irritation peppering his voice. "Who is this dreaded dream?"

Manchester said nothing. He rose from his chair and walked over to the tall object covered in the tarp. He stared at it for a moment, as if hoping he could wish it into something other than what it was. And then in a quick and violent movement, he flung the tarp away and revealed the object of his fear.

Bugbear dropped his third glass of lemonade, shattering it upon the stone floor. "By Snagglescruff's nose hairs! What is that bloody thing?" The goblin waddled from his chair and stood beside Manchester, both of them looking over the thing with a mix of awe and terror.

It was a suit of armor, black, gray, and white. It stood a good eight feet tall from toes to heads. Yes. The thing had two heads, one atop the other like a totem pole. In fact, the topmost head had arms, legs, and a body as well, as if it was small, goblin-sized creature sitting upon the shoulders of the larger figure. The lower figure held a terrible, dark sword, almost as tall as both figures combined.

Bugbear and Manchester were mesmerized by this fearsome weapon forged from Non-Logical Thought. They could do naught but stare. For there was no room for thought, only room for awe.

"Whittlegrip and Reginald crafted many weapons in their crusade against the Shadow Smith," Mother Twitchett explained. "Just as this place and myself are embodiments of the scroll, so this armor is an embodiment of one of their lesser regarded creations."

"Yes," Bugbear hissed. "I understand now. It wasn't just a game. It was a strategy. Alliances. Friendships."

"Apprenticeships," Manchester added.

"Yes," Bugbear continued. "All reflected on the game board."

"Whittlegrip and Reginald never called upon its power because they didn't have all the pieces in place," Mother Twitchett continued. "However, the events you two have moved can bring it to life. Do you understand what must be done? Do you know which final two pieces must be moved?"

Bugbear nodded as he began to speak the ancient rhyme: "*White, gray, and black stones scattered 'cross the board...*"

... while Manchester finished it: "*Now you must unite them to become the Noggle Lord!*"

CHAPTER 33
THE NOGGLE WAR

The patriots of Willow Prairie trudged through the frosted fields on the road to Tamarack, shoulders stooped and heads bent, the weight of unfamiliar weapons and unwanted war dragging them down. Only Riley seemed to move without hindrance, skimming across the snow like a skipping stone, ever alert and ever aware, barking back to Maga what he could smell on the wind.

"Siege engines!" he said. "Patchworks by the hundreds! Some were taken from Willow Prairie! Others from Chugwater, Brockville, and villages to the south! Goblins! And banderberry root! All this the wind tells us! These are the enemies we face!"

Maga gripped the pommel of her sword. She was the youngest of the dragon brides, and the last of them. When she was being trained, her sisters had told her of glorious battles of the past. Great wars against corruptive powers. Assassination plots. Border skirmishes. Campaigns that spanned the length and breadth of Annwfn. But she had experienced little combat in her own short lifetime... a few brawls with overly attentive aes dana dignitaries, and a handful of scuffles with overly curious ogres. This would be her first and last true war. She had only her training upon which to rely, and the great Dragon Spirit which dwelt within all her kind. She led these brave people to their deaths. The only thing that kept her from weeping with shame was knowing that she would die beside them.

As for their weapons, there was little. A few hunting rifles. Some pistols. An old Civil War cannon. Ceremonial swords. And pocketknives. Some of the patriots had military experience. Sagramore had fought in *The War Between the States*. A few others had participated in some *Range Wars* out West. There were also hunters and trackers among them. But most of the people were simple folk, used to small town life and small town problems. The larger world had seldom encroached upon them, and there had been little need to kill anything beyond the occasional varmint.

In all, roughly three hundred volunteers marched from Willow Prairie that morning. That would be enough in weapons and fighters to slow the Shadow Smith's hordes, giving the rest of the world a few more precious days of freedom. Yes, most would die on the snowy fields beneath Tamarack today. Others would be enslaved. But the Shadow Smith would pay for his victory. This Maga vowed in the name of the Great Drake.

She saw the steam from the Smith's siege engines rising from the peak of Tamarack, making it look like a great, primordial volcano. The enemy would have the advantage in equipment, numbers, and vantage point. But Maga and Riley had already worked out a plan that would tip the balance for at least the first encounter.

"Scouts ahead!" Riley warned as he came rushing back from the forest some fifty yards in front of them.

"Release the livestock," Maga ordered to her troops. "Herd them towards the woods. Then take cover in the brush and behind these knolls."

The patriots responded, unharnessing the some twelve heads of cattle and twenty sheep they had brought with them. They swatted their behinds and urged them towards the forests ahead.

"Hunters, calls to the ready," she said to a group that crouched with her behind an incline. They pulled up duck calls, turkey lures, and other hunters' tools. Maga watched as the cattle and sheep inched closer to the forest, her eyes narrowed as she waited for just the right moment. "Now," she whispered.

The hunters commenced their calls, sending out an awkward symphony of animal sounds. This went on for some time, as the rest of the army crouched in the brush. Then Maga signaled for the hunters to stop. She waited and she watched. Then came the slaughter.

Nearly two dozen patchworks swarmed from the forest at the foot of Tamarack. These were the most savage of their kind... the predators and carnivores set loose upon the wilderness as trackers and scouts. But the animal instincts that served them so well in their duties, now worked against them in Riley and Maga's trap. As the beast-men leapt upon the livestock, rending and tearing into the warm flesh, Maga rose up from her cover and waved the patriots to action.

"Cannons, rifles, and pistols!" she shouted.

The sounds of weapon fire echoed through the valley and the smell of gun powder laced the bitter winter air. Many patchworks fell, distracted by their bloodlust and unprepared for an attack. Bullets riddled fur and feathers, and cannon balls exploded in their midst. Those who survived fled back to the woods, wounded and traumatized. Many more lay dead or dying beside the slaughtered livestock.

Maga raised her hand and signaled for a cease-fire.

From the forest came all manner of unearthly screams and terrifying howls. Human misery and animal torment mixed into sounds that were meant to be heard only in nightmares.

"Hunters, sound your calls," Maga ordered.

"You think to draw them out again so soon?" a hunter asked.

"No," she said, turning away from the forest. "I hope to drown out that God awful noise."

Riley scampered up to Maga. "The plan works! They are confused! Man's mind fights with animal's instinct! They do not trust their own senses!"

Maga nodded. "The Smith will turn his own artillery on us now. Try to pound us into submission before he sends the rest of his troops down to finish us."

"We should move then," Sagramore suggested.

"No. We stay put."

"And let him destroy us?"

"My dear Mister Sagramore, why do you think I had Missus Yassberry and the rest of the elderly take all of the town's mirrors to the church bell tower? The Shadow Smith's spell has been broken in Willow Prairie, where the sun now shines bright. We shall share that sunshine with our neighbors atop Tamarack."

Maga motioned to a young bugler who then let out a long, awkward call in the direction of town. Suddenly from Willow Prairie a beam of light shot forth, blanketing the top of Tamarack with bright, white illumination.

And from atop the shrouded peak came more screams. And the sounds of artillery misfiring. And the cursing of goblins and the howling of animals.

"They'll never be able to aim," Maga said with a smirk. "With the sun in their eyes, they're firing blind. If they want to kill the people of Willow Prairie they shall have to face us here, on the battlefield. That way we shall at least ensure ourselves honorable deaths."

"So we wait?" one of the hunters asked.

"Yes and no," Maga answered. "Riley shall take a small party into the forest to finish off the surviving scouts. Then from there they shall set themselves up as lookouts, sending signals when the enemy approaches. I have more surprises in store for them. The Shadow Smith shall fight hard for his victory this day!"

Riley saluted Maga and scurried through the ranks, selecting his team of spies.

As the assassins went about their dark tasks, the long moments settled over the remaining troops on the field. Maga's sisters had described such waits as "*Wedding Eves*," the long, tedious torment before a warrior's marriage to war. This was a time for reflection. To put the affairs of mind and spirit in order. To steel one's nerves and settle one's fears. Maga used this time to come to terms with two emotions that had ruled her heart in the past few weeks... her love for Martin and her anger at Bugbear.

She found it ironic that Bugbear's last, self-loathing words to her and the king referred to a dream. "*I'm tired of living in someone else's dream*," he had said. Yet Bugbear had started the dreams. He had fanned the passion in Manchester, igniting boyhood fantasies of adventure and magic. He was responsible for Manchester's ascension to the throne of Willow Prairie. He had even given Maga the nudge she needed to accept her love for Martin. But when he abandoned the king and Willow Prairie, he proved himself an opportunist who would stand with the king only so long as his schemes played out to his advantage. This is what angered her. For she had seen a different side of him that proved he could be more than a typical goblin... more than a trickster and conniver. She recalled his sympathy and affection for Riley... the tears he shed when he discovered what Ollamh Cron had done to him... and the joy he shared when he realized how at peace the young patchwork truly was. His pain at Martin's rebuffs was a sign of true character as well, as was his remorse for his part in awakening the Shadow Smith. But pain and remorse did not excuse the abandoning one's friends.

Yes, she was angry at Bugbear. And the thing that angered her most was that he was not there beside her now. She missed him, despite all of his faults. Or perhaps because of them. He was unique. He was Bugbear. And she wished he had not died alone.

The king had died alone as well. But his was a better death, met with honor and dignity. He did not abandon Maga and Riley, but demanded that they abandon him. Therein was the great difference between Bugbear and Martin. Bugbear was the dream-starter, where Martin was the dream-protector. Bugbear fathered the dreams, and Martin raised them. How strange to suddenly think of them this way, yet how natural. As different as Annwfn and Earth, yet always meant to be together. Advisor and King. Teacher and Apprentice. Bugbear and Manchester. And although she loved only one half of the whole, her blade would sing for them both this day. Her life would end in defense of their dream. Here in the shadow of Tamarack, Bugbear and Martin would share in her glory.

A whooping crane called from the forest. Riley's signal. Maga motioned for the riflemen to ready their arms. She waved to the patriots manning the cannon to load their charge. She drew her sword and stood tall upon the white field, her keen eyes fixed on the tree line. The patchworks and gray goblins thundered forth from the forest, bearing fangs, claws, blades, and spikes. Maga swung her sword 'round her head and cried out with a voice thick with rage: "*Send them back to Hell!*"

The cannon thundered. The rifles barked. The patriots cheered.

Many fell in the first wave of enemy troops. The cannon took a large bite from the middle. The rifles and pistols sent many more to their dooms. But the goblins were heavily armored, and some of the patchworks took to the ground, running on all fours beneath the line of fire. The infantry would be hard pressed to handle those that survived, for they were the cleverest and hardiest. Maga motioned for the artillery to fall back to higher ground. She then marshaled her cavalry, which consisted of twenty good men and women on horseback.

"Ten riders on each side of the enemy!" she ordered. "The infantry will push from the front. Riley and his men will push from behind. We'll squeeze them like a fat tick!"

Maga waved her warriors forward as she ran towards the oncoming tide of savages. The patriots followed, crying out their defiance, waving their swords, knives, clubs, and pitchforks. The two waves of rage clashed, steel ringing and growls rumbling. Maga dispatched several patchworks... feral things concocted of coyotes and weasels, dogs and rats, opossums and bobcats. Sagramore made a good show for himself, slicing a goblin's throat and gutting an owl/cat.

But other townsfolk met their deaths on the snow. Maga saw a young feed store clerk fall beneath the jaws of a bear/stallion. The town librarian lost her hand to a goblin's ax. A stable boy died, torn to shreds between two warring wolf-things.

Eventually she ignored their plights. For she had already suffered several bites and scratches as a result of these distractions. If she was to waste any more time mourning the dead, she would soon join them. She silently prayed for their peace, and continued carving a path through the pitiless hordes.

Maga began to see the battle in colors and shades. Dark bodies falling on white snow. Red blood spraying across the dull gray sky. White teeth tearing into pink flesh. Silver blades slashing into dusky fur.

Then she began to notice spaces... empty spots where enemies should have been, yet were not. The enemy ranks were thinning. The cavalry closed in from the sides, mostly intact. Riley and his assassins fought towards them from the back. The remnants of the frontal assault trudged on, clashing with the bulk of the Smith's forces in the middle.

The patriots actually seemed to be winning. Maga's tactics had overcome the enemies' superior numbers and equipment. Many of the surviving patchworks fled, their instinct for survival stronger than their loyalty to the Shadow Smith. Those remaining were disorganized, confused, and frightened. The riflemen took advantage of this, firing their guns into the air to heighten the sense of terror.

Then a large, black shape fell upon Maga, swift as a bolt of lightning, and twice as powerful. It struck her with clawed hand, knocking her headfirst into the snow. Not allowing herself the luxury of pain, she flipped over to her back and held up her sword to block further attacks. Its face was inches from hers... a twisted, snarling thing with long, curved horns, a flat pig's snout, and long, yellow fangs. Its hot breath billowed before her, polluting the cold air with the stench of blood and dead meat. It plucked her badge from her vestments and gripped it tight until blood dripped from his paw. And it spoke.

"This is mine, witch!"

The voice was corrupted by Ollamh Cron's alchemy, but Maga still recognized it. It was Constable Pawe, now made to resemble the beast he had always been.

She brought her sword to bear against his head, but the creature turned, blocking the blade with his horns. Amazingly the sword shattered. And the patchwork Pawe laughed. "Cron calls me *the Barghest*. I'm her blue-ribbon boy. Unstoppable. Insatiable. And real grumpy."

Maga drew back, gritting her teeth and glaring at her foe. Several of her men attempted to put a stop to the beast, but their knives and pitchforks were useless against the bear's blubber and boar's muscle. The Barghest swatted them aside with his massive paws. He gorged them with his bloodstained horns. And he trampled them with his iron-shod hooves. Bull, boar, bear, mustang, and madman advanced upon Maga. A great, heaving mass of murder. A rank, rumbling engine of evil. A foul, fierce perversion of nature.

Riley Ratcatcher sprang upon the Barghest, his claws ripping and his teeth snapping. "Maga is not for you! Test your strength against us!" The boy was much smaller than Pawe, only standing at the brute's knee. But his courage and savagery dwarfed any patchwork in the Smith's army. He drew blood, clambering up the Barghest's razor back, and digging deep into the thick flesh with needle-teeth. Pawe roared and flailed. He reached around with thick, fumbling paws, trying to grab his tormentor. He bucked and shook and trembled. He stomped and jumped and jerked. But Riley dug in, holding on with a carnivore's conviction, his jaws clamping harder, his claws digging deeper.

In a final, desperate ploy, the Barghest fell backwards, putting his full bulk on the young patchwork. Riley yelped and fell silent. Pawe rolled over, and got to his hooves, leaving his defeated foe broken and bloody on the snow.

"Riley!" Maga screamed as she rushed to his side. He still breathed, but Maga could already see that he suffered several broken bones.

"You'll join the pup soon enough," the Barghest growled as his shadow fell over her once again.

As Maga balled her fist and readied herself for a final struggle, a greater shadow fell over the Barghest. Three shadows. Three huge shadows.

"Bad doggie!" a voice bellowed. "Nasterous doings are you imposing on these poor folks!"

A meaty arm took the startled patchwork monster by the neck, binding him in a headlock.

"Punishments time, boys! Get the belt, Dubbin!"

"With the greaterest of pleasures, Loomis!"

"Ogres?" Maga gasped as she watched the three huge brothers whip the frantic Barghest. "Ogres?"

"I trust you approve?" a familiar voice chortled from behind.

Maga spun about with delight and wonder. "Tudmire!"

Indeed, it was Tudmire, a bit more tattered and disheveled than when she had last seen him, but in good health and good spirits. She was somewhat surprised to find herself embracing the goblin, but the joy of the moment overwhelmed her.

"They do good work," Tudmire said with a smile as he accepted the hug. "Worth every penny it cost me. Well, every penny it cost the town, that is."

"That's why you raided the treasury?" Maga asked, pulling back from him with a smile on her lips.

"Couldn't really let anyone know about it. Hush, hush. Top secret. That kind of thing. No one would have agreed anyway. They don't understand ogres like me. It's not the money they like. It's the respect."

"Bad doggie!" Loomis yelled as the whipping continued.

Tudmire looked down to Riley's broken body. "Oh, merciful Heaven! Riley!"

Maga remembered herself, turning to the stricken patchwork and examining his wounds. "Watch my back, Tudmire."

"Well, I'm unarmed, but I'll certainly do my best."

Maga gently ran her fingers over the patchwork's body. He had some cracked ribs and a broken arm. Fortunately the snow seemed to have cushioned most of the impact. "He'll be okay. There are a few broken bones, but he mostly just had the wind knocked out of him."

"That's good news!" Tudmire said, as he looked out over the battlefield. "Seems the battle is going your way! Sorry I didn't get here sooner. Ogres are terrible about stopping for bathroom breaks." The goblin's bulging frog-eyes darted over the fallen foes and clashing combatants. "Where's the king?" he asked. "I'd like to offer my apologies for being all skullduggerish on him."

Maga turned away and began petting Riley's fur. "Martin is dead," she whispered.

Tudmire stared at her, unblinking and unbelieving. "No," he said with a shake of his head.

"Yes, he is," Maga said. "He died yesterday fighting a patchwork hunting party. Bugbear has fallen as well."

"No, they haven't," Tudmire laughed. "Not my wily cousin Bugbear! Not my good friend Manchester!" Tudmire laughed as he waddled out towards the dying battle. "Manchester! My dear boy! It's me! Tudmire! I've come back! You still owe me that jar of pennies from our Noggle Stones games, you know! Bugbear! I forgive you for those cruel things you said! Do you see how I proved you wrong? I'm more than just a gambler! Do you see?" Tudmire laughed a bit longer, turning around in circles, searching in vain, until he collapsed to his knees. "Manchester," he sobbed. "Bugbear. Do you see?"

Maga could not bring herself to look at the goblin. Her own grief was too fresh to share that of another.

Mercifully, Riley roused. "We are sorry for not killing it," he gasped.

Maga smiled, wiping away a tear with one hand while stroking Riley's head with the other. "Dear boy," she whispered, "you are all that is noble in this world."

The ravens circled. The fog drifted. The sounds of battle waned, until only the shouting of the ogres and howling of the Barghest remained.

Tudmire shuffled over to Riley and Maga, his head yet heavy with grief.

"Turdmore!" Riley blurted, then winced with the pain of too much movement.

"Riley, m'boy," the goblin murmured with a slight smile. "Quite an exciting day. Sorry I couldn't have shared more of it with you."

"*There is still much to share,*" the wind whispered.

"Did you hear that?" Maga asked, doubting her own senses.

"I believe so," Tudmire said.

Maga looked up to Tamarack where the thick, black cloud gathered on the peak. Slowly it descended towards them.

"The Shadow Smith!" she exclaimed. "To arms, patriots! Rifles at the ready! Load the cannon!"

Tudmire helped Riley to his feet as Maga took up a discarded sword and rallied the remaining troops. Rifles were leveled at the cloud as it settled in the midst of the battlefield, spreading its darkness out twenty feet in every direction. The cannon was aimed. Swords were drawn. Hearts were beating.

The cloud contracted and faded, and when finally gone, revealed Ollamh Cron, a savage goblin with a shovel, and a plain man in a black robe.

"This has been very pleasant," the man said. "I mean that with all sincerity. A wonderful show. Thank you very much." He smiled and nodded to Maga and her comrades. "But I'm afraid I'm going to have to ask you to die now."

"Three of you against sixty of us?" Maga laughed.

"Oh," the man said, his coal eyes sparkling with amusement. "You assume we're going to fight you? No. That's what the patchworks were for. Dreadful idea, I'm afraid. Don't worry. Cron shall be punished for her failure."

Cron bowed her head, quiet tears staining her cheeks.

"I prefer to let others fight for me," the man continued. "Especially after that dreadfully long imprisonment I just escaped. But, oh well. I suppose less nap time is the price one pays for ruling the world."

Maga scowled. "Fire!" she ordered with a drop of her sword.

The rifles thundered. And the Shadow Smith laughed. Cron and the gray goblin fell to the ground, their bodies riddled with bullets and stained with blood. But the Shadow Smith stood.

"You are an impressive tactician, Maga Ap Allherahiah," he said. "Your mother should be proud. But then your mother is dead, isn't she?"

Maga growled and rushed towards the Smith, her blade raised high.

"And death is an interesting thing, isn't it?" the Smith continued.

A hand took Maga by the ankle, tripping her into a pile of corpses. The dead hands clawed at her and the dead mouths moaned to her. She squirmed and floundered, trying to escape their cold grasps.

"They sometimes call death *the Land of Shadows*," the Shadow Smith said. "A rather poetic loophole that I'm more than happy to use to my advantage."

The battlefield awoke with the writhing, lurching, shambling corpses of humans, patchworks, and goblins, taking up arms to recruit the living to their ranks.

"We can't defeat him!" one of the townsfolk yelled as he dropped his rifle and ran. One by one, the patriots fled, until only a handful remained. And even they, Willow Prairie's most resolute defenders, trembled as their own dead staggered towards them.

Maga kicked the corpses off of her, rolling to her feet and slashing several more in a wide, violent arc. "Take up your arms!" she shouted to her troops. "They still fall like any other foe!"

The ragtag remnants heeded her call as they charged into the thick of the shadowed host, their mouths stretched into howls of defiance, their arms raised in wild rage. Riley found an abandoned bow and quiver of arrows, which he strung with his good arm and fired with his teeth. He proved quite proficient with the weapon, sometimes killing two or three with a single arrow. Tudmire took up a pitchfork, a clumsy weapon for a clumsy warrior fighting clumsy foes. Between his awkward stabs and blundering bludgeons he sent more than a few deadmen back to their graves.

And the ogres continued their struggle with the Barghest, oblivious to the other conflicts around them. The monstrous patchwork was worn to a thread by this time, his body thick with welts and his fur nearly rubbed from his body. His eyes fell closed and his muzzle dripped with drool. The fight had fled his frame and he seemed to surrender to his fate.

"Swats him in the arse!" Loomis ordered.

"Oh, we'll swats him!" Dubbin agreed.

"The snouts is good for swatsing too!" Nigel offered.

And the three brothers wandered off the field, taking their new pet into the woods for further torments and training.

In the midst of the gruesome battle, the Shadow Smith stood, the corpses of Ollamh Cron and the goblin gardener rising to stand beside him. "Corpses make for very effective warriors," he mused, turning to the undead Cron. "Why didn't we just kill our troops to begin with?"

Ollamh Cron opened her grotesquely distorted mouth, letting thick and putrid fumes roll out over her gray tongue and yellow teeth.

"Ah, yes," the Smith gasped as he turned away, covering his mouth and nose. "The smell."

The army of corpses soon had the patriots herded into a small circle where they stood back-to-back, fending off grasping, undead claws and snapping, supernatural maws. Maga, Riley, and Tudmire gathered together, defending and alerting each other.

"I never had a chance to say good-bye to Bugbear and Manchester," Tudmire sobbed as he swatted an enemy with the handle of his pitchfork. "But I won't let myself go without saying good-bye to you two. It's been an honor to fight beside the royal rat-catcher and the chief justice of Willow Prairie."

"The honor has been ours, Sir Seneschal," Maga replied as she cleaved a patchwork corpse.

"And ours," Riley said, his arrows piercing several goblin ghouls.

The last of their comrades fleeing or drafted into the undead enemies' ranks, the three dots of color struggled against the great tide of gray.

Then they heard it. A great horn, clear and deep and echoing over the field. It sounded three times. And then came the thunder. And the lightning. And the terrible wind.

The corpses stopped, their dim minds seeming to respond to an unheard command. They looked to the west. As did Maga and her companions. A wall of color approached, melting the snow and bringing green grass and living things with it. And at the base of this wall walked a figure nearly eight feet tall and covered in spiked black, gray, and white armor. It had two heads, one atop the other, and both wore terrible masks distorted into shouts of rage. As it entered the battlefield, the corpses fell before it like wheat before a scythe. Wild flowers sprouted in its footsteps and bees swarmed about its heads.

Maga readied her sword as it approached. "This doesn't look good, my friends."

Riley grabbed Maga's sword arm and urged her to lower it. "Stand aside," he said. "This is not our enemy."

"Are you serious?" she balked. "Look at it! It's horrific! It's monstrous! It's... it's... it's..."

"Mother Twitchett once told us: '*When God is angry He dresses His messenger accordingly,*'" Riley said as he guided both Maga and Tudmire off to the edge of the field.

The wave of color continued, overwhelming the army of undead, returning them to their rest. The Shadow Smith stood in the center of the field, defying the great winds that howled around him and ignoring the bolts of lightning that struck the earth. He glared at the armored figure as it approached.

The great warrior paused as it neared the knoll where Maga, Riley, and Tudmire cowered. The bright wave of color that sprang from its footfalls washed over them, and Maga could feel her wounds heal and see the injuries of her companions fade as well.

The bottom head turned to them, its eye slits glowing red.

"*Give it to us,*" a voice rumbled forth, bold as a thousand shouts, yet distant as a whispered dream.

"G... give you what?" Maga whimpered.

The top head turned, its eye slits glowing green.

"*The king's weapon,*" a different voice rang out, shrill as a cock's crow, yet tender as a mouse's sneeze.

Maga stared for a brief moment, her dragon bride poise shattered and swept away by the overwhelming menace of the creature before whom she trembled. She reached into her cloak and felt for it... the tickle of the feather and the point of the tip. She removed the quill and with hesitant, trembling hand offered it up to the warrior.

A thick, armored hand reached down and plucked it from her grasp. Then, one at a time, the heads turned back to look at the Smith.

A few more heavy footfalls brought the creature before the robed devil. Ollamh Cron and the goblin gardener crumbled to the ground, like puppets without strings. The Shadow Smith seemed so small and insignificant standing before this primordial creature. And the sunlight and color dwarfed the fiend all the more. Maga marveled to think that this little man had been the source of so much torment and struggle throughout the centuries.

"*The game has been played,*" the top head spoke.

"*We are victorious,*" the bottom head concluded.

"*White, gray, and black stones united on the board.*"

"*Now you must surrender to the dreaded Noggle Lord.*"

The Smith smiled as he pulled the scroll from his robe. "But I have this! The relic that divided the world all those eons ago!"

The eyes glowed red. The eyes glowed green. The scroll burst into flames and the Smith dropped it, his face suddenly streaked with terror.

"*Those lines have been written,*" the top head spoke.

"*Those lines have been read,*" the bottom head concluded.

The Shadow Smith fell to his knees, holding up his arms in surrender.

"Please!" he pleaded. "I only wanted to be free! I only wanted to live!"

"*Free to enslave,*" the top head said.

"*Living to kill,*" the bottom head concluded.

With one hand the Noggle Lord held up the quill. With the other it held the squirming and screaming Shadow Smith to the ground.

"*Hold still,*" the top head said.

"*This will only hurt forever,*" the bottom head concluded.

The Noggle Lord wrote strange script upon the Smith's forehead, the letters burning red and green into his flesh. Writhing and whining, the Shadow Smith faded, his body turning more and more into a shadow itself. Until finally, the sun washed away every trace of his existence.

The Noggle Lord raised its heads skyward, drawing the great sword that hung at its side and lifting it to sparkle in the fresh daylight. Then, with a sudden, violent motion, it drove the blade into the ground where the Smith had fallen.

"*Whittlegrip,*" the top head said.

"*Reginald,*" the bottom head said.

"*The mission is completed, the enemy defeated,*" they said in unison.

The Noggle Lord collapsed, its great form buckling like an ancient tower crumbling before the wind of a mighty tempest. The ground trembled. The remaining snow evaporated. The earth swallowed the dead. And color filled the world once more.

Maga, Tudmire, and Riley slowly rose from behind the knoll. They crept forward, towards the still and silent Noggle Lord.

"I wonder how much that armor would sell for?" Tudmire mused.

"Shush!" Maga demanded. She inched ever forward, extending her sword to poke at the metal hulk.

The companions jerked back as the armor stirred and a moan came forth.

"*Next time I get to be on top,*" an all-too-human voice said.

"Martin?" Maga said, her mind filled with disbelief, joy, and shock.

"*Maga?*" the voice echoed from within the steel husk.

"*Make yourself useful,*" another voice said, "*and pry us out of this bloody monstrosity!*"

"Bugbear!" Tudmire blurted, his fat face filling with delight.

With frantic hands Maga, Tudmire, and Riley pulled and pried at the bulky armor. It came apart with surprising ease, peeling away like a banana skin. Bugbear and Manchester spilled out, drenched in sweat and trembling with exhaustion.

"That was the hardest game of Noggle Stones I ever played," Bugbear gasped as Tudmire helped him to his feet.

Maga fell atop Manchester, smothering him in kisses and coos. "I thought I had lost you!"

"I thought I'd lost me too, Maga," the king said with a smile. "But I found myself again in my dreams." He kissed her before she could say another word.

"What did you write on that devil's forehead anyway?" Tudmire asked Bugbear as he eased him over to sit on a rock.

"*Hope!*" Bugbear exclaimed. "We wrote the Non-Logical word for *hope!* The silly sack of shadows was allergic to it!"

The greetings continued, and the explanations poured forth like lemonade from Mother Twitchett's pitcher. Hugs, laughter, and joy were shared, the sorrow and dread of the past few days melting in the sunlight.

Hours later, after prayers for the dead and rest for the weary, the companions set out on the trail for Willow Prairie. All save Riley who lingered a moment to look off into the thick forest.

"Riley?" Maga called as she stepped away from the rest to collect him. "We're going home now."

"And what of them?" Riley asked, pointing into the woods. "Where is their home? Where do the patchworks go now that the war is over?"

Maga placed a hand upon Riley's shoulder. "We shall speak with the king about that."

Riley looked up to her and smiled. He touched her hand and licked it gently. "You shall make a great queen."

And before Maga could offer protest, the beast-boy trotted off ahead of the others, laughing and rolling through the tall grass.

CHAPTER 34
BURNING THE TEA FIELDS

Bugbear watched the flames reach into the night sky, tickling the edge of the moon. The smoke rolled out over the plateau, skating off the top of Tamarack and fading into nothing over the valley. He watched, his eyes round and unblinking, his face empty of emotion. The tea fields burned.

It had been a week since the great battle that ended the Shadow Smith's threat and decimated the town of Willow Prairie. The dead had been mourned. The deserters had been pardoned. And the world had begun to heal. Yet as Manchester saw Bugbear standing before the flames, he knew some things had not been resolved.

While men tended the edges of the fire, the king approached his advisor.

"The smoke won't infect anyone?" he asked, standing beside his friend and watching.

"No," Bugbear answered, still unmoving. "It was made to humble goblins. I am now immune, and Tudmire is safely sleeping in Willow Prairie."

Manchester nodded. He had been through much with his mentor in the past months, yet now the goblin seemed to suffer in a place beyond his reach. He wanted to say something that would pull him from his somber mood. But he knew that standing here in the place of his enslavement stung Bugbear's memory and numbed his sense of self.

"That's where I saw him die," Bugbear finally said.

"Who?" Manchester asked.

"I don't know," Bugbear answered. "He was a goblin, like me, humbled and enslaved by the tea. He died out there, tending the tea fields, his life eaten away by shadow." He continued gazing at the flames, his eyes wide and blank. "I fed them tea, Manchester. I fed their addiction. They died for it. Yet I was spared. Just because I share Whittlegrip's blood. An accident of birth."

"No accident," Manchester said. "Fate. You stumbled a bit along your path. But you followed it all the same. Don't blame yourself because they fell. This was the Shadow Smith's sin, and he's paid for it."

An empty moment fell over them... a time for the words they had spoken to find their meanings... a time for hearts and minds to mingle and mend.

"You should marry Maga," the goblin said, turning away from the fire.

"What?" Manchester said, his thoughts suddenly scattered by this unexpected announcement. "You mean to secure my throne and provide an heir? Yes. That makes sense."

"No, you insufferable twit!" Bugbear spat, turning about with a look of disgust. "Because you love her! By Whittlegrip's beehive! Do I have to advise you in all things, including your heart?"

Manchester smiled. "Yes, I do love her. But I'd thought you were opposed to that. I mean, I could see you supporting a marriage for political reasons, but love..."

"'Twas your love for each other that saved Willow Prairie," Bugbear said, his fierce display giving way to calmer words and tone. "Saved us all, really. For your happiness and hers, you should marry. And yes, it would secure your throne. After all, the people love her now. But that is an entirely secondary benefit."

Bugbear paused for a moment in the middle of the Smith's camp. In the moonlight he looked at a phonograph on a table. With a quirky smile he turned the crank and set the needle upon the record. The music rose through the night, adding a sense of majesty and power to the fire.

"The Shadow Smith was a creature made of lies," Bugbear said, turning to Manchester. "But he told one truth. You humans are inspiring." Bugbear turned away again, as though the words came to him from someplace in the distance. "I have found the apprenticeship most satisfactory, Manchester. I dare say that you have taught me more than I have taught you."

"Nonsense!" Manchester protested.

"Hush!" Bugbear said, holding up a hand. "These words are hard for me. I may be cured of my addiction, but not my pride." The goblin took a deep breath and continued. "It has been my experience that a scholar is never more right than when he admits that he is wrong. I have been wrong, Manchester. I have said and done many hurtful and selfish things. Some can be blamed on the tea. But some is my own doing. I can erase none of it. I can only continue learning." He turned once again to Manchester, smiling in a small way, his eyes reflecting the fire from the tea fields. "Here, where I was enslaved by the Shadow Smith, I pledge to you, good King Martin, that I shall serve the throne of Willow Prairie and hold the good of the realm above my own needs."

Manchester returned the smile and bent down upon one knee. "And I pledge to you, my dear advisor, that I shall heed your counsel above all others."

They stood for a few moments and stared at the fire. The flames were dying now and the men used wet blankets to extinguish the outer edges of the field. The stars shimmered above and the music swelled.

"This is all too insipid," Bugbear sighed.

"I knew you were going to say that," Manchester laughed.

"Let's go dip Tudmire's hand in a bowl of warm water!" the goblin tittered as he broke away and ran towards the trails.

Manchester followed, feeling a warmth and ease he had not known since his Monkey Years.

CHAPTER 35
THE WEDDING

After changing his wet bed sheets, Tudmire began preparations for the wedding celebration. And within weeks an event unfolded which enveloped the town of Willow Prairie like a multicolored quilt... a lavish banquet with the finest food, rarest wines, and hardiest ales... a festival filled with the sounds of merry lutes, flutes, harps, and voices, carrying the songs of celebration and mirth.

All manner of folk attended. They came from the human settlements of Chugwater, Brockville, and Tilene. They journeyed from the goblin towns of Caer Coblyn, Tor Delbin, and Gul Dureen. They ventured forth from the aes dana kingdoms of De Doty, Tuathian, and Dulwitch. And they traveled from the Dwarven keeps in the Winestain Mountains. Even Loomis, Dubbin, and Nigel came, enchanting everyone with their pet Barghest's tricks.

The celebration attracted several patchworks, who sniffed around the edges of the town, as if remembering in some distant piece of their human minds that they were a part of this community once. Riley coaxed some of them inside the town limits and reintroduced them to their homes. Most townsfolk stayed clear of the feral interlopers, but the patchworks remained docile and courteous guests. Although they did tend to eat a bit much. And they did not use silverware. And one of them urinated on the ornate tapestry the Chieftain of Dulwitch had given Maga and Manchester as a wedding gift.

Still, most of the guests agreed it was an opulent display. *"The finest feast ever," "Even Paradise does not hold such pleasures,"* and *"A celebration worthy of King Oberon,"* were among the words bandied about by the celebrants. Needless to say, Tudmire's head swelled almost to the point of bursting.

Manchester, Maga, and Bugbear sat in serious councils during much of the celebration, informing various community leaders of their discoveries while also forging important alliances. Several peoples swore their allegiances outright to Manchester, including Brockville, the ogre brothers, the dwarves, and the goblin settlements. Others signed non-aggression treaties and secured border rights to their lands. In the end, through Bugbear's clever negotiations, Willow Prairie was positioned as the most significant and highly regarded of the realms in this new world... a pivotal and central kingdom, where all people were welcome and great knowledge was shared.

The wedding itself came upon the second day of celebrations. It was held in the church, the doors and windows open so that those unable to fit in the pews could observe from outside. The town minister, Doctor Glenn, presided, and Bugbear served as best man. Flowers filled the front of the church, many picked from the footsteps of the Noggle Lord at the base of Tamarack. An urn with Mother Twitchett's ashes was placed in the front pew, Riley and an uncomfortable Tudmire sitting beside. And Manchester and Bugbear stood at the front of the church, dressed in sharp, black suits, awaiting the arrival of the bride.

As Riley played his fife, Maga entered the church, her white gown catching the sunlight, filling with a glow that seemed unearthly. A small beagle/opossum patchwork scattered flower petals before her (despite Riley's protests of *"pouch-belly conspiracies."*) Maga's feet fell upon the long, red carpet, leaving not a trace of her passing. As the soft notes ended, she stopped at the altar, standing beside her king, looking into his eyes and smiling. Manchester returned the smile and took her hand.

Bugbear tried to keep from teetering and tottering with boredom as the minister droned on about love, and commitment, and sickness, and death. He waited and watched and waited some more. Finally, as he smiled to a bee that buzzed about a nearby bouquet of flowers, Manchester nudged him.

"Time for the ring," he whispered.

"Oh!" Bugbear gasped. He fumbled through his pocket for a moment and produced the gold band.

Manchester took it, and gently placed it on Maga's finger. Maga in turn, placed a gold band upon Manchester's finger. And Bugbear in turn, returned to watching the bee.

Doctor Glenn raised his arms and smiled to the assembly. "You may now kiss the bride! And you may now kiss the groom!"

Maga and Manchester pressed their lips together, holding one another by the shoulders, eyes closed and faces flushed.

A thud, yelp, and flying usher came from the back of the church. The crowd turned about, as did the wedding party. Ten armored women appeared from nowhere and everywhere, swords drawn, and eyes set upon Maga.

Maga gasped. "My sisters!"

"Dragon Brides?" Manchester said. "Wh... what do they want?"

"We wish to know why we were not consulted on this union," one of the warriors said, stepping towards the altar.

Bugbear bolted before the king and queen, setting himself between them and the intruders. "We sent word out where we could. The dragon brides have no homeland. And homelands are scattered and confused as it is. There was no way to know where to locate you and your kin."

"Regardless," the dragon bride said, "we wish to state our intentions here and now."

Maga stepped in front of Bugbear. "I protest! This man spared me from execution and saved the entire world from enslavement to the Shadow Smith! There is no shame in this wedding for he is of Reginald's blood and a true king!"

Bugbear stepped in front of Maga. "See here!" he barked at her. "I'm protecting you! Be gracious enough to stand back!"

"Enough!" the dragon bride commanded as her comrades joined her before the altar. "We pronounce our judgment!" In unison they moved forward, standing squarely before Manchester. All ten of them stared him in the eyes, still and silent. Manchester met their gazes, turning from one face to the next. Then they knelt at Manchester's feet, eyes cast down and swords poised before them. "Heir to Reginald, king of Willow Prairie, husband of our sister, we swear allegiance to thee and thine. We are your blade. We are your swift arm. We are your eyes in the world. Let all who hear these words know our place is ever in the service of King Martin and Queen Maga."

Bugbear jittered and jerked. He tugged excitedly at Manchester's coat. "Do you realize the importance of this? Do you know the significance? The dragon brides have sworn their allegiance to no power since the Great Drake himself! To have not only won the heart of one such warrior, but now the loyalty of her entire clan? It... it's unheard of!"

"What do I do now?" Manchester stammered.

"Accept their pledge and bid them rise!" Bugbear insisted. "Even I cannot stand to see such a proud people humbled like this for much longer!"

Manchester raised his arms. "Rise, noble sisters. My queen and I accept your gracious offer."

The dragon brides stood and once more looked Manchester and Maga in the eyes. "We are proud of you, Maga. Allherahiah is proud of you."

Maga took her sister's hand and smiled, blinking back tears. "Thank you."

CHAPTER 36
AS THE BEE FLIES

It was hours later amidst the celebration that Bugbear found Manchester performing silly card tricks for a group of children.

"You know," Bugbear said, coming upon the king, "that's the first time I ever saw you perform a magic trick."

"Not doing a very good job of it," Manchester chuckled as he handed the cards to the children. "It's a good thing I found that quill. I never would have made a living as a stage magician."

Bugbear laughed as he took Manchester by the sleeve. "Come with me, Manchester. I wish to discuss something with you."

"Certainly," Manchester said, following his mentor to a spot near the ruins of the library.

"You are to be congratulated, my king," Bugbear whispered. "Because of their loyalty to you, the dragon brides were willing to meet with me. Not since the time of Whittlegrip and Allherahiah have goblin and dragon bride held such council. They have told me some things." Bugbear peered about to make certain no ears but Manchester's heard his words. "Things about the Shadow Smith. About his origins. About his masters."

"His masters?" Manchester balked.

Bugbear waved him down. "Not so loud. This is delicate business." Bugbear made another quick scan of the area before continuing. "Yes. The Shadow Smith was truly but a shadow of a greater threat... a threat which was banished long ago by the dragons. The dragon brides had few details beyond this. After all, these events occurred even before the time of Allherahiah. But in their travels Maga's sisters have seen signs and portents suggesting this threat is trying to return to our world."

Manchester stroked his beard. "Cron mentioned a *subtler power* that the coranieid served at the beginning of time. At first I assumed she meant the Shadow Smith. But now..."

"Yes," Bugbear interrupted with his finger raised in the air. "A good foundation upon which to build my investigation."

"What investigation?" Manchester asked.

Bugbear looked to the ground, as if to hide some sliver of shame in his eyes. "I must leave you now, my king. I must explore and discover the secrets of this *subtler power*."

"So soon after the wedding?" Manchester said, his face drawn with disappointment. "There's so much left to do."

"Nothing you, the queen, and Tudmire can't handle," Bugbear said. "I shall go out into this new world. These *Scatter Lands*. Perhaps one of the other races has information. Or perhaps there are lost records detailing these ancient events." Bugbear took Manchester's hand. "I should leave now, secretly, while eyes and ears are distracted by the celebrations. No one must know of my mission. Only you and Maga... the queen."

"Yes," Manchester said with a grim nod. "Do you need supplies? A mount?"

Bugbear patted his coat and smiled. "I have my coat-of-many-pockets. And I have a mind filled with Non-Logic. Both shall provide me with what I need. I shall send word by messenger bee when I can."

Manchester took his friend by the shoulder and pulled him into an embrace. Bugbear struggled at first, but then surrendered to the sentiment. "Good luck," Manchester said. "You shall be missed."

"As shall you," Bugbear said. "Give my regards to Tudmire and Maga. And look after Riley. I made a promise to Mother Twitchett..."

"I did as well," Manchester said with a smile and a nod. "Maga's with the boy now, teaching him trick shots with the bow he picked up in the battle."

"Really?" Bugbear said, pulling out of the hug. "You know, by the markings I'd say it's a Nagonene bow. Possibly a relic from Reginald's time. You should encourage Riley in this new interest. Archery builds character."

"Agreed," Manchester grinned.

For a few moments they simply enjoyed one another... being beside each other, remembering the events they had shared and the world they had defended. Bugbear had never had such a friendship before. Not even with Duergar. In Manchester he had found someone his equal... a being at once majestic as well as ordinary. He was indeed *The Magnificent Manchester*.

"Good-bye, King Martin."

"Good-bye, Master Bugbear."

And so Bugbear parted from Manchester, wandering through the merrymaking crowds... gently pushing past pages carrying platters piled with pheasants, hams, turkeys, and beef... past strumming and crooning bards... past boasting warriors and tittering maidens. He stepped off the cobbled roads of Willow Prairie onto the dirt trails that led out of town and wound over the hills and past the peak of Tamarack into the wide and unknown world.

"It's wonderful to be free, isn't it?"

"Which way should I go?" Bugbear asked himself as he stood at a fork of three trails.

A buzzing flitted past his ear. Then past the other ear. The bee hovered before him, looking to him with its endless honeycomb eyes.

"I'll let you decide, my friend!" Bugbear piped.

And the bee flew west. Bugbear skipped behind, letting the burdens he bore ease away for just a few moments.

"It's wonderful to be free, isn't it?"

The End

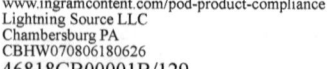